D0463516

The Neapolitan Streak

THE NEAPOLITAN STREAK

Timothy Holme

Coward, McCann & Geoghegan   NEW YORK

First American Edition 1980

Library of Congress Cataloging in Publication Data

Holme, Timothy.
  The Neapolitan streak.

  I. Title.
PZ4.H74869Ne 1980   [PR6058.0'45355]   823'.914
ISBN 0-698-11052-8   80-14145

Printed in the United States of America

To the two Johns who insisted that
Peroni should live

Achille Peroni

To some people the city of Verona means Romeo and Juliet. To police inspector Achille Peroni it meant bean soup. Peroni was Neapolitan and his native cooking was spicy and imaginative with an air of danger about it. So any town which could vaunt bean soup as its speciality – as Verona did – was not likely to appeal to him.

Not that food was everything. Peroni had an almost non-professional relish for crime which aroused his Neapolitan love of drama. And there was no shortage of crime in Verona.

It had not always been so. A couple of decades previously, when Peroni had been stationed in the south, Verona had been a quiet provincial town with a summer season of opera in the Roman amphitheatre (known as the arena), an agricultural fair and a disused cattle trough which served nicely as Juliet's tomb. Crime was almost non-existent then.

Now all that was changed. Verona was in the top league along with cities like Milan and Turin. A shrine for violence, drug-peddling and every imaginable sort of crime which brought its sleazy pilgrims from all over Europe.

There were reasons for it, rooted deep in the past. For one, the Americans, after bringing with them unprecedented wealth and the chromium cornucopia of the supermarket, had withdrawn almost overnight under President Johnson, leaving behind an aroused but unsatisfied craving.

And, of course, there had been the legislation, pushed through parliament by the lady senator with the unlikely name of Merlin, closing down the state-run brothels which had all the effect of opening an erotic Pandora's box to set a bizarre army of whores and pimps loose on the unprepared city.

Then there was political violence, as much an Italian speciality as pizza. Particularly there was the Red Brigade, the dreaded underground movement which had kidnapped and slaughtered the Christian Democrat president, Aldo Moro, in 1978.

Only the day before Peroni's current meditation a young Christian Democrat councillor in Verona had been shot in the legs while leaving his home. The attack – claimed as an act of Red Brigade justice in the usual anonymous communiqué with the five-pointed star at its head – had not been intended to kill. Just to punish and frighten. The doctors said the councillor would never walk properly again, and that did frighten a lot of people.

And the worst of it was that they would probably never get the gunman. Political criminals were rarely caught and even more rarely held, a fact which made Peroni nostalgic for England where punishment followed on crime like effect on cause, or so he chose to believe.

Earlier in his career, before the Peroni legend had been created by the media, he had had six months' special attachment to New Scotland Yard, and he had never got over it. He had scarcely checked out at Heathrow before he fell in love with the country and with all things English. He even persuaded himself that he liked English weather and English tea. And when he returned regretfully to Italy – loaded with clothes from Harrods and the Scotch House, sausages, baked beans, kippers and Cooper's Oxford Marmalade – he had acquired a fair amount of the language as well, wildly inaccurate and veined with a heavy Neapolitan accent, but recognisably English. He would sometimes talk it to the great admiration of his family and friends and, whatever the evidence to the contrary, he obstinately insisted on regarding England as the earthly Paradise.

In fact, of course, if he'd lived there for more than six months the climate would have killed him. Even in Verona, 1500 kilometres south of England, he was ill-at-ease, homesick for the Neapolitan sun and the Neapolitan sky. He missed the sheets hanging out over the streets like banners, the ripe, olive-coloured southern beauty which flowered and withered so quickly, the single rooms opening on to the street in which entire families lived, ate, worked, copulated, quarrelled, suffered and died.

Only in Naples, he felt, could Peroni be fully Peroni.

He had applied for a transfer before, but it was an official application and had gone the way of most official, unbacked applications. What he needed was a word in the right place from somebody who carried weight. What was more, he knew just the person. 'If ever there's anything you want doing,' the person had said, 'you only have to let me know.' But of course Peroni could never take advantage of the offer. A policeman with his position and background (especially background) could never ask favours of such a man.

Or couldn't he?

He lit a black-market English cigarette. Its smoke seemed to trickle lazily from the crater of Vesuvius. He listened as temptation whispered to him. Then he reached for a piece of paper.

At that moment a phone on his desk rang.

It was a summons from *dottore* Guerra.

Practically everybody at the *Questura* was a *dott*. Not a *dott*. of medicine, but of law, since that was the easiest to get and the most appropriate for a policeman. Peroni was a *dott*. himself.

This proliferation of *dotts* was convenient. It gave them all a simple, non-committal manner of addressing each other. '*Buon giorno, dottore!*' '*Buon giorno, dottore!*' 'Oh, *dottore*, a man hanged himself from a parapet over the river during the night. See to it, will you?' 'Certainly, *dottore*.'

If you are not an *Eccellenza*, a *Santità*, a *Commendatore* or even a lower-case *professore*, then a *dott*. will do very well.

But *dott*. Guerra was above the common run of *dotts* for he was also the *questore* or police chief of the city.

If Peroni was the essence of the south, Guerra was the essence of the north. People who liked him said he was efficient, those who didn't called him Germanic. But even his enemies had been unable to dredge up any scandals about him for his integrity was unshakeable. He was a bachelor in his late forties, tall, athletic and good-looking in a melancholy way. Moreover he had had a brilliant career and was tipped for one of the top police jobs in Rome or Milan, a promotion he had well earned by the cool-headed daring he had displayed on numerous occasions. He was scrupulously polite and punctiliously fair. Moreover, he had never shown a trace of prejudice against Peroni's southern-ness as most northerners invariably did, perhaps because he had held a senior police job in Naples himself some years previously.

Secretly Peroni envied Guerra. Guerra was upright while Peroni, though he usually did his best, had a tendency to bend. Guerra was consistent while Peroni was not. Above all, Guerra was bold in action while Peroni's stomach turned to water in the proximity of danger.

'Come in.' Guerra's voice came almost musically courteous as Peroni knocked at the door of his office.

Peroni went in. It was a large, dark, stately office. Guerra sat behind a massive wooden desk, above his head the regulation crucifix, on either side of him glass-fronted bookcases with legal and scientific tomes, in front of him a formidable mass of correspondence, forms, documents and photographs, all arranged as if by computer. (Guerra's efficiency was another quality Peroni envied.)

'*Buon giorno, dottore,*' said Guerra. 'Forgive my disturbing you. Please take a seat.'

Peroni sat and waited, reflecting that the precise psychological moment for writing to that person had passed with Guerra's summons, and who knew when it might return?

For a second *dott.* Guerra seemed to study Peroni, then he started to speak again. 'I've just received a missing-persons report I want you to look into. It concerns a certain General Piantaleone.'

'Piantaleone,' said Peroni, 'the wartime hero?'

'Precisely,' said Guerra, as though approving Peroni's perspicacity. 'It seems that he left his house on Monday evening and has not returned since.'

'Three days ago,' said Peroni.

'The family,' said Guerra, answering the unspoken query, 'didn't report his absence until now as they believed they could trace him themselves.'

'He must be getting on a bit.'

'He is seventy-four years old,' said Guerra, who liked to be precise. He then handed Peroni an official sheet of paper with the details.

'I'll go and see the family right away,' said Peroni, standing up when he had studied the sheet.

'*Buon giorno, dottore,*' said Guerra, also standing and holding out his hand which Peroni took. 'Oh, *dottore,*' he went on when the handshake was concluded.

'Yes, *dottore?*'

'The family have asked for our discretion. Naturally you will act as you think best, but perhaps you may wish to bear the request in mind.'

Scrupulous as always, thought Peroni. Now if they had been in Naples, Guerra would already have been on his way to the bank with a million lire and Peroni would have received strict orders to hush the whole thing up.

'Yes, *dottore,*' he said.

Peroni went through the ornate doorway of the *Questura* and down the marble steps which countless dead *contessine* and *marchesine* had trod on their way to and from balls. For the place was a seventeenth-century palace, which was romantic, though there were times when its inmates would have preferred the functionality of New Scotland Yard.

It was hot outside. Today, even by Neapolitan standards, the sun was bright. It beat upon the roofs of the police cars waiting to speed off to murder, kidnap, hold-up or whatever the home town of the star-crossed lovers might offer next in the way of crime and violence.

Peroni and his driver got into one of them and they set off for General Piantaleone's address. Reluctantly Peroni decided that the circumstances didn't warrant the use of the siren. He enjoyed the siren. The ugly wail, when he was riding with it, sent an adrenalin surge of excitement through him. And he liked the turning of open-mouthed heads, especially when they were female and pretty.

As they went he tried to remember something about General Piantaleone. Roman profile, heroism, uprightness. He'd been a fascist, of course, but then so was everybody else in those days. After the war he had become a symbol of incorruptibility. As things went from bad to worse, as corruption mounted and scandal followed scandal, people would sigh and say 'If only General Piantaleone were in charge!' or 'The Italy of General Piantaleone was very different from this!' By which, of course, they didn't mean the Mussolini era, but some vague, legendary golden age which no historian would certainly be able to discover.

For some time now General Piantaleone had been out of the public eye, though he was still looked on as a symbol of all the virtues that were so conspicuous by their absence on the Italian political scene.

The car stopped in the heart of the medieval part of the city in front of what appeared to be a fortress, four-square in thirteenth-century hostility. Peroni got out and studied it. It had been built to withstand a siege and the dull red brick of its façade glowered on the world as an enemy. The windows had heavy iron grills before them and there was a massive wooden front door.

Peroni went up to it and pulled a hand-bell which jangled threateningly a long way inside. As he waited, he had the uneasy feeling that a cauldron of boiling oil might descend on him at any moment.

Sixty seconds passed before he heard the grinding of locks within. He pictured to himself the door being opened by a funereal-looking butler, chilly and disapproving, and was therefore the more surprised when it in fact opened to reveal one of the prettiest little maids he could have wished to see, a dimpled little Veronese with demure but sparkling eyes.

'*Buon giorno,*' she said with a nice balance of respect and provocation.

'*Buon giorno* to you,' said Peroni, drinking her in. '*Questura,*' he went on and noted with satisfaction the excitement his announcement evidently caused her.

'Come in, please.'

She held the door open while Peroni stepped into the large, dark hall, then closed it behind him. Heavy, old-fashioned pieces of furniture loomed up at him as though they were guardians of the place. You could almost hear them growl.

The little maid led Peroni across this hall and then held open a door for him. As he passed her to go in, his right hand flicked towards her bottom in a little arc, the eternal gesture of the Neapolitan male. It was, of course, an old Peroni, long since officially dead, who was responsible, and the gesture was firmly halted by the police inspector. But only just in time.

'I'll tell the *signora,*' said the little maid, but the look she gave him as she went out said that her instinct had told her of that other Peroni.

Inside the room was as dark as the hall had been. It was overcrowded with furniture, including a grand piano entirely covered with ornately framed family photographs, ordered like the graves in a military cemetery. Peroni recognised the lofty Roman profile of General Piantaleone in several, sometimes posed in military uprightness with Mussolini or other leading figures of the fascist era, sometimes less formally with children and other members of the family whom Peroni was able to identify from their Roman profiles similar to those of the clan patriarch.

Peroni heard the door opening and turned to face a nervous, faded woman in her sixties. He could just see that she had once been beautiful, though she was now worn and lined and had a nervous tic in her left eye. She seemed desperately worried and helpless. But in spite of her emotional state there was something aristocratic in her bearing, and Peroni seemed to remember that the General had married, or practically inter-married, into the old nobility from which he sprang himself.

'*Commissario?*' she said, moving towards him with her hand outstretched.

Chameleon-like, Peroni's character, and sometimes even his appearance, seemed to change according to the person he was interviewing, and he had the knack of establishing his new personality at the very outset with a single phrase or gesture. So now, touching his lips to her oustretched hand, he announced himself as a sympathetic figure of old-world courtesy.

'Peroni,' he said, introducing himself. She had, he realised, instantly categorised him as a southerner, though not a trace appeared in her voice or expression.

'Please sit down, *commissario*.'

'I understand,' he said, sitting, 'that your husband disappeared on Monday evening?'

'Yes.'

'Perhaps you would tell me everything that happened.'

'We had dinner as usual shortly after eight o'clock. After dinner my husband said that he was going out. He did so and – didn't return.'

'Is he in the habit of going out after dinner?'

'Yes. He goes out most evenings.'

'Returning at what time?'

'It depends. Ten o'clock, eleven. Sometimes even midnight.'

'Where does he go?'

'He walks. Sometimes he calls in at a bar.'

'Any particular bar, *signora*?'

'The Bar Dante in Piazza dei Signori. But he didn't go in there the night before last. It was one of the first places we asked at.'

'You only informed the police of his disappearance this morning?'

That embarrassed her. 'Yes,' she said, avoiding Peroni's eyes. 'We were anxious to avoid publicity.'

'But presumably you've taken steps to trace him?'

'Oh, yes. You see, the Piantaleone family is an extremely large one. We have relatives throughout the town and the province.

14

It seemed advisable to make enquiries through them before disturbing the authorities.'

Peroni had come across families like that before. They spread out through a city like an oak tree spreading its roots until they have infiltrated in all directions and at all levels. They formed a Mafia of brothers-in-law and sisters-in-law and cousins and aunts and nephews and nieces. In the end, he reflected, families like that were the most effective power in Italy.

'But none of your family knew anything of him?'

'No. It's as though he had disappeared without trace.'

'*Signora*,' said Peroni, 'has your husband been in any way upset or preoccupied recently?'

'No.'

The answer was too quick, and Peroni knew she was hiding something. Whatever it was might explain the delay in informing the police of the General's disappearance.

'Is there anybody who might for any reason have a grudge against him?'

'My husband is loved by everybody!' she said with more than a touch of aristocratic haughtiness.

'Forgive me,' said Peroni, as suave as a papal legate, 'but political passions run very high in Italy and your husband was – ' He paused delicately.

'A fascist!' she said, finishing the sentence for him. 'Everybody was in those days. The only difference being that my husband has never been ashamed of his allegiance. He believed in the cause, and it was no fault of his that it became corrupted.'

'But he has had no political involvement in recent years?'

'He has grown above politics!'

Could anybody grow above politics in Italy? Peroni wondered. If things always came down to sex in France, in Italy they always came down to politics. Or nearly always.

'How does your husband pass his time, *signora*?'

'He spends much of it in Rosaro.'

'Rosaro?' queried Peroni, to whom the name was new.

'It's a village about half an hour's drive from Verona. The family once owned a villa there which was abandoned long before the war. It's no more than a ruin nowadays. But we also have an estate there and that's still used for wine production and fruit growing. My husband goes up there practically every day. He's very proud of the Piantaleone wine and he often says that he only feels completely at his ease in the company of the peasants there.'

Peroni thought he could almost see the General, a patriarchal landowner, indulging in dialect and drinking in peasant kitchens. Aloud he said, 'And of course you've made enquiries up at – ?'

'Rosaro,' she supplied. 'Yes, they have seen nothing of him there.'

'Does he drive himself up there?'

'No, he's always driven by our eldest son, Loris.'

'What other members of your family were present at dinner the evening before last?' asked Peroni.

'Paolo, that's our younger son, and our nephew, Gabriele.'

Peroni sensed antagonism at the mention of the third name.

'Yes,' she said, the antagonism plainer. 'His parents were both killed in an accident when he was small. He has been brought up with us.'

'Your elder son – Loris I believe you said? – was not present at the dinner?'

'He was in Milan. He returned the next morning as soon as he heard what had happened.'

'I'd like to speak to all three of them if I may.'

'Certainly. I'll send them to you immediately'.

Peroni rose with her and once again touched his lips to the hand she offered him.

When she had gone he listened with a Neapolitan-trained inner ear to the medieval fortress about him. He heard the scufflings of powerful emotions in the air and decided there was certainly enough latent conflict to precipitate a tragedy.

There was an unexpected knock at the door.

'Come in,' he called, hoping it was the pretty maid.

It wasn't. It was a shy, good-looking young man – scarcely more than a boy – in jeans and T-shirt. He seemed very agitated and Peroni wondered whether it was the understandable nervousness most people felt on being sent for by the police or whether it was something more.

'I'm Paolo Piantaleone,' said the boy. 'Mamma said – '

'Yes, of course,' said Peroni, suddenly all paternal geniality. 'Nothing to be alarmed about. I just wanted to hear your account of what happened last Monday.'

'Well, I was out for most of the day – '

'Where?'

Still in paternal vein, Peroni put the question good-naturedly. The result was interesting. Paolo flushed. 'Nowhere special,' he mumbled. 'I went for a drive outside Verona to get some air. It was terribly hot.'

'Anywhere special?'

'No, no – just about.'

'With friends?'

'No, by myself.'

For the second time Peroni had the distinct impression that something was being hidden. He nodded understandingly and stored the information away for future reference. 'What time did you come back?' he asked.

'About half past seven – time to change.'

'Change?'

'Pappa always expects us to change for dinner. Suit and tie.'

'I see. And then?'

'I came down for dinner about eight, and then when it was over I went into the garden. That's about all.'

'What was there for dinner?' asked Peroni, who was curious about culinary details.

Paolo looked startled for a second, then frowned in concentration. 'Risotto, I think, to start with, or maybe it was spaghetti – And then – no, I can't remember.'

'Never mind. How did your father seem during the meal?'

'All right – nothing special.'

'What did you talk about during dinner?'

'I can't remember.'

Whatever was the subject of Paolo's agitation, the interrogation had plainly moved away from it for he was noticeably

17

calmer now. Peroni continued to question him, but learned nothing of practical value. And when he had cordially shaken the young man's hand and watched him out through the door, he was merely left with the certainty that both mother and son were concealing something.

Almost immediately the door opened again, without any preliminary knock this time, and Peroni found himself faced once more with the now familiar Piantaleone profile. But the spirit animating it was different. Somewhat short with black hair and eyes, the man who now came into the room gave an impression of burning internal fervour and driving nervous energy. He made Peroni think of a black panther.

'Loris Piantaleone,' he introduced himself stiffly, without offering his hand.

Peroni was now a southern bureaucrat who carried out regulations to the letter because he was too ignorant to deviate from them, was not above taking bribes, but above all had secure state employment with a pension at the end to which he was sticking come what may.

'Name?' he asked.

'I've already told you.'

'I must have things in order, if you don't mind. Name?'

'Piantaleone. Loris.'

Laboriously and quite unnecessarily, Peroni wrote it down. 'Residence?' he asked.

'I live here!'

'The address please, *signore*.'

Peroni kept it up for ten minutes, and even Loris Piantaleone's arrogance was powerless against the sheer dead weight of it.

'Now we come to the day of the disappearance,' said Peroni. 'I understand you were absent?'

'I was in Milan.'

'When did you leave Verona?'

'The same morning.'

'By what means?'

'By car.'

'Did you see your father before your departure?'

18

'Briefly.'

'Did he appear in any way unusual to you?'

'Not in the least.'

'What was the nature of your business in Milan?'

'I was buying agricultural machinery for the family estate.'

'Did that necessitate staying overnight?'

Loris looked at Peroni with cold dislike. 'I had to visit a number of firms,' he said, 'and I don't see what that has to do with my father's disappearance.'

'I have to follow the correct procedure, *signore*,' said Peroni with all the doggedness of stupidity. 'At this stage anything may be relevant.'

After a number of questions about the General's habits which confirmed what he had already learned, Peroni asked, 'What sort of a man is your father?'

'My father is a great man!'

When Loris had gone Peroni reflected what a useful disguise stupidity could be. If he had not appeared so obtuse, Loris would probably never have betrayed the emotion he showed at the last question and answer. As it was, Peroni had been able to see on his face a glow of fanatical worship. Which might be interesting.

The cousin, Gabriele, of whom the General's wife had so obviously disapproved, had the features of a decadent Greek god beneath a wild mop of golden hair. He was dressed in hand-chafed jeans which bore a famous sartorial signature on the back pocket. On his feet were the sort of sandals that are usually displayed one at a time in shop windows on a revolving mirror, and round his neck he wore what appeared to be an Aztec deity on a golden chain.

'I understand, *commissario*,' he said, 'that you are investigating the mysterious disappearance of Uncle Orazio. I shall be delighted to assist you in any way I can.'

More Neapolitan than a garlic-flavoured pizza, Peroni looked at the young man and winked. Was it a wink of complicity from one performer to another? Or was it an involuntary contraction of the eye? Whatever it was, it had the desired effect.

'Gabriele Piantaleone?' he said, having got the young man at a disadvantage. 'The son of the General's deceased brother?'

'Quite correct.'

'And you live here?'

'I do.'

'You were at dinner on Monday night just before your uncle disappeared?'

'That's right.'

'Anything in your uncle's manner which seemed unusual?'

'There's always something unusual in my uncle's manner, *commissario*.'

'Oh?'

'He's a great hero, didn't you know that? There's always something unusual about great heroes. Look at Napoleon.'

'You're not an admirer of your uncle's?'

'How can you say such a thing? Everybody in this house is an admirer of my uncle's. It's the *sine qua non* of our existence.'

'Do you know of anybody who bears him ill-will?'

'Oh, these great heroes always have their enemies.'

'Names?'

'No idea. Uncle Orazio's political activities are a closed book to me.'

'I thought he had no political activities?'

'In the past I mean.'

'He still holds extreme right-wing views?'

'Indeed he does. All the Piantaleones are fascist pigs. It's in the family blood.'

'Even yours?'

'No, I'm the black sheep. Or I suppose I should say the white sheep. I'm quite apolitical, which is very un-Piantaleone.'

'Do you think that your uncle might have gone off on his own accord for some reason?'

'Before the first of August? Never! '

'What's so special about the first of August?'

'You don't know? You must have arrived very recently from Naples, *commissario*. The first of August is the traditional date for the annual ball of the Veronese nobility, the great families stretching back to the days when the Holy Roman Empire meant something. It's a big do – coloured lanterns, an orchestra, French champagne (none of your Italian spumante), caviare titbits and eighteenth-century costume *de rigueur*. Uncle Orazio believes in it with all the fervour of his upright and heroic soul. Nothing would induce him to miss it.'

'Odd to make such a fuss about titles when there's no longer a monarchy,' said Peroni, who was a republican when he thought about it.

'You don't know the nobility, *commissario*,' said Gabriele. 'Their ranks closed with the abolition of the monarchy. They were transformed to a sort of secret society – not unlike your Mafia, come to think of it.'

Ignoring the possessive, Peroni reflected that this was the second time the idea of the Mafia had cropped up in this investigation. He wondered if it was to be that sort of affair. Had he come all the way north only to be involved in the secret specialities of the south? He pictured a vision of *omertà*, protection and bribes falling about him like autumn leaves. He didn't quite know whether to like it or not.

'So you can make no helpful suggestion about your uncle's whereabouts?' he said.

'You might try dragging Lake Garda,' said Gabriele.

There was some resistance when Peroni asked if he might speak to the servants. But, emanating southern charm, he got his way and was led down to a dark, stone-flagged kitchen where he saw an ample cook, two gardeners, a sour-looking female, an immaculate male servant and, to his great inner contentment, the pretty maid.

The sitting-room of the domestic staff was put at his disposal, and there he received the cook. He put all the right questions to her and received all the right answers. The General was a hero, it was a privilege to work for such a man and she was most upset by his disappearance. But she knew of nothing that might account for it.

Next came the vinegary female, and she was most upset about the General's disappearance, too. Again Peroni put all the right questions and got all the right answers. He went on to put the right questions to the gardeners and the smooth gentleman with no better results.

Last of all, the pretty maid came in and, seeing how unprofitable the right questions had been, Peroni decided to put a couple of the wrong ones for a change.

There was spaghetti for lunch with mussel sauce. Back in Naples the mussels would have been fresh from the polluted waters of the bay. Here they were preserved, but Peroni's sister, Assunta, managed to make the dish taste Neapolitan all the same.

Between brother and sister the past in Naples moved like a ghost which none of the others could see. And perhaps even she was beginning to see it less clearly now. Her husband, Giorgio, was an effective exorciser precisely because he didn't believe in ghosts. He was a rolling, jolly northerner, an architect by profession, with oodles of affection for his entire family, including Peroni.

He and Assunta had two children. The younger, Stefano, was a ten-year-old, bespectacled chess genius. The elder, Anna Maria, was fourteen and looked like the spirit of Naples. Peroni adored them both.

'Any good problems today, Uncle Achille?' asked Stefano.

'I don't know,' said Peroni. 'Somebody called General Piantaleone disappeared from his home on Monday night.'

'Piantaleone?' said Giorgio, long trails of spaghetti dangling like streamers from his mouth. 'Isn't he the war hero?'

'That's the one,' said Peroni.

'I remember him,' said Assunta. 'Very handsome – they used to have his picture everywhere.'

'Murdered?' asked Stefano, blinking solemnly through his spectacles.

And why not? thought Peroni. If the large, Mafia-like network of the Piantaleone family hadn't been able to trace him in three days, it was certainly a possibility.

'I don't know,' he said cautiously.

'Does he have a family?' asked Anna Maria.

'Oh, indeed he does. An enormous one. It seems that there are Piantaleones everywhere.'

'But an immediate family?' Anna Maria pressed.

'Yes. There's a wife, two sons and the General's nephew who all live in the same house.'

'And what do they have to say?' asked Stefano.

Peroni's family were always avid for details about his investigations, and he was usually ready to give them. The children, he had found, could be particularly helpful, Stefano with his chess-trained mind and Anna Maria with an often uncanny instinct.

'Well,' he began. He launched into a detailed report of the various interviews, keeping nothing back except the bit about the Piantaleone maid. They wouldn't have approved of it – he didn't approve of it himself – and it would have put Assunta fairly and squarely back on the saddle of her favourite hobby-horse which concerned the necessity of his finding a wife.

'You know what I think, Uncle Achille?' said Anna Maria when he had finished.

'No,' he said, looking at her quickly. 'What?'

'All this stuff about him being a great hero – there's something wrong with it. It's like – ' She searched for a simile. 'It's like a mask. I believe that the face behind is quite, quite different.'

After lunch, Peroni drove up to Rosaro, the village where the Piantaleones had an estate. The atmosphere of the place made him reflect that time went slower here than in the city. Violence, pornography, drugs, abortion and pressure salesmanship of the *Encyclopaedia Britannica* had plainly not come to Rosaro which still lingered peacefully and, on the surface at any rate, happily in the last century.

Everywhere on the walls were strips of coloured paper saying 'Long Live Our Parish Priest!' Hens pecked about in the single street, ancient crones dressed in black doddered peacefully about unspecified business, snotty-nosed children with apple cheeks played outside a bar where their fathers and their grandfathers and so on back had drunk wine and played cards and shouted at the tops of their voices.

Peroni went in and asked a cheerful, barrel-like woman who came out of a back kitchen hung about with infants if she could direct him to the Piantaleone estate. Then, to the best of his ability translating her instructions which were given in heavy dialect, he got back into his bright red Alfa Romeo which he preferred to official transport.

The estate was some way out of the village and, as he drove towards it, he saw a still majestic, but crumbling ruin of a villa which he guessed was the one referred to by *Signora* Piantaleone. It stood some way off the road and was surrounded by a jungle of vegetation which must have once been a garden.

He came to a small group of houses grouped round a court-yard where the Piantaleone peasants lived. The place seemed deserted, but then a large and fierce-looking dog came bounding out barking. Peroni was terrified of dogs and contemplated a dash back to his Alfa, but realising that would only make matters worse, he tried to look bold and keep on walking. Then fortunately a woman came out of one of the houses.

'*Ehi*, Bobi!' she called. 'Lie down!'

The dog obeyed immediately.

'*Buon giorno*,' said Peroni gratefully.

'*Buon giorno*,' said the woman, eyeing him with evident approval.

'A fine-looking dog,' said Peroni.

'He's a good watch-dog,' said the woman, and then went on almost coquettishly, 'Come in and have a glass of wine. It's hot out here.'

'With pleasure,' said Peroni.

He followed her into the cool, stone-flagged front room and accepted a glass of sharp red wine. Everything went splendidly until he announced his business and immediately saw her expression transformed by alarm.

'Did you hear,' he asked, 'that General Piantaleone disappeared from his home in Verona last Monday?'

'Yes,' she said evasively, no longer even looking him in the eyes. 'Yes, I did hear something of it.'

As he continued to question her, the evasiveness grew stubborn. She had no idea where he might be. She didn't know when or how often he came up to Rosaro. She never saw him because she was always in the house and her husband and sons told her nothing.

Perhaps her husband would be able to help, she said, and directed him to the field where they were working. But before he went she insisted on his taking another glass of wine, and as he drank it her eyes seemed to say how willingly she would discuss anything with him except the doings of the Piantaleone family.

Her husband, as Peroni expected, was no better. Courteous dumbness reigned throughout the estate.

Peroni recognised the pattern. It was the Mafia all over again. Eyes which didn't see. Ears which didn't hear. But why? Loyalty to the Piantaleone family? Or were they hiding some more specific knowledge?

Then suddenly Peroni had an idea.

Don Adriano adjusted his mask carefully and tucked in his soutane so that it should not interfere with his movements. He was removing a superfluous queen from one hive to another and that was a job you couldn't afford to take chances with. He had been keeping bees for forty years and had become a leading authority on the subject, not to mention the fact that his honey was the most delicious to be had throughout the Veneto.

Don Adriano was also the parish priest of Rosaro and he played a dominant role in the village life. He welcomed the villagers into the world, instructed them, reproved them frequently, married them and sped them on their way into eternity. And then he accompanied their remains to the village cemetery with its flowers and little lights and photographs of the dead.

As Don Adriano opened the hive, bees swarmed angrily about

25

him. Then he sprayed them with smoke which would put them to sleep and enable him to remove the second queen. He had just finished the spraying when he heard a voice behind him saying, '*Buon giorno, reverendo.*'

'Stay away!' he roared without turning round. 'Bees sting!'

He had immediately recognised the accent as southern. Southerners in his experience were all idle good-for-nothings and he firmly believed that a dividing line should be drawn right across the country somewhere just south of Rome.

He finished transferring the queen, set the hives to rights and only then turned. Through the eye-piece of his mask he made out the southerner who was suspiciously good-looking. A danger for the entire female population of the village.

'*Buon giorno,*' said the southerner again. 'Forgive me disturbing you.'

'*Buon giorno,*' Don Adriano vouchsafed. The southerner certainly seemed agreeable enough, he thought, taking off his mask and unhitching his soutane. Not that that made him less dangerous – quite the contrary. 'How can I help you?' he said.

'*Questura,*' said the southerner, holding out his hand.

A policeman, thought Don Adriano, taking the hand warily. Aloud he said, 'You'd better come into the presbytery.'

'Thank you,' said the southerner.

'Margherita!' shouted Don Adriano as they went into the house. 'A bottle of wine and two glasses! This way,' he went on. 'Sit down. Now then, what can I do for you?'

'Is it true that a queen can lay as many as a million eggs in her lifetime after only a single mating?'

For a split second Don Adriano was taken aback. The southerner was interested in bees. That changed everything. 'Indeed, it is true,' he said. 'Now if I were to tell you some of the things I've learned about bees in the last forty years, you wouldn't believe your ears. For instance . . .'

Don Adriano was launched upon his favourite subject. He talked happily on. When his elderly housekeeper, Margherita, came in with the wine he scarcely noticed her. Automatically he filled the glasses, drank and re-filled them. The southern policeman asked the most discerning questions. He seemed to have an instinctive understanding of bee-keeping. Don Adriano decided that here was a glowing exception to his general rule about southerners.

After about half an hour he brought himself to a somewhat sheepish halt. 'You must forgive me,' he said. 'You got me on to my favourite subject and I'm afraid I do tend to run on about it.'

'Quite the contrary,' said the southerner, 'I find the subject enthralling.'

'Yes, but you're a busy man. You haven't got time to waste. Now, tell me how I can help you.'

'Perhaps you've heard that General Piantaleone has disappeared from his home in Verona.'

'Yes, yes, yes – poor man! An extraordinary business! Somebody mentioned it to me only the other day. It seems the family were making enquiries about him. May the Lord grant that nothing untoward has befallen him.'

'You knew him?'

'We were not what you might call close acquaintances. I knew him slightly.'

'He spends much of his time up here?'

'That is so. Until about eighteen months ago.'

Don Adriano felt as though a charge of electricity had been put through him by the sudden galvanisation of the hitherto languid and friendly southern policeman.

'Until about eighteen months ago you said?'

'Yes,' said Don Adriano, wondering why the statement was so dramatic.

'You mean,' said the southern policeman, 'that for the last eighteen months General Piantaleone has not been coming up here frequently?'

'Very far from it. Of course, I don't necessarily see him every time, but I should imagine that he doesn't come more often than once a month. I remember thinking that he seemed to have lost all interest in the family estate.'

Like most Neapolitans, Peroni had a deep veneration for St Janarius, the patron saint of Naples whose blood still miraculously liquefies twice a year. He wore a medal of St Janarius wherever he went and invariably appealed to him in moments of danger. And he was happy in the knowledge that so far St Janarius had never let him down.

Apart from this, however, his religious beliefs tended to be a bit incoherent. But he did have a theory that a good priest will always tell you the truth if he knows it and is handled correctly. And once again, he thought as he drove swiftly back towards Verona, this theory had proved true.

For a year and a half General Piantaleone had been regularly leaving his house in the company of his son, Loris, with the official intention of going to Rosaro. And equally regularly he had been going somewhere else.

If Peroni could find the answer to where that somewhere else was he would almost certainly know why the General had disappeared.

And he had high hopes that his next interview would tell him exactly that.

Trembling with excitement, Samantha was tempted to put on the eye shadow too quickly and ruin the whole effect. But she forced herself to go slowly, shading each eye with the care of an artist at work on a major canvas.

Finally she was done. She examined the overall effect with critical approval, picked up her bag and left the house. Her eyes were modestly lowered, fixed on the pavement ahead of her, but she didn't miss one of the male looks which were shot at her from all directions. The rapid, sideways glance of the priest, the hard appreciative stare of two *Carabinieri*, the cheeky appraisal of a refuse collector, the old man's lingering look of regret. She filed them all away for further examination at leisure.

For all the excitement of the outing, though, she remembered her resolution not to say anything indiscreet. They had been

28

specially asked to be careful what they said, and one had to remember where one's loyalties lay.

She arrived at her destination with male eyes raking her from all directions, but she had already spotted the only man in Verona who interested her at the moment. He was the best-looking man she had ever seen. Very southern-looking, of course, but it suited him. Cook said that the papers called him the Rudolph Valentino of the Italian police.

And what a way he had with him! When she had gone in to be questioned by him that morning she had been expecting him to ask almost anything except what he did ask. Did detectives usually make dates while they were on duty? Experience on television and at the cinema offered nothing comparable.

Now he had seen her. He jumped up and held out a chair for her. She smiled and sat. Yes, an ice-cream would be lovely.

As he ordered it together with something called a Chivas Regal for himself she felt as though everybody were looking at her, and that made her feel a tiny ice sliver of fear that word of her meeting with him might get back. But the sliver melted in the glow of his sun.

He wanted to know all about her – where she came from, her family, her schooldays, the songs she liked. He even asked her what her favourite flowers were, and when she said violets a boy seemed to pop up from nowhere with a basket of them, and he bought her a bunch.

The questions went on so softly and gently that she almost felt as though they were caresses. He started to ask her about the family, too.

'Of course it's a privilege working for such a great man,' she said. 'Mamma used to have a picture of him hanging up in the living-room when I was a little girl. I think she was a bit in love with him. It would be a shock for her if she knew what he was like now.'

In the far distance there was something which sounded like an alarm bell, but the southern policeman was watching her lips in such a way that she ignored it.

'Well, of course, it's his age,' she went on. 'Old men do get a bit funny, and you can't blame them. Arterio-sclerosis and that sort of thing.'

'What exactly does he do?' the Policeman asked.

'Well, as far as I'm concerned,' she said blushing slightly, 'the worst of it is the touching. I have to be very careful never to be alone with him. And even in company he sometimes tries to – well you know what I mean. And then we always have to be sure that the spirits are locked up. And the scenes! He's terribly touchy – the smallest thing puts him into a rage. Just as well the walls are thick, I always say, or else people would hear. But as Cook says, what a man's like in his old age can't alter what's gone before. General Piantaleone was a hero, and the family's quite right to protect his memory.'

How long had he been like that?

'He's only been really bad these last few months. When I first came into service with the family he was perfectly all right.'

But he still went up to Rosaro, didn't he?

Yes, as far as Samantha knew, he did. Mr Loris drove him off practically every day. No, she couldn't say what the General did up there as she'd never been. And she certainly didn't know of anywhere else where he might go to. Why should he go somewhere else? Cook said he went up to Rosaro, and Cook always knew everything.

Yes, another ice-cream would be a lovely idea.

The ending had been awkward. As he finished his questioning and the spell began to wear off Peroni noticed sadly how she regained her powers of reasoning, rather like someone coming to after an anaesthetic. He was accustomed to this experience with attractive female witnesses, but the sense of loss that accompanied it never diminished.

He saw her eyes slowly widen in panic as she realised she had told him all the things she had resolved to keep secret. Her stare of pleading made him recall the English phrase about killing a sitting bird.

So first of all she had to be reassured. Then she had to be got rid of. Not that Peroni was averse to the suggestion that her eyes, once the first panic was passed, were so insistently making. Indeed, the old Peroni was all for falling in with it. But the *dott.* wouldn't hear of such a thing. With reluctance and an undignified internal struggle Peroni wrenched himself free from Samantha.

So Anna Maria had been right, Peroni reflected on his way back to the *Questura.* The face behind the mask was a different one indeed, the face of a testy and lecherous dotard. This explained the evasiveness of the General's wife, too – she was protecting the heroic image.

But the problem of Rosaro remained intact. Where did the General go to? There was one person who knew, even if he would certainly never say. Peroni decided that a great deal more would have to be learned about Loris Piantaleone.

General Piantaleone

It took Peroni a couple of hours next morning to telephone all the agricultural machinery factories in Milan. In the process he got a fair haul of wrong numbers including the planetarium, a *Signora* Martini who sounded as though she were expecting something tenderer than the *Questura* of Verona, a chemist's and a little girl who said she was sorry Mamma wasn't at home.

At the end of it all, Peroni was hoarse, exhausted and quite certain that Loris Piantaleone had not visited any agricultural machinery factory in Milan on the day of his father's disappearance.

The cumulus of doubt that hung over Loris's head thickened perceptibly. Could he have abducted his father? Peroni remembered the glow of fanatical worship he had seen on Loris's face and decided that – in conjunction with what he had learned from Samantha – it might somehow be so. Certainly it was possible that Loris knew where the General was and, if he were kept under discreet surveillance, he might just lead them straight to him.

After consultation with *dott.* Guerra, a round-the-clock watch on Loris was organised. The man chosen for the first shift was Lenotti. Lenotti, who was a martyr to his stomach and apparently lived on camomile tea, seemed to carry trouble about with him and had the mournful expression of a bloodhound wrongfully accused of urinating on the sofa. It was even said that his baleful influence extended to the weather. Although superstitious like most Neapolitans, Peroni had never believed this and would have dismissed as mere coincidence the fact that, shortly after Lenotti had parked just down the street from the grim medieval façade of the Piantaleone home, there came a low rumble of thunder and the first fat drops of rain spattered heavily on the road.

A militant feminist seethed in the bosom of Franca Verdi, but Franca was too timid ever to let her out and the result already, at the age of only twenty-five, was a ruined digestive system. Franca worked for the *Arena*, the daily paper of Verona which was dominated by male chauvinist pigs, and she mainly handled stories which her colleagues felt beneath their dignity like exhibitions of African handcraft organised by missionary fathers and occasional features of strictly female interest. When she was given these assignments the feminist within her stormed an indignant refusal while Franca meekly smiled and accepted.

At the moment she was alone in the office with an elderly sub-editor who was mechanically fitting bits of agency material into an early page like a jigsaw puzzle which he had already done several thousand times before.

The telephone rang and the sub moved to answer it, then recalled that there was a female slave in the office and said without looking up, 'Get it, will you, Franca.'

'Yes, of course,' said Franca with a smile he didn't even notice, while the feminist screamed unheard, 'Answer the bloody thing yourself!'

Franca picked up the receiver. 'The *Arena*,' she said sweetly.

'The Red Brigade here,' said a flat, male voice without regional accent.

At first Franca thought it was a joke. This was something that happened on big newspapers like the *Corriere della Sera*. The dreaded band of ruthless political killers would surely not bother with a rather dreary local rag like the *Arena*.

Meanwhile the voice was continuing. 'Go out of the front entrance of your office,' it said, 'and turn right. Twenty metres ahead of you there's a litter box. Wedged behind the litter box you'll find a communiqué.'

The voice stopped and the line clicked dead.

'What was it, Franca?' asked the sub.

'The Ursuline nuns want me to go and see their new chapel,'

Franca improvised wildly to the silent applause of the feminist within.

'Fine, fine,' said the sub, finding a piece about a hotel blaze in Aberdeen which just fitted the hole he was trying to fill.

Trying not to hurry, Franca got up, went out of the office and down the stairs. It was raining heavily outside and thunder was rumbling ominously, but she was too excited even to look about her for an umbrella. Going outside was like stepping under an enormous shower turned on to the full. Immediately outside the entrance she turned right and there, sure enough, just ahead of her through the driving rain, was a litter box. She must have passed it hundreds of times without noticing it. Her heart beat wildly as she ran up to it. She had read how a Red Brigade messenger always watched while a message was picked up. Was a Red Brigade messenger watching her now? The young man in the doorway opposite? The girl in a car parked outside the bar?

Her hand shaking she felt behind the litter box. At once it came into contact with paper. She pulled out a common, orange-coloured envelope of a type widely used in commerce and opened it, sheltering it under the roof overhang to keep it dry. Inside was a single gestetner sheet of rough paper. She unfolded it and saw at the top the notorious five-pointed star of the Red Brigade. If this was a hoax it was a complicated one.

She started to read. 'The enemy of the people, General Orazio Piantaleone, having been tried by a proletarian court for crimes against the people, was found guilty on all counts preferred against him. The sentence of death was passed. Said sentence has now been carried out. The servants and hired assassins of the multinational lackeys will find the corpse of the fascist murderer in the uninhabited building scheduled for demolition on Lungadige San Giorgio. This marks the anniversary of 31st July.'

The last sentence was obscure, but the rest was clear enough. Do what they liked now, the men could never undo the fact that Franca had brought in the news of the first Red Brigade killing in Verona. She walked back through the driving rain with her head high.

Peroni had no hesitation about using the siren this time, and the police car in which he was riding with two colleagues surged with a wild, banshee wail through the rain-washed streets. But heads were turning less than they used to do, he noticed with disappointment, and it wasn't only the weather. It was over-familiarity. The Italians were getting so accustomed to tragedies and disasters that their appetite for sensation was becoming jaded. And, as if that wasn't enough, there were far too many ambulance drivers who used their sirens to cut through tiresome traffic knots when they were on their way back to the station without so much as a sprained ankle in the back.

It didn't take long to get to the Lungadige San Giorgio and the siren was decrescendoing to a bass hum as Peroni and his colleagues jumped out of the car. There was no mistaking the building referred to in the communiqué. It was a crumbling, two-storey house, boarded up at the door and windows. But when they got up to it they saw that the boarding was not nailed hard in place and had obviously been removed recently. They opened it up again and went in.

The first thing they noticed was the smell, a nauseating, pungent odour of advanced decay. Peroni, who was fastidious about such things, lit one of his black-market English cigarettes. The room they were in was dark and bare with an ancient sink full of rubble and plaster and two barred and boarded windows. If it hadn't been for the smell and the Red Brigade's communiqué they might have taken the shape on the floor for old sacking. It was, in fact, covered with sacks, but when they were removed Peroni immediately recognised the Piantaleone Roman profile.

The decaying General wore a dark suit, black shoes, tie and a once white shirt. In the shirt-front were five perforations with blackberry stains around them.

'The first Red Brigade killing in Verona,' said Peroni.

'Wonder why they picked on him,' said one of the other two.

'Because he stood for something,' said the second who tended to belong to the old school himself. 'They always pick their victims carefully.'

Peroni thought of Samantha's revelations and wondered. Though, of course, with his family so carefully covering up the General's arterio-sclerotic goings-on they didn't perhaps make so much difference to outsiders. The General still did stand for something.

'Why did they wait until today?' asked the first man, 'they must have killed him several days ago.'

'They explained that in the communiqué,' said Peroni. ' "This marks the anniversary of 31st July." This day last year two of their key-men were killed in a gun battle with the police – remember?'

The other man nodded. 'They're great ones for anniversaries, the Red Brigaders,' he said.

'And they never do anything without a reason.'

That was true, too, thought Peroni. They were such ruthless followers of their own peculiar reason as to be completely un-Italian. And, of course, even though they were Italian by nationality they had been trained by the Germans and the KGB. A lot of work lay ahead. Endless checking and re-checking, road-blocks, swoops on apartments. And for the smallest Red Brigade fish the police net pulled in there would be a massive heap of other stuff that would otherwise have been left in peace on the bed – every variety of small-time racket imaginable, and it would all have to be sifted through and then sorted out to the competent departments.

And then Peroni realised that the Piantaleone killing was no longer his business. With the Red Brigade so evidently claiming its paternity, it passed to the political squad. He felt a surge of relief.

There was, of course, still the loose end of Loris's day in Milan, but there was presumably some other explanation for that.

There came the howl of approaching sirens, then a shrieking of tyres and the sound of engines braking to a sudden halt followed by a slamming of car doors outside. Peroni looked out and saw a small army of *Carabinieri* with machine guns taking up positions about the house and keeping the fast-swelling crowd on the far side of the road.

The officer commanding the *Carabinieri* detachment was a Sicilian and he and Peroni shook hands with a certain complicity, fellow countrymen recognising each other in an alien land.

'Is it true then?' asked the *Carabinieri* officer. Peroni nodded. 'Looks like a lot of sleepless nights ahead,' went on the officer.

A dark blue, ministerial-looking Fiat drew up and *dott.* Guerra, as unruffled as if he had been arriving for the opening of a new post-office block, stepped out. He looked interrogatively at Peroni, who nodded.

'Kindly see that the magistrate is informed at once,' he said.

The police doctor gave his unofficial opinion that the General had been shot two or three days before and said that the appearances were quite consonant with the shooting having taken place on the night of his disappearance. He believed that the body, however, had only been moved to its present resting place within the last twelve hours.

Questioning of people who lived thereabouts produced nothing useful beyond the fact that there were various reports of car engines stopping and starting during the night, but as there were traffic lights about a hundred metres away this didn't mean much.

The magistrate arrived, examined the body and took formal note of the affair on behalf of the judiciary authority. He then gave permission for the body to be removed to the police mortuary while *dott.* Guerra gave instructions for the clothing to be examined by the scientific squad.

'I shall be holding a conference in my office in half an hour,' said Guerra to Peroni and the *Carabinieri* officer. 'Both you gentlemen will kindly attend.'

'Yes, *dottore*,' they said.

Unlike most Italian officials, *dott.* Guerra when he said half an hour meant exactly thirty minutes, and it was already long past lunchtime. The Red Brigade had disrupted the country

37

indeed, Peroni reflected, when one had to sacrifice one's midday plate of spaghetti.

He drove back to the *Questura* and just had time to call in at the nearest bar for a toasted sandwich with a slice of pink blotting paper called ham and yellow blotting paper called cheese, accompanied by a glass of detergent called Valpolicella wine.

Dott. Guerra's office was full for the conference. There was the head of the DIGOS, the political police, an unexpectedly roly man who looked like Father Christmas without a beard, but possessed behind his genial appearance one of the steeliest brains in the peninsula; there was the *Carabinieri* officer Peroni had met that morning with two colleagues and an irascible *Carabinieri* General; there were various DIGOS functionaries as well as the deputy police chief and *dott.* Guerra's secretary.

'For some while now, as you are all aware, gentlemen,' *dott.* Guerra began, 'the Red Brigade has been active in Verona. We have had various "punishment" lamings of prominent Christian Democrats and, recently, armed assaults on the Mondadori printing works and the Aquarama clothing factory. Now we have a murder as well, and furthermore the murder of a man who represented all that is best in our rapidly degenerating body politic.'

Peroni wondered whether Guerra, who seemed to know everything that went on in Verona, was aware of the General's catastrophic decline.

'The Minister has been in touch with me already,' Guerra continued, tapping one of the telephones on his desk with solemnity and looking around the attentive faces before him, 'and he expects rapid and satisfactory results.'

Once more Peroni congratulated himself on being out of it. A policeman's lot was not a happy one (surely that was English?) when Ministers expected rapid and satisfactory results.

'We are certain, I take it,' said the *Carabinieri* General, 'that this assassination is the work of the Red Brigade?'

'I have not yet received a detailed report on the communiqué found behind the litter box this morning,' said *dott.* Guerra suavely, 'but a preliminary examination indicates that it is perfectly genuine. The typewriter is probably not the one used in the most recent Red Brigade communiqués, but presumably they possess more than one machine.'

It wasn't often that *dott*. Guerra made a joke, and the observation produced a respectful murmur of amusement. Only when it had passed did Peroni wonder whether the remark had been intended as a joke.

'Besides,' Guerra was continuing, 'all the other aspects of the affair bear the clear stamp of the Red Brigade.'

'Hurrumph,' went the *Carabinieri* General, implying that he would allow himself to be convinced for the time being.

'As far as our general campaign is concerned,' said Guerra, 'the Minister has called for total collaboration between the DIGOS and the *Carabinieri*. The DIGOS will infiltrate, conduct undercover enquiries and generally act in complete freedom as the circumstances warrant.'

The Father Christmas DIGOS chief looked rounder and more genial than ever and Peroni wondered what thoughts of secret interrogations and treachery were going on inside his large, snow-covered skull.

'And your men, General,' Guerra went on, 'will set up roadblocks, comb selected areas and make raids according to plans predisposed between ourselves or acting on information from the DIGOS.'

The General and Father Christmas nodded stiffly at each other. They were not friendly. The balance of power between the *Carabinieri* and the public security police (from whose ranks the DIGOS were drawn) was a delicate one. Each believed the other had too much power. The *Carabinieri* suspected the PS Police – often correctly – of being Communist-infiltrated. The PS said that the *Carabinieri* were retrograde and reactionary and went about in pairs so that, while one would be able to write, the other would be able to read.

As Guerra continued to outline plans for the massive Red Brigade hunt, Peroni began to feel remote from the whole business. It was no longer his affair. The DIGOS and the *Cara-*

binieri would share the kicks and the glory together. All that would come Peroni's way were the various side-products of the investigation. He was so sure of this that the effect of Guerra's next announcement was cataclysmic.

'Preliminary investigations into the General's disappearance were carried out by *dott*. Peroni who will therefore remain in charge of the investigation.'

In consternation, Peroni felt all eyes in the room shift to him and convict him by an overwhelming majority of being Neapolitan. He sought out the pair belonging to the Sicilian *Carabinieri* officer which flashed him a message of solidarity.

His initial alarm gave way to an irresistible wave of self-satisfaction that he had been chosen to head such a spectacular enquiry as this. Obviously Guerra, for all his northern reticence, was not entirely impervious to the Peroni legend.

However, Peroni recognised cautiously, it was by no means going to be one long pizza party. The situation risked being a dangerous one with him as scapegoat if things went wrong and the *Carabinieri* General and Father Christmas getting all the glory if they went right. Cards would have to be carefully played. But, as Peroni was well aware, Neapolitans – and particularly Neapolitans with his background – were versed in the art of keeping aces, not only up their sleeves, but in every available space afforded by the human body and its coverings.

Peroni's appointment confirmed, Father Christmas was asked to give an up-to-date briefing on Red Brigade activity in Verona. He got to his feet looking as though he were about to distribute toys to all present.

'The so-called Veronese column of the Red Brigade which has been active for more than a year,' he said, 'was formed in the university, though its founders and key men and women are now independent. We have uncovered two lairs, one thanks to an informer's tip, one due to the suspicions of a member of the public living in the same block. But in both cases the occupants got away in time, taking with them any really dangerous material they had, leaving behind arms, false documents, gestetner equipment and so on. No great loss for an organisation which finances itself with ransoms and bank robberies worth many billion lire.

'We've made various arrests, too, but so far they've only been flank-men or sympathisers with no more than call-box contact with the inner core.

'Our real problem with the Red Brigade, though, was that we just weren't a match for them. We still aren't. They had prepared for years in the most highly specialised schools of terrorism in the world when our men were just about a match for football hooligans. It was like sending squadrons of vintage aircraft after a space rocket.

'But we're learning. Infiltration is the primary essential. We must learn to infiltrate them as they have learned to infiltrate us.' He looked about him with eyes as genial as ever which nevertheless seemed to be asking if somebody in that room was a Red Brigade spy.

Quite possibly, thought Peroni, who wouldn't have put it past any of them.

The *Carabinieri* General cleared his throat angrily, as though indignantly refuting the charge.

'But to infiltrate,' went on Father Christmas, 'you need time. First time to prepare your infiltrators. They need to be well prepared. The least hint of suspicion and all you're left with is a dead policeman. Then time for the infiltrators to work their way in, become accepted and finally gain information which is really worth having.'

Next he passed round three identikit pictures of Brigade fighters in the Verona column. One had a heavy, drooping moustache and slit eyes. Another had a round, heavy-jowled, clean-shaven face, while the third was ascetic-looking with steel-rimmed spectacles and short hair. Instinctively Peroni mistrusted the whole identikit technique which he considered a monstrously overrated scientific fraud. He was bound to admit, however, that it occasionally produced results. So when the meeting came to an end he asked the DIGOS chief for copies.

'Oh, *dottore* – ' Guerra stopped Peroni as he was on his way out.

'Yes, *dottore*?'

'The media are anxious for a statement. Of course, the strictest reserve must be maintained concerning our enquiries, but we shall have to let them have the outstanding facts. I have called a press conference for five o'clock and I shall be greatly obliged if you will conduct it.'

'Certainly, *dottore*.'

Five o'clock, Peroni was thinking. Too late for the evenings, but just in nice time for the eight o'clock television news which was peak viewing time. With any luck he should make the lead story.

The room with its magnificent windows overlooking the river, its stuccoed pillars and high ceiling on which faded and cracking nymphs and fauns still gambolled, had once been the ballroom. Now the police used it as a bar, and their bawdy, raw or merely banal exchanges had taken the place of the witticisms, the high society chit-chat and the amorous whisperings which had once sounded there.

As Peroni entered, he summed up his audience at a glance, in spite of the already dense cloud of smoke. There were telecamera teams from the RAI and, he noticed with satisfaction, the Monte Carlo and Swiss television networks. There were also correspondents from the *Corriere della Sera, La Stampa, Il Giornale, Il Giorno,* the Communist *Unità* and all the other leading circulation dailies.

Peroni moved through the crowd shaking a hand here, smiling and nodding. He was in his element with the media. And its representatives liked him. Not for nothing had they nicknamed him the Rudolph Valentino of the Italian police. He was their idea of what a policeman should be – cordial, outgoing, full of surprises and with a professional understanding of what makes a good headline.

And this was going to make one. The men of the DIGOS, who had an almost morbid passion for secrecy, had confiscated the Red Brigade communiqué and obliged the *Arena* newspaper to silence with the direst legal threats. So Peroni had the stage to himself and intended to make the most of it.

'Good evening, ladies and gentlemen,' he said, taking his place on a platform at one end of the room. The cameras whirred encouragingly.

'At thirty-seven minutes past eleven this morning,' he went on giving it to them straight, 'a body was found in an abandoned building on the Lungadige San Giorgio. It had been shot five times. It is the body of General Orazio Piantaleone.'

Accustomed as he was to causing sensations, even Peroni was taken aback by this one. There was a gasp, then a sort of electrical hum went round the room, pens scribbled frenetically, cameras zoomed in on him. Monte Carlo got his right profile, Switzerland his left and the Italian RAI his full front view.

'Responsibility for the murder was claimed by the Red Brigade in a communiqué following a telephone call to a girl journalist on the Veronese daily, the *Arena*. The communiqué was stuck behind a litter box just outside the newspaper offices.'

With the sort of Neapolitan smile that always charmed press and public Peroni let it be understood that his statement was over and questions could begin.

'Is the communiqué genuine?' With the question a microphone shot out under Peroni's chin.

'A full examination hasn't been completed, but the experts consider it genuine.'

'Who discovered the body?'

'I did, in the company of two other functionaries of the *Questura*.'

'Was he shot in the abandoned building?'

'No.'

'Where was he shot?'

'We are enquiring into that at the moment.'

'When was General Piantaleone last seen alive?'

'On Monday evening.'

That set off another babble of excited comment in the stately, smoke-filled room.

'He'd been missing for three whole days?'

'That is so.'

'Where was he last seen?'

'At his home. He had dinner with his family and then went for a walk from which he didn't return.'

'Kidnapped?'

'I'm not in a position to say.' It was just one degree better than, 'I don't know.'

'Is anything known of his activities after he left home?'

The short answer to that was no, but it wasn't in keeping with the Peroni legend. 'I'm afraid that must be covered by the reserve surrounding enquiries.'

'Why General Piantaleone?'

Peroni was beginning to think that when he knew the answer to that he would be a good deal nearer home.

'Because he represented all that is best in our rapidly degenerating body politic,' he said, thinking that *dott.* Guerra might be pleased.

The English or American press would never have taken a line like that, he reflected, but the Italians were all busily copying it down which just went to show that, in spite of the Red Brigade, they were a deeply sentimental race. And even the Red Brigade combatants must have mammas tucked away somewhere.

The questions went on. Peroni ducked, shielded, parried, riposted. It was a consummate performance and, as he made his way out to enthusiastic applause, he marvelled, not for the first time, how easy it was to satisfy the media.

If you knew how to go about it.

There was a mirror in the waiting-room of the *Questura* at Verona into which people rarely bothered to glance. The back of it, however, which was in another room, was frequently peered into, for it was a two-way mirror, and policemen sometimes liked to examine their clients before confrontation.

Through this mirror Achille Peroni now observed the members of the Piantaleone family whom he had convoked. They looked, he decided, like characters in search of an author. Four not six. They were all in formal mourning except for the cousin,

Gabriele, who was dressed with the same casual luxury as the day before.

Appraising them professionally, Peroni calculated that the nerve-jangling process of being kept waiting in the *Questura* had done its work, at any rate with the widow and the two sons.

He went to his office and sent for *Signora* Piantaleone, jumping up when she came, kissing her hand, pressing her into a chair and murmuring condolences.

'I am anxious,' he began, 'to find out all I can about your husband's activities in case there should be anything about them which might have attracted the – attention of the Red Brigade.'

'I've already said that he spent practically all his time on the estate up at Rosaro.'

'*Signora*,' said Peroni, 'for the last eighteen months of his life your husband scarcely went up to Rosaro at all.'

The effect was dramatic. Her mouth fell open as though the jaw-bone had suddenly become too heavy. She recovered quickly and shut it again, but she couldn't prevent consternation, fear and bewilderment appearing in her eyes. It was too spontaneous not to be genuine.

'I appreciate this must be a shock,' said Peroni, 'but can you think of anywhere – anywhere at all – your husband might have spent the time when he said he was in Rosaro?'

'No, no – I can't.'

But Peroni had speared the thought which flashed through her mind to be instantly hidden away with the other embarrassing truths about General Piantaleone. He had spent all that time, she believed, with another woman.

And why not? thought Peroni. In view of Samantha's testimony it was a good probability.

He continued to question the widow without learning anything more, so finally he got out the three identikit pictures he had had from the DIGOS. He put the first before her. 'Have you seen anyone resembling this man?'

She looked at it with distaste, but forced herself to examine it before shaking her head in the negative. She followed the same pattern for the other two. Peroni collected the pictures together, put them in his top drawer and then accompanied her to the door, bowing slightly as she went through it.

Paolo, the youngest son, was able to throw no light on his father's activities. As far back as he could remember Pappa had always spent his time at the estate and the news that he had been going there scarcely at all during the past eighteen months plainly baffled him completely.

With no expectation of recognition Peroni laid the three identikit pictures in front of Paolo, and was therefore the more surprised when he saw the young man's face contract for a second at the sight of the third face, the ascetic one with steel spectacles. Peroni thought he could sense fear.

'Remind you of someone?' he asked.

'No,' said Paolo.

'Are you sure?'

'Quite sure. I've never seen it before. Or perhaps I've seen it many times. It's a common sort of face among young people nowadays.'

There was truth in that, but Peroni didn't believe it was the explanation. He felt a lift of excitement.

But the recognition was not confirmed by Gabriele. Peroni watched him carefully as he looked at the ascetic-faced young man, but there was no reaction. Either he had unusual self-control or the face meant nothing to him.

'You know what they remind me of?' he said. 'Every other identikit picture I've ever seen. I believe you make them up.'

Two to one, thought Peroni as he waited for the elder son.

'Sit down,' he said, without looking up when Loris came in, and he went on scribbling away, industriously bureaucratic.

'One elephant went out to play,' he wrote, copying out for want of anything better the words of a song which had taken his fancy while he was in England. 'Upon a spider's web one day. He found it such enormous fun/That he called for another elephant to come.'

'Where did you take your father,' he said when he judged Loris to be sufficiently exasperated, 'when he was supposed to be in Rosaro?'

46

'What do you mean, supposed?' said Loris. 'I did take him there.'

'That's not my information.'

'Then your information is wrong.'

And he stuck to it. Peroni added stubbornness to fanaticism and denseness in his inventory of Loris Piantaleone.

'Then perhaps,' he tried, 'you would like to tell me where you were on the day of his disappearance when you said you were visiting agricultural machinery factories in Milan?'

Almost perversely he hoped that Loris would cling to his original story of this, too. And he was not disappointed. An interesting query now posed itself. If the killing was so obviously the work of the Red Brigade, why should Loris continue to lie so doggedly and stupidly in the face of facts? Could it be that the killing was not so obviously the work of the Red Brigade after all? Was Loris somehow involved. Or was it something completely different he was trying to conceal?

In his wisdom Peroni decided that the surveillance was more likely to get at the truth than insistence on his part. He puffed in bureaucratic annoyance and reached for the identikit pictures.

'Do you recognise any of these pictures?' he asked.

This time there was no mistaking the reaction. Loris clutched the third picture and studied it slowly with an expression of pure malice.

'Yes,' he said after gloating over it for an eternal thirty seconds, 'I recognise that face. It's Policarpo Pillipopoli.'

Immaculately suited, the young man picked up a glass of red wine, but before it reached his lips his elbow was jogged by his little boy and the wine splashed darkly on his shirt. His face contorted with irritation.

'That's an impossible stain!' he snorted.

'No, dear,' his wife corrected him, large-lipped, smiling and cool. 'With Bio-Movi no stain is impossible!'

'With Bio-Movi,' repeated a male voice more emphatically as the camera moved in on her frozen smile, 'no stain is impossible!'

The picture faded and the screen became silent and featureless. The next programme was the news.

After the interview with Loris Piantaleone, Peroni's next move was obviously to track down Policarpo Pillipopoli. Loris had either not wished to go any further than his initial revelation, or else he had been unable to. The face, he was sure, was that of a certain Policarpo Pillipopoli, a former school companion. He could and did provide Policarpo's address, but denied knowledge of any link between him and General Piantaleone.

'But they're Communists!' he added with some venom. 'All the Pillipopolis are Communists!'

Peroni put Loris down as one of those people who saw Communists under the bed, but found the information interesting none the less.

Recalled, Paolo admitted having attended the same school and allowed that the face could be that of Policarpo Pillipopoli. He denied having noticed the resemblance before, but his ill-concealed agitation made this seem implausible.

Also recalled, Gabriele repeated that the face meant nothing to him, but as it turned out that he'd been to a boarding school, which the General had hoped would reform his indolent and generally reprehensible character, there was reason to believe that he was telling the truth. What interested Peroni, however, was the expression of amused malice which the name Pillipopoli brought to his face.

The General's widow started when she heard the name, though she insisted that the identikit picture meant nothing to her. Apparently Policarpo had only been a remote school acquaintance of Loris and Paolo, so why did his name arouse such distinct reactions in all the family? The answer would have to be sought at the Pillipopoli home.

When these interviews were finished it was nearly time for the eight o'clock news and Peroni decided to catch it at home on the way to the Pillipopoli residence. He couldn't resist watching the effect on his family.

The television erupted into the fanfare announcement of the news. TG 1 spun on to the screen and off it again. And then there was Peroni's face, appearing before that of the newscaster, an honour usually reserved for the Pope.

'At thirty-seven minutes past eleven this morning,' he heard himself saying, 'a body was found in an abandoned building on the Lungadige San Giorgio.'

Normally only Giorgio, Peroni's brother-in-law, watched the news, but the familiar voice quickly brought the rest of the family around the set, and there were cries of 'Uncle Achille!', 'Why didn't you tell us?' and 'You might have telephoned!' Well satisfied with the effect he had achieved, Peroni baked in the waves of hero-worship which emanated from the other four people in the room.

'Is that *all* you've found out?' asked Stefano when the Piantaleone story had given place to the price of spaghetti.

'No, no,' said Peroni, 'I know quite a lot else, but you can't go round telling everything to the newspapers and the television.'

'You *are* clever, Uncle Achille!' said Anna Maria. 'Tell all!'

'Not now,' said Peroni. 'I've got to go and see someone called Policarpo Pillipopoli.'

'What a stupid name!' said Stefano. 'Did someone really call him that?'

'Must have done,' said Peroni. 'It's probably an old family name.'

The Pillipopoli residence turned out to be a magnificent Palladian-style villa standing in its own grounds with two stone lions *couchant* before an imposing entrance and carved stone balconies in a façade decorated by a now almost vanished fresco; here and there you could still make out the haunches of nymphs, coronets of vine leaves and a trickle of wine pouring from nowhere into a golden cup. It was a pleasant building, full of light, with roses blowing about its face.

A discreetly modern speaker with bell had been fitted into the ancient wrought-iron gate. Peroni pushed the bell and waited.

'Who is it?' came a smooth voice from the speaker.

'*Questura*,' said Peroni.

The voice found nothing to say to this, but the gate clicked open. Peroni walked up the gravelled path admiring the velvety lawns, which reminded him of those he had seen in Oxford colleges, and the immaculate flower-beds. It would require a lot of labour to keep such extensive grounds so perfectly, he thought, and wondered if there could be any truth in Loris's story about the Pillipopolis being Communists.

When he had climbed up the steps and passed between the two stone lions the front door was opened to him by a butler who looked as though he had been specially raised in England for export only. The butler raised his eyes interrogatively.

'*Questura*,' Peroni repeated. 'I'd like to speak to Policarpo Pillipopoli.'

'Master Policarpo is not in residence at the moment.'

'Oh? Where is he?'

'I am not in a position to say, sir. Perhaps you would like to speak to *il signor conte*?'

A count indeed, thought Peroni, a Communist count?

'*Il signor conte* is Master Policarpo's father,' the butler explained smoothly.

'Then perhaps I would like to see him,' said Peroni.

'If you'll come this way, sir.'

Peroni stepped inside. The furniture in the hall was discreetly and expensively contemporary. There was a Persian carpet on the floor as big as a football pitch and a picture on the wall, lit by a suffused glow, which Peroni didn't have time to study long enough to identify as Canaletto or school of.

The butler took him up in a gleaming carpeted lift to a first-floor corridor where he showed Peroni into a room, announcing that he would inform *il signore conte*.

It was a light-blue room. The furniture was light blue. The flowers, newly picked, were light blue. Even the pictures were dominated by light blue. There was an Angelo Dall'Oca Bianca, the nineteenth-century Veronese artist, of a Lake Garda scene and there was a pencil sketch of a girl with a light-blue wash by Renato Guttuso who was practically speaking the official artist of the Italian Communist Party.

Pondering the implications of this, Peroni found himself calculating that the two pictures together would be worth several million lire, and what was more he knew just how they could be carried to the right person in Switzerland, where –

Hastily the old Peroni was pounced on and silenced just as the door opened and *il signor conte* came in. He was a big man with a silvery-grey mane of hair and a handsome, slightly puffy, incisively lined face. He wore an open-necked silk shirt through which the silver hairs of his chest played like spring wavelets, and his trousers were dark crimson corduroy.

'Pillipopoli,' he introduced himself. 'Gino Pillipopoli.'

'Peroni,' said Peroni, a courteous senior police official who knew far more than he was saying. He took the outstretched hand and felt the palm sweaty with panic.

'I understand you are from the *Questura*?'

'That's right,' said Peroni quietly.

'Please sit down,' said Pillipopoli, motioning to an enormous powder-blue armchair. He was badly flustered by Peroni's failure to state his business, but he didn't dare enquire further.

'Thank you,' said Peroni, letting himself sink into the armchair. He accepted an English cigarette and some Chivas Regal whisky which Pillipopoli telephoned for. While they were waiting for it, *il signor conte*, with an obvious effort, made small talk. Had Peroni been in Verona for long? Did he like the city? Had he been able to admire the panels on the doors of San Zeno?

There was a knock at the door and the English butler appeared with a bottle of Chivas Regal on a silver tray with superb crystal tumblers which he put between the two of them.

'*Signor conte*,' he said in a respectful murmur as he was doing so, 'the costumes have arrived for the ball. The man is anxious that you and *Signorina* Francesca should try them on as soon as possible in case any adjustment should be required.'

'Ah, excellent,' said the Count. 'Kindly inform *Signorina* Francesca, and I will be down shortly.'

'Certainly, *signor conte*,' said the butler going out.

'The ball?' queried Peroni.

'Yes, it's an annual ball held on 1st August for certain of the older Veronese families. An outdated sort of affair, probably, but amusing. . . .' The speech trailed away.

'Of course,' said Peroni, letting the silence rest heavy. This was the second time the 1st August ball had been mentioned. He wondered whether it might be worth attending.

'How can I help you?' asked the count, unable to bear it any longer.

'Yes, of course,' said Peroni. 'Forgive me. I am anxious to contact your son, Policarpo, but I understand that he's not living here at the moment?'

'That is so.' Pillipopoli avoided Peroni's eyes.

'Perhaps you can tell me where I can get in touch with him?'

The Count downed his whisky. 'I'm afraid I don't know where you can get in touch with him.'

'Oh?'

'He left home nearly a year ago, and I've heard nothing of him since.'

'Under what circumstances did he leave home?'

The Count licked his fleshy lips. 'I'm sure there's nothing to it that could constitute a police matter,' he said. 'Policarpo is highly strung, and it would do more harm than good to run after him. Can we not leave it like that?'

Then Peroni saw that Pillipopoli had opened his jacket and was fingering a cheque book which projected from the inner pocket. So the incorruptible north was bribing the depraved south. Or trying to.

The depraved south eyed the cheque book hungrily. Well, why not? Bribes were part of a policeman's life, weren't they? And this particular one would be able to buy a lot of the things that Peroni liked best. Expensive English shoes and cases of Chivas Regal. So what about a couple of million for a start?

'Why did he leave home?'

It was as though a stranger had spoken. There were times like that when it was the *dott.* who seemed to be a hostile alien, intervening at crucial moments and spoiling everything. And at such times the old Peroni longed for nothing so much as to meet the *dott.* in some dark alley of his mind and finish with him for

52

ever. *Ciao*, Chivas Regal!

Pillipopoli sighed. The cheque book withdrew. 'He was going through a difficult period,' he said. 'I think he needed to be on his own for a while.'

'Did you discuss the matter before he left?'

'Not in any detail,' he said warily, his small eyes darting about as though searching for some way of escape.

'He just left?'

'You could say that.'

'Was he in any way upset?'

'A little emotionally disturbed – very natural at his age.'

'And yet you didn't inform the police?'

By now Pillipopoli was sizzling like a large trout on the grill. 'He is of age . . .'

'And you've heard nothing of him since?'

Pillipopoli contented himself with a defeated gesture.

'Didn't it occur to you that something might have happened to him?'

'No news is good news . . .' He said it wretchedly, then suddenly he could bear it no longer. 'Why are you making enquiries about Policarpo?'

'Before I answer that, may I see a photograph of him?'

Pillipopoli looked at him uncertainly, then got up and went out of the room. He returned a few minutes later with two photographs which he handed to Peroni in silence. One of them showed a young man wearing steel-rimmed spectacles with a dark, pretty girl. They had climbed up into the lower branches of an olive tree and were sitting there together, their arms about each other's shoulders. She was laughing, while his expression was serious. But the photograph wasn't detailed enough for comparison with the identikit.

'A friend of his?' said Peroni indicating the girl.

'His sister.'

The other photograph was a passport head and shoulders. Serious, stiff, embarrassed. Recalling the identikit feature by feature, Peroni decided that they might be the same person and they might not which was more or less how it always was with

53

identikit pictures. He opened the brief-case he was carrying, took out the identikit and put it before the Count.

'Could this be Policarpo?'

The Count looked alarmed. 'Possibly,' he admitted. 'I don't know. Why?'

'This is the identikit of a Red Brigade combatant.'

Pillipopoli went white. 'No,' he said. 'No . . .'

Peroni poured Chivas Regal for both of them and held out a glass to Pillipopoli who took it with shaking hands and drank it avidly, spilling yellow drops down his heavy jowls.

'Under the circumstances,' said Peroni, 'I think it would be best for everyone if you were to collaborate with us completely.'

Pillipopoli no longer offered any resistance. 'It's true,' he said, 'that Policarpo's political thinking had become – extremely radical. But he's a very sensitive boy, not ruthless at all. He isn't the sort of person you associate with the Red Brigade.'

What sort of person do you associate with the Red Brigade? Peroni wondered. They liked music too, and had mothers and sisters, and bit their nails.

'I remember when he was small,' Pillipopoli was going on, almost pleading a case by now, 'one day my wife – she's dead now – was killing some insects with a spray when he came into the room. The sight of them curling up and jerking made him physically sick. Somebody like that doesn't join the Red Brigade!'

'Then what else might he be doing?' asked Peroni.

Pillipopoli raised his arms and then dropped them helplessly.

'What about his friends?'

'He has never easily formed friendships.'

'Girls?'

'None that I know of.'

'You say his political thinking was extremely radical. How did that come about?'

'Well, as you know,' said Pillipopoli, 'I am an active member of the Italian Communist Party.'

Peroni wondered why he should know, but let it pass.

'The Pillipopolis have always been politically committed and still are. But my children seemed to be the exception to this rule. Apolitical, I considered them. But that changed when Policarpo went to the university here in Verona. He was indoctrinated. All the family passion for politics was roused in him, but unfortunately in the wrong cause. He adopted militant, extra-parliamentary Communism which is, of course, a totally different thing from true Communism and, indeed, opposed to it. We had various discussions about politics. Heated discussions. It was following one of these that he – walked out of the house.'

'Do you know the Piantaleone family?' asked Peroni.

An expression he couldn't identify – bewilderment? Surprise? Anxiety? – appeared on the Count's face and then, as quickly, left it. 'Distantly,' said Pillipopoli, 'though it would be more true to say I know of them.'

Then, violently, a new thought struck him. 'You're not suggesting that Policarpo was involved in that?'

Peroni was certain that the mention of the Piantaleones had evoked some more distant emotion in the Count *before* Policarpo's possible involvement in the General's death had occurred to him.

'I've no idea,' he said truthfully. 'We're just trying to trace anybody who may have connections with the Red Brigade.'

The Count nodded dumbly.

'You said it was your daughter in the photograph just now,' Peroni went on. 'Does she live here with you?'

The Count nodded again.

'Do any other members of your family live here?'

'No, I've lived here alone with the children since my wife died.'

'Then perhaps I might have a word with your daughter?'

'Of course.' Pillipopoli rose. 'When you've finished just touch that bell and I'll show you out.' He moved heavily towards the door.

'Was there any reason,' said Peroni, halting him, 'for calling your son Policarpo?'

'It's an old family name,' said Pillipopoli colourlessly and went out.

As soon as the girl came in Peroni recognised her as the one in the photograph. She was about seventeen and wore a tartan kilt which he identified as genuine Scotch House.

Instantly he became his newspaper profile and, holding out his hand, he gave her the warm southern smile which was of such deadly infallibility.

To his consternation it didn't work.

'Good morning,' she said, taking his hand and shaking it politely, but without a trace of passionate or even timid melting.

'Good morning, *signorina*,' he said.

She sat modestly as though she didn't want the flow of her body to give too much away. Peroni watched her with a sense of frustrated lechery and then sat himself.

'May I have your name please, *signorina*?'

'Francesca Pillipopoli.'

He was going to say that Francesca was a pretty name, but decided against it. 'Have you any notion,' he said instead, 'about your brother's whereabouts?'

'No,' she said sadly. 'No.'

'Are you close, you and your brother – does he tell you things?'

'He used to, before this.'

'Did he tell you he was going away?'

'No.'

'Have you heard anything of him since he left? A telephone call? A message through friends?'

'No,' sadly again. 'Nothing.'

'I understand that your brother had extreme political views?'

'Yes. He got them from people at the university. They changed him.'

'How do you mean?'

'They made him a different person – not my brother any longer. It was because of politics that he went away. He and Pappa used to quarrel.'

56

'Did he ever talk to you about politics?'

'No.'

'*Signorina*,' said Peroni, 'do you know the Piantaleone family?'

This time he had the disconcerting feeling of having struck the bull's eye without knowing what the target was. For a split second Francesca looked terrified. It passed immediately, but it had been there.

'No,' she said quickly. 'That's to say I've heard the name. It's the General who was – ' Then she made the same inference her father had done and her large, dark eyes widened with horror. 'You don't think – ' she said.

'I don't think anything, *signorina*,' said Peroni, 'I'm just trying to find out.' He took out the identikit picture. 'Might this be a picture of your brother?'

She studied it carefully. 'I suppose it might be,' she said. 'Who is it?'

'It's an identikit of a Red Brigade combatant.'

'Oh, no!' she said. 'Policarpo wouldn't do that! He may have strange political ideas, but he's far too gentle a person to join anything as horrible as the Red Brigade!'

'Then knowing him as you do, *signorina*, can you think of some other explanation for his disappearance?'

'I think he fell in love,' she said slowly.

'Do you know any of his girl friends?'

'No – he's always been very shy with girls. But that might account for his suddenly going off without saying anything to anybody.'

'Don't you think he would have told you?'

'You never know in love,' she said. 'People in love do the most unexpected things.'

Driving back to the *Questura* in his red Alfa, Peroni pondered Francesca's theory. He was inclined to agree, but with a difference. Very possibly Policarpo had fallen in love, but not with a person. With an idea. The sort of idea that makes its worshippers shoot anyone who doesn't share it.

But there was something else which interested him – the expression which had appeared on Francesca's face and on her father's at the mention of the Piantaleone family. In both cases it had appeared *before they had made the connection with Policarpo*. This puzzled Peroni.

Back at the *Questura* he was told that *dott.* Guerra was waiting for him.

'A deputy public prosecutor has been appointed by the magistrature, *dottore*,' said Guerra. '*Dott.* Spinelli.' Spinelli was one of the most awkward magistrates in Verona, arrogant and hostile towards the police. His appointment would make things even more difficult. 'Any further developments, *dottore*?'

Peroni told him of the identikit lead to the Pillipopoli family, of his talks with the count and Francesca and of his various deductions.

'The Pillipopolis,' said Guerra. 'Hum. A large family with branches spread throughout the city.'

'The same sort of family as the Piantaleones,' said Peroni.

'Precisely, *dottore*. It's something of a coincidence, isn't it? Always assuming, of course, that this Policarpo and the subject of the identikit are one.'

'And both families are attending a costume ball tomorrow night.'

'The annual ball of the Veronese nobility.'

'I thought it might perhaps be useful if I were to attend it.'

Guerra looked quickly at him, and Peroni wondered whether there was a sparkle of dry amusement in his eyes. If so it didn't appear in his speech. 'It might indeed,' he said. 'It so happens that I am invited in my official capacity and you could perfectly well go as my representative.' He studied Peroni for a second as though assessing his capacity for undergoing a major ordeal. 'You'll have to wear costume,' he said at length.

'In that case I'll wear costume, *dottore*,' said Peroni.

He sounded stoical, but he was secretly rather pleased at the prospect.

'The breeches are too tight,' said Peroni.

'You should eat less pasta,' said his sister Assunta, unkindly.

'I haven't got a stomach,' said Peroni, looking carefully in the mirror.

'Not yet,' said Assunta. 'Put on the coat and wig and we'll get the overall effect.'

The overall effect was good. Anna Maria said that he looked beautiful and Assunta grunted approval. Peroni thought he would like to have lived in the eighteenth century. There would have been no police to speak of for him to work with, but he could probably have done some spying for the various European powers.

'So really the whole business is quite straightforward now,' said his brother-in-law Giorgio. 'The Red Brigade shot him and that's all there is to it. Glass of wine, Achille?'

'Thank you, Giorgio.'

'Put it on the table, Uncle Achille,' said Anna Maria. 'Otherwise you'll spill it all down this lovely red satin.'

'I don't know if it is quite as straightforward as all that,' said Peroni, doing as he was told. 'For a start there's the odd business of General Piantaleone pretending to go up to his estate in Rosaro every day. Where was he?'

'With a woman,' said Assunta pragmatically. 'Hand me the pins, Anna Maria, please.'

'Then there's the matter of Loris saying that *he* was visiting agricultural machinery factories in Milan on the day his father disappeared when he obviously wasn't.'

Stefano looked as though he were pondering a chess problem.

'I am inclined to agree with you,' he said. 'There is something distinctly questionable about that family.'

'Just the phrase I was looking for,' said Peroni. 'Ow!'

'I'm sorry, Achille, but you must keep still!'

'I can't see the Red Brigade bothering to kill an old man who was three-quarters senile,' said Anna Maria.

'But it was what he stood for,' said Giorgio.

'Oh, nonsense, Pappa!' said Anna Maria. 'I don't believe in all this standing-for stuff! It doesn't *mean* anything. The Red Brigade is very wicked, but it doesn't kill without a good reason.'

'What about the communiqué?' asked Stefano, as though he were giving check, but by no means mate.

'Oh, that could have been forged,' said Anna Maria. 'Couldn't it, Uncle Achille?'

'Well, it seems genuine enough,' said Peroni, 'but we can't be a hundred per cent certain. It wasn't the same typewriter as any of the ones they've used before, but that doesn't mean a great deal. It was the same make, though – an IBM.'

'What about this Policarpo person you were going to visit last night?' asked Stefano. 'I was extremely eager to hear about that, but unfortunately I was in bed when you returned.' He looked at his mother with owlish reproach.

'I was coming to that,' said Peroni. 'Policarpo Pillipopoli walked out of his home nearly a year ago and has not been heard of since.'

'Significant,' said Stefano.

'What's more,' Peroni went on, 'the Pillipopolis are all Communists – ordinary, respectable ones, though – while Policarpo seems to have been brain-washed by extreme, extra-parliamentary Communists while he was at university.'

'Highly significant,' said Stefano.

'And his father – a rather flabby, rhetorical-looking count – tried to bribe me to forget the whole business.'

'You didn't accept?' said Assunta alarmed.

'No, no,' said Peroni. 'The idea did occur to me, but I dismissed it.'

60

'So,' said Stefano, 'Policarpo Pillipopoli would appear to be our outstanding suspect?'

'You could say that,' Peroni agreed.

'Lift up your right arm, Uncle Achille.'

'I suppose you're looking for him?' said Stefano.

'Well, not personally,' said Peroni. 'I'm too important. A functionary of the DIGOS is trying to trace him.'

'What line are you taking?'

'Well, I'm going to this ball, aren't I?'

'I'm inclined to question the utility of that,' said Stefano.

'Oh, stop being so calculating, Stefano!' said Anna Maria. 'Uncle Achille is using his instinct, and Uncle Achille's instinct is unerring. That's what the newspapers say.'

'Put up your left arm, Achille.'

'I'm suspicious of instinct,' said Stefano. 'One thing, however, seems to me of vital importance.'

'What's that?' asked Peroni.

'You must find out what General Piantaleone was doing when he was meant to be up at Rosaro.'

'I entirely agree with Stefano about that,' said Anna Maria. 'He may have been killed by the Red Brigade and he may not. But there's something very suspicious about that family altogether. About both families in fact. I think we need to know a great deal more about them.'

'I'll do my best,' said Peroni.

'There, that's done,' said Assunta, standing back and eyeing her brother critically. 'Take it off now, Achille, or you'll get it all splashed with meat sauce.'

Patti admired herself in the full-length mirror of her cupboard. The high, powdered wig, the full powder-blue satin dress, tight at the waist, discreetly low-cut at the neck and at the hem revealing a tantalizing hint of ankle when correctly swirled – they were far from her usual style, but she was bound to admit they suited her.

She looked at her watch. Nearly nine o'clock. It was time for Gabriele to collect her. Of course, he was late as usual – you had to discount at least an hour when you were dealing with Gabriele. She sighed. If it had been anybody else, she wouldn't have put up with it.

She went into her small, expensive living-room with its 1930s posters, Swedish furniture and slim, stream-lined television set. The room also contained a large, glass tank in which some oily dark-blue liquid tossed slowly backwards and forwards for ever like a miniature, sunless sea. It was a present from Gabriele, and like everything from Gabriele it left her in two frames of mind. There were times when she thought she hated it, rolling hypnotically backwards and forwards, the curve of each wave identical to the one before. But there were other times when it fascinated her, and she could sit there for long minutes watching the slow pitch and toss. It was wonderful when she had a headache. She watched it now, wondering, as she did every time, why Gabriele had chosen just that, how much he had paid for it (a lot certainly) and where he had got the money from. Then she blinked herself free of it and went to make an American Martini.

She had time to drink two glasses before the doorbell rang. It was Gabriele looking just like a Goldoni hero in his eighteenth-century costume.

'We both look straight out of a Goldoni comedy,' he said with the disconcerting way he had of seeming to read her mind. 'Florindo and Rosaura. What's that – Martini? It's hardly in keeping, but I'll have some just the same if I may.'

She poured him a glass. 'Oughtn't we to be going?'

'No hurry. It's really a very dull affair, you know. It's just that people think it's glamorous because of all the coloured lights and free champagne.'

'Why do you go then?'

'It can be very useful. With all the nobility of Verona gathered together in a garden full of bowers and glades and summer houses, there's no end to what one can pick up. It was the year of my first communion when I first overheard something at the August ball. It got me a thousand lire, I remember, and not a year has gone by since without my picking up something or other. Prices have gone up, of course.'

'You are frightful.'

'What about you?'

'Well, at least I don't brag about it.'

'Hypocrisy – that makes it even worse.' He looked at her for a second with the expression of a little boy who knows he is going to shake you and wants to make the most of it. 'But this year,' he said, 'I shan't dissipate my energy on small stuff. This year I'm going to save it for something important.'

'What?' she said quickly, leaning towards him excitedly, her breasts straining in the powder-blue satin which only partly concealed them.

Again he paused for effect. 'It so happens,' he said, 'that I've found out where Uncle Orazio went on the night he disappeared.'

She gave a low whistle. 'Somewhere interesting?' They both attached the same significance to the word; for them it meant not so much curious as susceptible of gain.

'Very interesting, I should say.'

'How clever you are, Gabriele, and however did you find out?'

'Well, you know how I always like to glance at the post before the others see it. It's usually very dull, but every so often there's something which rewards one's perseverance. Today was one of those days. There was what you might call a letter from the dead.'

'A letter from the dead?'

'It was addressed to Loris, and I recognized the handwriting at once. It was heroic Uncle Orazio's.'

'Written before – ?'

'Exactly. The old man had gone very badly at the edges, as you know, but he was still cautious. Just in case anything happened he thought that Loris should know where he'd gone. So he wrote him a letter.'

'Why didn't he just leave it in the house?'

'Ironically enough, I imagine, because he didn't want me to get hold of it. He thought the post would be safer.'

'But it took five days!'

'Patti, my treasure, I can see you don't correspond. And as for Uncle Orazio, he lived in a past where Mussolini made the trains, and consequently the posts, run on time. Five days is nothing for the Italian post in the days of Christian Democracy.'

'All right. But tell me – where did your heroic Uncle Orazio go?'

Gabriele took a letter from the pocket of his long-tailed velvet coat. 'Read it for yourself,' he said, 'I've steamed it open.'

She took out the letter and read it slowly. When she had finished she whistled again. 'You're right,' she said, 'it is very interesting indeed.' Then suddenly she looked alarmed. 'But it's dangerous, Gabriele,' she added.

'I know,' he said, 'I've already thought of that.'

'Well?'

'Tomorrow morning – no, not tomorrow, it's Sunday – on Monday morning I'll put this letter in with the post. When Loris sees it, I know just what he'll do. He's thirsting for revenge like a character in a Greek tragedy – there's nothing Goldonian about him – and he'll plunge straight off there. I'll keep an eye on things from a safe and discreet distance. That way he runs all the risks and, with a bit of luck, I find out who's behind all this.'

'You *are* clever, Gabriele,' she said, her eyes heavy with invitation.

'I know,' he said, enthusiastically moving in to accept the invitation.

It would have come as a surprise to most of the Veronese if they could have seen the grounds in which the annual 1st of August costume ball was held. They were the property of a noble family who threw them open no more than once a year, and then only to a select number of their peers. Hidden from the public gaze at the front by the family palace and on either side by high walls, they stretched down to a terrace overlooking the river. Many generations of the family had spent their childhood here, playing endless games of hide and seek in the unkempt

64

walks and overgrown avenues, discovering mysterious worlds unknown to adult view.

As Gabriele and Patti came into these grounds through the house they saw a long table with a gleaming white cloth bearing a bewildering variety of snacks and drinks. Coloured lanterns were hanging from the trees, white-coated waiters walked among the guests offering trays of champagne, and somewhere in the distance a café-orchestra played tinkling, sugary tunes. Everywhere creaking dowagers, counts, barons and marquises of a dead chivalry communicated together like grave birds, all dressed as though they had stepped from a Guardi or Canaletto canvas, while further away towards the river could be heard the excited screams of laughter of the *jeunesse dorée*.

As the champagne began to mingle amicably with the martinis, Patti decided she was going to enjoy herself. Maybe it was a bore if you'd been coming all your life, like Gabriele, but when you saw it for the first time it was quite delightful. And if on top of that one was accompanied by the most desirable man in Verona . . .

Just as she was thinking this Patti was suddenly made to wonder, for the first time since she had known him, whether Gabriele really held that title after all. For her eyes had fallen on another man who, to say the very least, ran him closely for it. He was a southerner and looked like an eighteenth-century rake at the peak of his career. She wondered why on earth he was unaccompanied.

'Who's that?' she asked Gabriele.

He gave her one of his crooked smiles. 'Do you want to be introduced? Be careful, though. There's more to him than that irresistible southern profile. He's the policeman investigating Uncle Orazio's death.'

'Introduce me.'

'Good evening, *commissario*,' said Gabriele. 'May I introduce an admirer of yours?'

Patti felt her hand taken in a pleasantly virile grip as the policeman said his surname. Peroni. She murmured hers, accompanying it with what was intended to be a dazzling smile.

Certainly, she reflected, examining him carefully, she was not a girl to consort with policemen. All the same there was something oddly equivocal about this particular policeman which she felt strongly, but couldn't quite define. It wasn't exactly that he gave the impression of being corrupt, but rather you felt you might expect anything from him, even the most unexpected and un-policeman-like actions.

'Alone, *commissario*?' Gabriele was saying. 'Or are you too busy investigating to be bothered with women?'

'I could never be too busy for one such as the *signorina*,' said the *commissario*.

Suddenly Patti felt herself torn between the two. She wanted to accept the policeman's implicit invitation more than she had ever wanted anything, and yet she was frightened. She had always considered Gabriele dangerous, but this *commissario* was more so. It was therefore a relief as well as a disappointment when she felt Gabriele's hand touching her arm, re-claiming her.

'We must find somebody for you,' said Gabriele. '*Noblesse oblige*. Let's set about it straight away, Patti. *Arrivederci, commissario!*'

'*Arrivederci*,' said the southern policeman politely.

As she moved off with Gabriele, Patti felt she had missed the chance of a lifetime.

Peroni looked after the long-legged, expensive-looking girl with honey-coloured hair and wondered if he had been right to let the moment pass. He could easily have taken her from Gabriele, and Gabriele would have deserved it. But the *commissario* within reminded him that he was on duty, and he turned his thoughts reluctantly to business.

Just what business he didn't know, but he felt surer than ever that at this exclusive gathering of the Veronese nobility he could learn something about the strange half-world in which the Piantaleones and the Pillipopolis lived and, perhaps in consequence, something about the General's death.

As he moved restlessly from group to group an instinct,

sensitised years ago in Naples, told him something was about to happen.

He saw Gino Pillipopoli, magnificent in a dark-green velvet frock-coat with a laced handkerchief like frothed snow. A pure Goldoni aristocrat. What made such a man a Communist? Idealism? The Count didn't look idealistic, and anyway there were no ideals left in the Italian Communist Party, as power-hungry and self-seeking as all the others. Interest? Hardly. If the Communists came to power it would mean goodbye to pale-blue drawing-rooms and smooth English lawns. What then? The air of Italy which makes men mad, Peroni decided, mentally excluding himself.

Pillipopoli must have felt Peroni's scrutiny, for he turned uncertainly, recognised Peroni with a slight but visible start, and then gave him a smile and a little bow which were imbued with the embarrassment of their earlier interview. He turned away again as quickly as he politely could.

A moment later it was Peroni's turn to feel he was being looked at. He ignored the impression for a while, then took advantage of one of the brightly lit windows of the house which he used as a mirror. In it he saw Loris Piantaleone, and even the reflection showed him clearly that he had an enemy. He wondered what Loris was doing there. Searching for his father's murderer among the Veronese nobility?

Looking about him, Peroni came to recognise the classical Roman Piantaleone profile in a number of people and felt that he was acquiring an eye for the family characteristics. The Piantaleones tended to be darker than most northerners; their men were often good-looking while the women went scrawny in middle age.

He saw the Pillipopoli girl, Francesca, looking charming in her costume. She was just as Goldonian as her father, and Peroni thought that she resembled one of those delightful little maidservants who dart about in his plays like birds.

It was then that Peroni heard a Neapolitan accent somewhere behind him. The voice was a girl's, and she was saying, 'Oh yes, we do Spanish, too. We've got four languages – English, French, German and Spanish.'

What could a Neapolitan be doing at this exclusive Veronese gathering? He looked where the voice was coming from and saw a girl with high cheek-bones in a thin face with large dark eyes. She had black hair which poured quite straight down her back. Like everybody else she was wearing eighteenth-century costume, but somehow she didn't evoke the lace-cuffs world of Goldoni's nobility. Something about her made Peroni think rather of a Goldoni actress. She was talking to an elderly lady with a Piantaleone profile.

'How interesting,' said the old lady with a clear Veneto intonation, 'I must certainly tell my niece about it.'

'Tell her to give me a ring if she wants to know some more.'

'I will indeed. How very kind of you.'

The conversation ended and Peroni, ignoring a protest from the *commissario* within, went up to the girl. 'You're Neapolitan,' he said.

She looked at him with surprise, and then assumed the expression of a girl who doesn't intend to be picked up. 'As a matter of fact I am,' she said, and turned to move away.

'Forgive me,' said Peroni, moving beside her. 'It's just that I'm from Naples myself, and unexpectedly hearing you just now in the midst of all these northern accents – well, it conjured up visions of the Vomero and Marechiaro and Posillipo and Vesuvius across the gulf. I had to introduce myself.'

She smiled, at least partly won over by the argument, and accepted his outstretched hand. 'What brings you up here?' she asked.

'The same as brings most southerners north,' he said. 'My work. What about you?'

'My parents died a few years ago,' she said, 'and there wasn't much for me in Naples, so as I have some relatives here – the Piantaleones – I came up to Verona.'

Mentally Peroni whistled – a Neapolitan connection. Could this be what he was looking for?

'Uncle Orazio,' the girl went on, ' – at least I called him uncle,

68

though he wasn't really as close as that – General Piantaleone –
you've probably heard of his death – ' Suddenly her voice broke
and she turned away.

'Yes,' said Peroni. 'Yes.'

She made an obvious effort to control herself, and then continued in a steadier voice. 'Well, he was very good to me. He
helped me to start life here, got a flat for me, paid for me to
take an interpreter's course – '

'Ah, yes,' said Peroni, speaking his own highly individual
English, 'it is of this you are speaking when I hear your accent.
You are studying English, true?'

'Yes, of course,' she said, also in English. 'First and foremost.
One can do nothing without English these days.'

Her accent, he realised with chagrin, was almost perfect.

A waiter passed by with a tray of champagne glasses. 'Can
I get you a drink?' said Peroni, reverting to Italian.

'Thank you.'

'Chin-chin,' said Peroni when they had their glasses.

'Chin-chin,' said the girl gravely.

Just at that moment Count Gino Pillipopoli passed by and
noticed Peroni just too late to avoid him. 'Good evening,
commissario,' he said.

'Good evening,' said Peroni.

'*Commissario!*' echoed the girl, her eyes enormous, when
Pillipopoli had gone.

'Yes,' said Peroni. 'Does it matter?'

'Of course not,' said the girl. 'It was just a surprise.'

'And since you know,' Peroni went on, 'then perhaps I should
add that I'm in charge of the investigation into your uncle's
death.'

'Oh.' She looked at him in awe. 'Well, I hope you catch them
– whoever they are. Uncle Orazio was such a *good* person – he
didn't deserve to die like that.'

'I understand,' said Peroni, feeling his way delicately, 'that
he hadn't been entirely himself lately.'

'So you know about that?'

'Yes – something.'

69

'It was very sad. But it doesn't alter what he was before.'

'No, no – of course not.' Suddenly Peroni felt he wanted to hold her, and the music gave him an excuse. 'Shall we dance?'

'If you like.'

'What's your name?' asked Peroni when they had been dancing for a minute.

'Regina.'

'I like that.'

'And yours?'

'Achille.'

'That's nice, too, though I suppose you get jokes about your heel.'

'It does happen.'

For a while they danced in silence, then Regina said, 'It is strange . . .'

'What?'

'This little world – ' She gestured at the Canaletto scene about them.

'It's your world, isn't it?' said Peroni. 'You're a Piantaleone.'

'Only a distant poor relation. I don't feel part of all this. I come from outside like you.'

He liked the note of affinity. 'You're right,' he said after a second, 'it is a strange world. It's intrigued me ever since I became involved with it. That's why I came tonight. I wanted to know more about these people.'

The music finished and they went to sit under a tree. Regina seemed to be pondering something. 'I think,' she said at last, 'that the important thing about all of them is the past.'

'The past?'

'Uh-hum. They're dominated by it. In the past they were a vital and eminent part of the whole world order. Now they're an anachronism. But their background is too long and too compromising to be shaken off in a couple of generations. They can't just become ordinary *Signor* Rossi or *Signor* Verdi.'

Peroni found himself absorbed in her reasoning. This was what he had come to find out.

'Go on.'

'Well, it's as though they felt the presence of their ancestors, reproving them for not being great any longer, urging them to recover their greatness – which, of course, they can't do. They're obsessed by the dead.'

'Tell me some more.'

'I can't. Really I can't. If you want to know more, the person to talk to is the Dowager Countess Augusta.'

'The Dowager Countess Augusta?' repeated Peroni, puzzled.

'Yes. She knows more about these people and their past than anybody else.'

'But who is she?'

'She's the mother of somebody called Count Gino Pillipopoli. Oh, but of course you know him – he's the one that went by just now.'

This took Peroni off balance. The mother of the millionaire Communist. And the grandmother of pretty little Francesca and her brother, the suspected Red Brigade combatant, Policarpo.

'Do you know the Pillipopolis?' he asked.

'I don't exactly know them. I know of them. But the Dowager Countess is a sort of legend. I don't think she's been out of doors for years, but all the Veronese nobility know of her.'

'Where does she live?'

'With her son, Count Gino.'

This was another surprise. Pillipopoli had stated clearly that he had lived alone with his two children since the death of his wife. Why should he lie about his mother?

'I'll take your advice,' said Peroni, 'I'll go and see the Dowager Countess Augusta.'

'I'm sure you'll find her very interesting,' said Regina.

Peroni stayed late at the ball, and then drove Regina back to the riverside block of flats she gave him for her address.

'Can I see you again?' he asked.

'Yes,' she said, 'I think I would like that.'

'When?'

'Let me fix it, will you? The Piantaleones are a gossipy lot,

71

and with you involved in the business of Uncle Orazio, it might be best if we were just a little discreet. Umm?'

'Yes, of course,' said Peroni.

'Give me your telephone number – tell me when I can call you. . . .'

He wrote the number of the *Questura* and his own internal extension, together with the number of the flat. She folded the paper carefully and put it in her bag. Then she gave him her hand.

'Good night, Achille.'

It was a warm, firm handshake. He thought it promised more to come.

'Good night, Regina.'

He drove back to the *Questura* where there was work to be done, and when he had finished he spent what was left of the night in his office with his head on the desk, dreaming fitfully of Regina and the Dowager Countess Augusta who, in his sleeping fancy, took the form of an ancient fortune-teller staring into a crystal ball in which numberless dead Pillipopolis and Piantaleones whirled away into space like gigantic snowflakes on a high wind.

There were now two divergent lines of speculation in the Pianta-leone affair. One concerned Policarpo Pillipopoli, presumed Red Brigade combatant and suspected killer of General Orazio Piantaleone. The other involved Loris Piantaleone, the General's obtuse and fanatical elder son. Both were being dealt with. A round-the-clock watch was being kept on Loris – who scarcely moved from the Piantaleone home, however – and the DIGOS were doing all they could to trace Policarpo.

Neither of these lines of speculation were uppermost in Peroni's mind when he woke to find a beautiful Sunday morning clamouring outside his office window. His thoughts were occupied with the problem of the Dowager Countess Augusta raised by Regina the previous evening. This problem followed him down the street and into the bar where he had coffee, and then into the barber's. It receded briefly while he looked through the papers in the barber's chair and noted with satisfaction that he was still occupying the front pages, though tending to drop towards the bottom half. From a news point of view the affair needed fresh momentum. But even Peroni could not have envisaged the development that lay just around the corner.

Then when the barber started to pat on after-shave lotion (an English brand kept especially for him), the problem of the Dowager Countess presented itself with renewed urgency. He decided to deal with it immediately.

All about him as he drove to the Pillipopoli home, Verona was springing with the new day. The river was shining in the sun. Early, inexorable tourists were setting off in search of culture and snapshots. Waiters flicked napkins and brushed up basic phrases of enticement in English, French and German. The

73

pigeons set about their daily summer routine of gorging and posing for photographs. The churches, like venerable dowagers, composed themselves to receive.

At the Pillipopoli home Peroni was shown once more into the blue drawing-room where he was joined a moment later by the Count who looked both irritable and worried.

'Why didn't you mention that your mother was living here?' Peroni asked.

Pillipopoli flushed lobster red. 'My mother is a very old lady,' he stammered. 'She has nothing to do with the disappearance of my son and besides – well, to tell you the truth, she is not entirely in her right mind.'

Peroni's resolve to confront the Dowager Countess wavered slightly. He had an almost superstitious horror of mental illness. But the *dott.* kept up outward appearances. 'I should like to speak with her,' he said.

'It really can serve no purpose,' blustered the Count. Then, as Peroni continued to look inflexibly conscientious, his resistance crumbled. 'Please come with me,' he said heavily.

They went out of the blue drawing-room and into the gleaming lift which carried them in complete silence up to the third floor. Here there was a stairway with a door at the head of it on which Pillipopoli knocked when they had mounted.

The door was opened by a wiry woman in her sixties, dressed entirely in black and with her white hair tied into a bun.

'Good morning, nannie,' said the Count unexpectedly. 'Is Mamma up?'

'Yes, sir,' said the nannie, eyeing Peroni uneasily.

'This gentleman would like a word with her.'

'But – ' the nannie started to object.

'This gentleman is from the police.'

The nannie stepped reluctantly aside.

'I'll leave you,' said Pillipopoli, turning to go down the stairs. Peroni wished he wouldn't, but didn't see how he could very well detain him.

'If you'd step in here, sir,' said the nannie.

In Peroni's ears the phrase had an unpleasant ring of the

74

spider's invitation to the fly. He stepped in and found himself in a dark sort of hall. He felt as though he had passed into a different world.

'If you'll wait in here,' said the nannie, preceding him into a pitch-dark room leading off the hall where she turned on a lamp.

Peroni went in reluctantly and heard the door close softly behind him. By the light of the lamp he saw that the room was crowded with furniture. There were glass cases filled with porcelain statues of birds and animals, shepherds and shepherd-esses, fruit and flowers. Museum-pieces and worth a fortune, but his normal reaction was deadened by an acute sense of apprehension. He didn't relish the prospect of being assailed, physically or even verbally, by a crazy old woman, so now, as he waited, instead of letting his mind dwell on illicit thoughts concerning the porcelain, he murmured a quick invocation to St Janarius, the patron saint of Naples.

The door opened and he watched nervously as a wheel chair was pushed through it.

The occupant of the chair was an old woman, so small and frail that Peroni marvelled she should have produced so large a son as Gino Pillipopoli. But though age had shrunk her body, it had not affected her spirit which had a quality he recognised instantly as regal. The slightly hooked nose, the bird-like eyes exceedingly bright.

'Good morning!' she said and the voice, though quavering, had command in it.

'Good morning,' said Peroni, going to her and feeling greatly reassured.

She held out her hand, and he understood at once that it was for kissing not shaking. He kissed it.

'Leave us, Trombetti!' the Dowager Countess Augusta commanded.

The nannie bobbed and went out.

'Please be seated,' said the Dowager Countess. 'I understand you are from the Police Force. I suppose that is all right now-adays. From your appearance I observe that you are also from the South.' Key words she pronounced with audible capital

75

letters. 'What part of the South?'

'Naples.'

'We have many connections in Naples. Prince Tagliabosco, the old Princess Pasquini, the Marquis Bagnacampi. You know them? No, I suppose not. Not the same Circle, though you are Exceedingly Good Looking. How long have you been in Verona?'

'Rather over a year.'

'You like Our City?' She made it sound as though it really were hers.

'I'm devoted to it,' said Peroni. It wasn't true, but to say otherwise would have been *lèse-majesté*.

'It has been Our Family Home for as far back as it is possible to trace. Indeed, I daresay you have heard of Our Ancestors.'

'Not that I know of,' said Peroni politely, now quite at his ease and wondering why on earth Pillipopoli had said his mother was not in her right mind. She was obviously perfectly sane.

'Oh, yes you have!' she said sharply. 'The Capulets. There was a gel in the Family called Juliet who had an Unfortunate Affair. It caused quite a stir at the time. Surely you have heard of That?'

Now Peroni understood what Pillipopoli had meant.

Eyeing the Dowager Countess Augusta nervously, he realised that her imperious bright eyes were demanding comment. 'I had always thought,' he managed at last, 'that the story was invented by Shakespeare.'

'Rubbish! It is little good being in the Police Force if you don't know any better than That! Our Ancestors, the Capulets, are Perfectly Verifiable Historical Figures, every bit as real as *Signor* Shakespeare himself – indeed, considerably more so, as I understand there is some doubt as to his very existence. There is no such doubt about my Ancestors. They were living in the City at least three hundred years before the Alleged English Poet got hold of his somewhat garbled version of Facts which were anyway a Strictly Confidential Family Matter.'

'I didn't know,' said Peroni weakly.

'Indeed,' the Dowager Countess swept on, taking no notice of him, 'The Matter would never have come out at all if it hadn't been for that Imbecillic Archer.'

'What imbecillic archer?' asked Peroni.

'Pellegrino, the man's name was,' she said, adding with contempt, 'A Mercenary. He had gone to fight in Friuli under the command of Count Luigi da Porto, an Excellent Man, I understand, and a Valorous Soldier who laboured, however, under the Melancholy Delusion that he had a Vocation for Literature – not the first time, I may say, that such a Delusion has been the cause of Trouble.'

'How was that?' asked Peroni, beginning to be caught up in it in spite of himself.

'Because he Wrote It All Down, of course!'

'Wrote what all down?' asked Peroni.

'My dear man,' said the Dowager Countess Augusta, 'I can see I shall have to Start at the Beginning.'

'It would be very kind,' said Peroni with a belated bid at Neapolitan charm.

'When the man Pellegrino served under Count Luigi he blabbed out the story of Our Unfortunate Family Scandal which, being Veronese by origin unlike the Count, he had learned during his childhood. Shortly after that the Count was wounded in battle and was obliged to retire from Military Activities. In retirement, having nothing better to do, he decided to exercise what he considered to be his Literary Gift. And the first subject that came into his head was the story told him by that same Veronese archer, Pellegrino. And he wrote it down, which might be considered Behaviour somewhat Discourteous towards my Family in a person otherwise tolerably Well-bred. It became known throughout Italy and then throughout the World.'

'And the other family?' said Peroni as an awful suspicion leapt fully formed into his mind. 'The one from which Romeo sprang?'

'The Montagus,' said the Dowager Countess. 'Highly Unpleasant People, Violently Disposed and Crude in their Manners. They were Hunted out of the Town, you know, in the early thirteenth century, and if they hadn't come back The Whole

Unfortunate Business would never have occurred. But the Montagus are like Weeds, however much you uproot them, they always Spring Up again. Back they came. They were chased out again in 1324, but of course it was Too Late by then as It had already happened. The very fact, however, that they were banished for a second time shows quite clearly that it was All Their Fault.'

'But what I mean is,' said Peroni, 'do they have any descendants alive today?'

'Of course they do. The Piantaleones they are called now. And I may say the centuries have done Nothing to improve them!'

'But isn't seven hundred years rather a long way to trace back one's family tree?' asked Peroni as delicately as he could.

'Nonsense!' she said, 'I have many acquaintances amongst the Nobility who can trace their origins back to the Emperor Charlemagne, and that is all of five hundred years earlier. Besides, in the unlikely event of any member of this Family forgetting Our Past, the Feud would quickly remind him of it again.'

'The Feud?' said Peroni, unconsciously echoing her capital letter. 'Do you mean that it continued?'

'Well, of course – the Montagus, or the Piantaleones as they now call themselves, have always seen to That!'

'But I seem to remember something about a reconciliation and – what was it? – statues in pure gold?'

'Sentimental Piffle!' snapped the Dowager Countess, 'invented by *Signor* Shakespeare! Can you imagine how much gold it would require to erect one, let alone two, statues in pure gold?' Peroni felt bound to concede her a point. 'There was some Formal Reconciliation for the sake of the Authorities,' she went on, 'but can you imagine the Montagus respecting it? Remember, too, that our Poor Tybalt had been Murdered by Them! Would you expect us to leave that Unrevenged? And Juliet – the Poor Gel not yet Cold in her Tomb – could we Forget Her?'

'But she killed herself,' objected Peroni.

'Because she was Driven To It! If that Worthless Young Cad Romeo hadn't Seduced her, she would have got peacefully married to Paris and the whole Unfortunate Business wouldn't have occurred!'

'But she loved him – Romeo I mean – didn't she?'

'Love!' the Dowager Countess Augusta snorted, 'at the age of fourteen what do you expect a Gel to know about Love? Her Head was Turned, that's what it was!'

'And didn't he love her?'

'Ha!' The exclamation contained a world of scorn. 'We all know very well what that sort of love means! No, no, my dear man, the whole thing was a Quite Unforgivable Slur on our Family Honour, and if he hadn't had the good sense to kill himself, it would have been very properly done for him!'

The frail but indomitable old lady was as wrought up as if she were herself taking part in the drama. There was a flush in her cheek, her eyes were wild and her skeletal fingers coiled and weaved like demented snakes.

'You say the Montagus – the Piantaleones – have kept the feud alive,' Peroni went on, curious in spite of himself. 'How have they done that?'

'There are many examples,' she said. 'When the dispute between the Guelfs and the Ghibellines arose, My Family was naturally Guelf. It was the only Sustainable policy at the time when the Empire was Crumbling, and indeed Subsequent History has shown it to have been so. But naturally the Montagus, Reactionary as ever, were Ghibellines. And not content with holding such Absurd, Outdated Views, they continually provoked Us as the Leading Guelf Family in the City. You could hardly expect Us to Overlook That, could you?'

'I suppose not,' said Peroni.

'At the time when Garibaldi was Nobly Striving for the Unification of Italy,' she went on, 'My Family naturally supported him to the Utmost. Did not the Future lie in Unification? Of course it did! But the Piantaleones, as they were already known by then, continued to support the Austrian Tyrants, giving balls for their officers at which the women of the family, as they have done throughout the centuries, behaved Quite Shamelessly. Few families in Italy can equal the Pillipopoli partisan record during the Recent Conflict, while the Pianta-leones were Black Shirts to a man!'

Suddenly Peroni felt he couldn't stand any more. 'You've been very kind,' he said rising. 'I mustn't tire you any more.'

'I am not in the least tired,' she corrected regally, holding out her hand to be kissed, 'but I daresay you must be going about your Duties.'

'I'm afraid I must,' said Peroni, kissing her hand.

The Dowager Countess Augusta rang a little silver bell at her side and the nannie appeared with suspicious promptness. 'Show the *commissario* out,' ordered the Countess.

When he was out in the sun again Peroni felt as though he had passed through a black hole and come out the other side. Only then did it occur to him that Regina must have known the story that the Dowager Countess Augusta was going to tell him.

'In the name of the Father and of the Son and of the Holy Ghost,' said the priest, opening the Mass at the main altar of the church of SS Trinità.

Peroni, his sister, his brother-in-law, his nephew and his niece all crossed themselves devoutly.

'But surely the whole Romeo and Juliet story is pure legend?' whispered Giorgio to Peroni who had just finished outlining his interview with the Dowager Countess.

'Of course it is!' Peroni whispered back. 'Obviously that's the form her madness takes.'

'So the whole thing's just a red herring?' whispered Giorgio.

'Shh!' said Assunta, 'I confess to Almighty God . . .'

But her mind must have been going over the episode just as much as everybody else's, for, under cover of the Gloria, sung by a group of boys and girls accompanying themselves with guitars, she took it up again with her brother.

'What about the archer, Pellegrino?' she hissed, 'and Count Luigi da Porto?'

'What about them?' Peroni hissed back. He had rather feared

that his sister, an incorrigible lover of the marvellous, might try to sustain the authenticity of the Dowager Countess's story. But fortunately, he had calculated, he would have the good sense of Giorgio and the children on his side.

'Well, they do seem to bear the story out, don't they?' Assunta whispered.

'It's probably no more than a mere literary device,' said Peroni a little pompously under the covering swell of the Gloria. 'And anyway, something like that in a twentieth-century murder enquiry – '

'Shh!' said Assunta again.

'The first reading is from the book of Kings . . .'

'Achille's quite right, you know,' said Giorgio between the first and second readings.

'Thank you, Giorgio,' whispered Peroni between the second reading and the gospel, thinking how his common-sensical attitude would be applauded at New Scotland Yard.

Silence was imposed on them during the sermon, and Peroni wondered vaguely why Anna Maria and Stefano had not given him vocal backing. He got his answer during the sung Credo.

'I suppose you realise, Uncle Achille,' Anna Maria murmured to him, 'that the Capulets and the Montagus are mentioned in Dante? Quite factually, I mean,' she went on, 'and he was a contemporary. He quotes them as an example of the terrible feuds that went on in those days. *Purgatory* somewhere or other, I think.'

'The sixth canto of *Purgatory*,' specified Stefano, 'verses 106 to 108. It's part of an invocation to Albert 1 of Hapsburg, who was then Holy Roman Emperor, to visit Italy in order to witness and put a stop to the internecine feuds that were dividing the entire country. "Come and see Montagus and Capulets" are the precise words.'

Peroni was shaken. Assunta he had been prepared for, but that Anna Maria and Stefano should rally to her was an unexpected blow.

'Thank you very much,' he whispered in a tone laden with irony.

'Don't mention it, Uncle Achille,' said Stefano politely, either ignoring or failing to perceive the irony.

'. . . and the life of the world to come. Amen.'

Peroni didn't have his defence ready until the Our Father.

'Even assuming,' he whispered fiercely, 'that the Capulets and the Montagus did exist, it certainly doesn't mean that their descendants are walking about the streets of Verona seven hundred years later!'

'Why not?' Assunta hissed out of the side of her mouth.

'Because it's impossible!' he said.

'Of course it is,' mumbled Giorgio.

'Shh!' imposed Assunta, perhaps because they were saying the Agnus Dei, perhaps because she didn't like a united opposition.

'After all,' she got in quickly when the choir started a communion hymn, 'there are older families than that in existence.'

'If you put it like that, we all go back to Adam,' said Peroni, 'but if my reasoning in this specific murder enquiry is to be based on literary-cum-legendary theories I'm never going to get anywhere. Or rather I'm going to get everywhere except where I should be!'

Anna Maria was wrapped in prayer, having returned from communion, but she emerged from it to say, 'A little imagination doesn't hurt, Uncle Achille. If you don't use it, you might overlook something vital.'

That put an end to the discussion until Mass was over when, having passed from the cool darkness of the church into the shimmering heat outside, Stefano pronounced his final verdict.

'From a purely pragmatical point of view,' he said, 'this new disclosure cannot be overlooked in our calculations.' Peroni looked at him gloomily. 'It is indisputable,' Stefano went on, as though viewing an imaginary chess board at a crucial point in the game, 'that General Piantaleone has been murdered and that Policarpo Pillipopoli has vanished from home. It is also beyond doubt that the former was a leading figure on the extreme right political wing while the latter held, or holds, views of an equally extreme left wing nature. Add to that an identification of the General with the unquestionably historical clan of Montagu and of Policarpo with the no less historical clan of Capulet, and we are led to a single and all but inescapable conclusion.'

'What's that?' asked Peroni helplessly.

'That the old family feud has broken out once more.'

Loris

To Peroni's surprise and consternation, even *dott.* Guerra was not entirely sceptical of the story.

'I appreciate, *dottore*,' said the Veronese police chief, 'that with your pragmatical approach' – (Stefano had used the same word, Peroni remembered, deciding that he must look it up in the dictionary) – 'such an idea must seem absurd. On the other hand, it is unquestionably true that many families of the Italian nobility do trace their lineage back an extraordinarily long way. And the historical reality of the Capulets and the Montagus appears to be beyond dispute.'

'But, *dottore* – ' Peroni began without great conviction.

'Let us put it like this, *dottore*,' said Guerra with a manicured hand raised in a courteous gesture of authority, 'while not allowing our thinking to be unduly influenced by historical or literary considerations, it may be useful to bear in mind the possibility of ancestral ties playing some role in these events. Shall we leave it like that, *dottore*?'

'Yes, *dottore*,' said Peroni, reflecting that public opinion had it all wrong when it looked to the south for exaggerated use of the imagination and to the north for sober common sense. Things were just the other way about.

Lenotti, that woeful connoisseur of camomile tea, had done various shifts of observation on Loris Piantaleone without learning anything of the remotest interest. And the reports of his colleagues were all equally negative. Loris scarcely moved from the fortress-like medieval Piantaleone home. And indeed, thought Lenotti, if he hadn't been in such a humble position he would have felt called upon to make some sort of criticism.

Why was the watch being continued? After all, it was public money that was being spent. Taxes. His own taxes apart from anything else. It was that *Commissario* Peroni. Not, of course, that Lenotti would say a word against his superiors, but you had to remember that the *commissario* was a Neapolitan, and the Neapolitans were generally known as wild and thoughtless. True, the *commissario* had a reputation for sensational successes, but it was all based on the newspapers and Lenotti well knew you couldn't rely upon a word they said. Besides, all these successes had been achieved – if achieved they had been – *before* the *commissario* came to Verona. Since then he hadn't done anything. And he got his cigarettes on the black market. Of course, it was none of Lenotti's business, but you couldn't help noticing certain things. And now that the *commissario* had been given a job of some importance, what did he do? Waste valuable manpower on following somebody who didn't go anywhere.

At this point Lenotti's reflections were interrupted by the sudden appearance of Loris Piantaleone who hurtled out of the massive wooden front door in an obvious state of mental agitation and ran to a grey sports car parked outside. It was the first time since the watch had started on him that he had driven anywhere.

Anticipating that he would surely lose his prey in the traffic and consequently be made to look a fool before the Neapolitan *commissario*, Lenotti waited until Loris had turned the corner at the end of the road before shifting into gear and moving after him. Fortunately, the traffic in town was heavy that morning and Lenotti had no difficulty in staying fairly close behind him without any risk of being seen. Indeed, Loris was in such a state of agitation that he would scarcely have noticed if he had been followed by an identified police car with its siren on.

What Lenotti did not see was that he, in his turn, was being followed by a young man with golden hair who Peroni would have instantly recognised as Gabriele Piantaleone.

Loris surprised Lenotti – though not Gabriele – by driving out of Verona and then heading in the direction of Lake Garda.

Now things were going to start going wrong, Lenotti decided with gloomy satisfaction.

But just outside the village of Lazise, the lake appeared like a vast and burnished silver saucepan on his left, and Lenotti felt a rare wave of optimism. After all, he had managed to stay with Loris, and he had not been observed. Perhaps things would work out well after all. Perhaps he would return to the *Questura* with information to put *Commissario* Peroni's nose out of joint.

It was at this moment that a car pulled out of a hotel gate on the right of the road just ahead of him. Waving cheerfully to some people behind him, the driver swung his car to the left.

Lenotti didn't need to see the GB plate behind the car to realise that the fool at the wheel was English and, distracted by his farewells, was driving off on the left of the road straight towards Lenotti's car. To swerve on to the other side of the road would have meant instant death under the wheels of an oncoming juggernaut. The best Lenotti could do was brake as hard as he could which didn't prevent a head-on crash with the English car.

He just had time to tell himself that he had known all along things would go wrong when the force of the impact knocked him out.

He didn't know that Gabriele Piantaleone, who was driving a couple of hundred metres behind him, was able neatly to overtake the pile-up and continue, unobserved, on the tail of his cousin, Loris.

The fat girl had often wondered exactly how one was recruited into the ranks of the Red Brigade. She didn't expect to be one of the leaders, and indeed, she would have been more than wary of such a dangerous honour. But she would have liked to be an active sympathiser, one of those who left messages, one of those who made telephone calls to anonymous voices to report that a certain car had passed a certain way at a certain time. It was in the hope of being recruited for such a mission that she had been hanging round extreme left-wing university circles for more than a year now. So far nobody had said, 'Psst!

Are you ready to help the cause of the proletariat?' but she hadn't given up yet. At this very moment, she was sitting with a group of left-wing students outside the Costa Pizzeria in Piazza Dante. All the tables were full, mostly with camera-hung tourists, red, peeling and exhausted, and the students, ostentatiously tattered, stood out in clamorous contrast.

'The trouble with university politics today,' said an aggressive girl with a moustache, 'is that they're ninety-nine per cent a game. Spraying slogans on walls – that's what it amounts to! That and a lot of talk!'

'Not always,' said a lean, gangling boy with enormous spectacles. 'Look at Curcio and Margherita Cagol and Paola Besuschio.'

'That's the one per cent,' said the girl with the moustache, 'Or rather it was – they're ancient history now. Who's really *doing* something on the university scene today?'

'In a savage, repressive police state like this,' ventured the fat girl, 'anybody who *is* doing something takes good care to keep it quiet.'

The girl with a moustache looked as though she were going to say something, and then changed her mind.

'There *are* people just the same,' said a very young-looking boy called Toni.

'Who, for example?' asked the girl with a moustache pugnaciously.

'Well, for example – ' said the boy called Toni, pondering the question. 'For example, what about Policarpo Pillipopoli?'

'Ha!' snorted the gangling boy with the enormous glasses, 'with his family's money? Don't you believe it! He's just another daddy's boy who plays at political theorising!'

Again the girl with a moustache looked as though she wanted to say something, and again she changed her mind.

'He hasn't been around for a long time,' said Toni thoughtfully.

'He's probably gone for a round-the-world cruise!' sneered the gangling boy.

'I wonder,' said the fat girl. In fact, she had been wondering for some while about Policarpo Pillipopoli. She knew he was the son of a count and belonged to one of the richest families in Verona, but his thinking had been highly explosive, and he had disappeared. Could he have gone underground? Could he, perhaps, be the real blood-boultered thing?

'There's nothing to wonder about!' said the gangling boy, 'Policarpo Pillipopoli would faint at the sight of a gun.'

This time, whatever she was thinking was too much for the girl with a moustache. 'As a matter of fact – ' she began, the words sounding as though they had been squeezed out of her.

The others looked at her interrogatively. She couldn't go back now. She hesitated a second, then leaned forward. 'Policarpo *is* an active Red Brigade combatant!' she whispered.

'How do you know?' asked the gangling boy incredulously.

'I can't tell you,' she said.

'Go on, Giulia!' said the boy called Toni, laughing, 'you're making it up!'

'I'm not!' said the girl with a moustache, going brick red. 'Listen, if you don't believe me,' she went on like a goaded beast, 'but keep quiet about it!' The students' heads moved into an even tighter circle. 'You remember that Christian Democrat pig they lamed last week?' Yes, they all remembered it. 'Well, I was there when it happened!' She paused. 'I was collaborating!'

The fat girl felt a hideous lurch of jealousy in her stomach. Why should they ask Giulia and not her? No wonder the cause of the proletariat was limping so badly! She thrashed about in her mind for a way to spite them.

'Somebody,' Giulia was going on, 'had asked me to stage a car breakdown at a precise position on a road junction at twenty to eight that morning so as to keep the traffic blocked for at least three minutes, and to go into the phone box opposite and pretend to call for help. From the phone box I saw the whole shooting. It was done by a red-headed girl and a man. And the man was Policarpo Pillipopoli – there was no doubt about it!'

'*Pizze, signori!*' announced the waiter, arriving with plates stacked up his arms like an exhibit in the Art Biennale at Venice.

They looked at each other in awe while the steaming pizzas

were placed before them. Then, thoughtfully, they began to eat, the mozzarella cheese stretching out of their mouths like chewing gum. When they had finished the group broke up and its separate members set off for various destinations.

The fat girl, having excogitated the perfect revenge, went to the local headquarters of the Christian Democrat Party to sign on.

The girl with the moustache walked home, deciding for the umpteenth time that she really would at last start actually to read Karl Marx.

The gangling boy went to see a pornographic film which was deviationist and reactionary, but nice.

The boy called Toni, having made quite sure that he was unobserved, went to the *Questura*.

The boy called Toni was the youngest member of the DIGOS in Verona, and he looked even younger than he was, which was why he had been selected and trained for infiltration of student groups. He was also one of the small army of people whose most immediate and pressing aim was the finding of Policarpo Pillipopoli, the presumed slayer of General Pianta-leone.

And Toni now had information which moved things forward appreciably. Policarpo and the Red Brigade combatant of the identikit *were* one and the same person. And less than a week before Policarpo, in the company of a red-headed girl, had carried out a 'punitive' laming in Verona.

'A Neapolitan,' said Peroni, 'shouldn't ape northern rationalism.'

'Have you been aping northern rationalism, Uncle Achille?' asked Anna Maria.

'Like the fool I am,' said Peroni in a rare moment of humility, 'I have. I tried to assume that there was no such thing as a jinx on certain people. But any Neapolitan beggar could have told me that Lenotti was unlucky. And it had to be him on watch outside the Piantaleone home this morning when Loris finally made a break for it. Lenotti went out on his tail. They took the road towards Lake Garda. At last we might have been on the brink

89

of discovering where General Piantaleone went when he should have been up at Rosaro – the key to the whole business. And what happens? An Englishman, driving on the wrong side of the road if you please, smashes into Lenotti's car and knocks him unconscious! Would that have happened to anybody else at the *Questura*? Of course it wouldn't!'

'If I were you, Uncle Achille,' said Stefano, 'I should withhold judgement on the validity or otherwise of superstition until a moment of greater objectivity. One thing at least seems evident.'

'What's that?'

'If Loris's movements this morning are pertinent, it would seem that General Piantaleone was going somewhere on Lake Garda.'

'Lake Garda is a very big place,' said Peroni ungratefully.

'Nevertheless, it's a step forward.'

'And what are you going to do about it in the meantime, Uncle Achille?' asked Anna Maria.

Peroni gave an epic, gloomy shrug. 'There's not much I can do about this side of it,' he said. 'We'll just have to wait until we see Loris again.'

He couldn't know that they were not to see anything of Loris alive again. And precious little of him dead.

Having put the General's posthumous letter amongst the Monday morning mail, Gabriele had sat back over his third coffee of the morning to await results. They weren't long in coming. As soon as he started to read the letter, Loris went deathly pale, and then a slow flush started to spread over his face.

'Something the matter, Loris?' Gabriele had asked amiably.

Loris had shot him a look of pure venom which Gabriele received with a baffled but forgiving smile.

'I'm going out . . .' Loris had spluttered, stuffing the letter into his pocket.

Gabriele had watched from the house as Loris drove off. A few seconds later he saw another car, parked further down the road, starting to move off behind Loris. He recognised the driver as the same who had parked in the street on various other occasions in recent days. A man like that exuded his calling like sweat, and Gabriele was in no doubt that he was a policeman. This was a nuisance. Not that he expected to discover immediately the person he was looking for (the same person who had killed Uncle Orazio? Possibly, very possibly), but it would be a pity if the police got on to the same track as he was.

There was, however, nothing to be done about this, so Gabriele took his time in order to allow both cars to get comfortably on their way, and then went out to his own. As he had expected, Loris took the lake road. And then, just outside Lazise, there was a quite unforeseeable stroke of luck. The policeman was run into by an English car driving on the wrong side of the road. As he overtook the accident Gabriele felt a surge of elation. Now he had the field to himself again.

He arrived at the village of Garda just in time to see his cousin turn off on to a smaller road leading up into the hills where it would be impossible to follow him without being recognised. So Gabriele went round by another way to a vantage point in the hills above Garda which he had chosen on previous visits of observation. It was a quick run, and when he got there he saw Loris's car below him stop outside a heavy iron gate. Loris got out, said a few words into a speaker, then climbed back into the car. The gates opened for him and closed immediately behind him.

Gabriele took off his shirt and lay on his stomach to sunbathe, giving the impression (just in case anybody happened to be observing him, and one could not be too careful) of an innocuous tourist. But at the same time he observed the villa below him.

Not for the first time, he wished that he could see it from the inside, inspect it room by room. But he knew that any attempt to do so would have been suicide, and so he contented himself with watching from a distance. The place was well protected from peepers. Apart from the high walls and the solid, unassailable gate, there were trees about the villa itself which almost entirely hid it from view, and even from his eyrie Gabriele could only make out parts of the building and small patches of gravelled walk or lawn.

Some weeks before, his suspicions having been awakened about General Piantaleone's visits to Rosaro, he had succeeded in following his uncle and cousin to Garda, and it had not taken him long after that to realise what was going on. But his conclusions had been based, not so much on *what* he saw, as on *whom* he saw passing through the heavy gate.

The situation had instantly appeared to him as the most 'interesting' that had ever come his way, and he was in the process of studying it to see how it could be made to yield a maximum profit when the General's death had changed everything, bringing with it the possibility of even greater gain, but also requiring further knowledge which only Loris could lead him to.

As Gabriele mulled all this over and observed the villa beneath him, chain-smoking four Swiss Mercedes cigarettes, the sun sizzled down on his already near-coffee tanned back and crickets chirped noisily all about him.

Suddenly a new thought struck him. If Loris was confronting an unknown somebody in the villa with the evidence he had that General Piantaleone had gone precisely there on the night of his death, then that unknown somebody could hardly allow Loris to leave the villa alive.

Not that Gabriele would have minded his cousin's death; indeed, under other circumstances, it would have been a pleasure. But now it would have meant losing the only direct lead he had to the unknown somebody. The search would have to begin all over again, and without a blundering and blinkered cretin like Loris it would be much more difficult.

And then, slowly, the gates opened and Loris's car re-emerged. Gabriele thought it must have been the first time in his life he had ever been relieved to see his cousin again. He put on his shirt and drove quickly down to the main road where he saw Loris emerging from the small road leading to the villa.

Again he allowed some traffic to pass before setting off himself. For once nobody seemed in a great hurry. Perhaps it was too hot. Or perhaps everybody was enjoying the spectacle of the lake, glittering blue at the feet of the mountains opposite.

Gabriele himself had no time for nature except in so far as it expressed itself in the female form, and he leant forward on the steering wheel, whistling through his teeth and wondering where Loris would take him now.

Just as they were passing Bardolino he heard some way in front of him a noise which sounded like a muffled and gigantic burp, and at the same time he saw a flash of light so brilliant that it momentarily dulled the lake. For a split second he wondered bewilderedly whether it had something to do with the volcanic nature of the nearby Monte Baldo.

In front of him chaos broke loose. There was an agonised screaming of brakes, cars swerved about on the road like demented dodgems, and there were a series of rending metallic crashes as they catapulted into each other. At the same time the roar and the flash which had started it all resolved themselves into a single pyre of leaping flames.

Gabriele managed to stop on the verge of the road without running into anybody or being run into. He got out of the car and quickly took shelter in a hotel forecourt until the lethal waves of traffic came approximately to rest. Then he edged cautiously up the road towards the flames which still continued to claw at the sky. He knew now what he would find.

It was impossible to get near, but you didn't have to be near to see that little remained of Loris's car and less still of Loris himself. Gabriele recognised with regret that his enquiries would have to take a new turn.

People were running about in all directions, screaming and gesticulating. But soon they would begin to reason coherently, and then there would be telephone calls and wailing sirens and police, fire brigade and ambulance. Gabriele decided he had better be away before that started to happen. He got back into his car, flipped it neatly round (no question of driving through all that and back to Verona for the moment) and headed again in the direction of Garda.

When he had put several kilometres between himself and the nightmare scene of the explosion, he began to work out the probable course of events leading up to Loris's death. Loris had confronted somebody in the villa with his evidence of General Piantaleone's presence there on the night of his death and demanded satisfaction. The somebody had then realised that Loris must not reach Verona alive and, unable or unwilling to kill him on the spot, must have temporarily lulled his suspicions (with an imbecile like Loris that can't have been too difficult) and persuaded him to drive back to Verona, having previously placed, or had placed, the bomb in the car.

So what would somebody now do? Gabriele decided that, under the circumstances, they would prefer to get out of the immediate area of Lake Garda as quickly as possible and would therefore close up the villa and make for somewhere else. It might just be worth returning to his vantage point, he decided, to see if anybody did come out.

And he had not been there for long when somebody did come out.

Somebody's car turned up towards the hills, presumably with the intention of avoiding the principal lake-side road into Verona. Gabriele contemplated following it, but decided that, on the less frequented mountain road, there was too much danger of being spotted.

So he did the next best thing.

The DIGOS files were hopelessly inadequate. This was no fault of the benign, Father Christmas-like DIGOS chief, but was due to the fact that Communist pressure in the early seventies had forced the government virtually to dismantle its political espionage service which had been so painstakingly evolved, and with it had gone much of the information the service had built up. Only in 1978 when, as a result of the Moro kidnapping and killing, the Communists put themselves forward as the sworn defenders of law and order was the creation of a new secret service undertaken. But the mass of reserved information, secret, scurrilous, absurd, explosive, improbable, double-checked and spiteful by turns which is the vital food of such an organisation was pitifully insufficient.

Nevertheless Toni turned to what there was of it in his

search for the red-headed girl who had teamed with Policarpo Pillipopoli in the punitive laming which he had learned of in the pizzeria. In the group of known terrorists and active sympathisers he could find nobody who could be made to fit the role.

But there was another, far larger category of people in the half light between the known political criminals and their associates on one hand and the pure-as-lambswool ordinary citizen who votes Christian Democrat, runs a Fiat and indulges in mild tax-dodging when possible. There are hundreds of names in this category. Names of people who have been brushed, perhaps quite fortuitously, by the shadow of suspicion and whose personal details have been left to grow dusty in an archival limbo until the shadow, or something more than the shadow, falls on them again and causes their file to be transferred to the first category.

Here Toni found three red-heads who had been suspected at one time or another of association with the extra-parliamentary left, which probably meant no more than that they had once distributed stencilled leaflets outside a school or helped in the organisation of a student protest march.

At the address of the first one, he was confronted by an unshaven, hostile father.

'She went off the best part of a year ago,' he growled reluctantly when Toni had finally persuaded him to talk.

Even if he wasn't as young as he looked, Toni was still young enough for enthusiasm, and his heart checked with excitement at the answer which almost exactly squared with Policarpo's disappearance from home.

'Where did she go?' asked Toni.

The man spat. 'One of them organisations,' he said with disgust.

'You know about it?' asked Toni with surprise.

'Well, of course I know about it!' said the man. 'You can disapprove as much as you like, but there's no way of not knowing if your daughter becomes a bloody nun!'

If he had been Peroni, Toni would have reflected that this

was a typically Italian ending to the lead. But as he wasn't, he just turned his attention to the second red-head.

From the spattered flesh and the assortment of limbs that had been blasted about the Verona–Garda road just outside the village of Bardolino, more famous for wine than violent death, it would have been a slow and laborious process to arrive at an identification of the victim as Loris Piantaleone. But Lenotti, who had recovered from concussion in hospital, confirmed that the shattered car was the same he had followed that morning when Loris had driven it towards Garda.

'Of course, it is always possible that some other person may have been at the wheel during the return journey,' said *dott.* Guerra.

He and Peroni had been at the scene of the explosion for more than an hour, and Guerra had just climbed back into his official car preparatory to returning to the *Questura.*

'We shan't have positive medical evidence until this afternoon,' Guerra went on, 'but in the meantime I think we may assume that the driver was indeed Loris Piantaleone.'

'Yes, *dottore,*' said Peroni, leaning down and speaking through the car window which made him feel at a disadvantage. 'And to think,' he went on in exasperation, 'that if Lenotti hadn't smashed into that English car – '

'I was given to understand that it was the English car which smashed into Lenotti,' said *dott.* Guerra, who liked to get facts straight.

'Well, whichever way it was, *dottore,*' said Peroni, restraining his impatience, 'if it hadn't happened, we might know by now what this was all about.'

'We might indeed, *dottore.* And what do you propose to do now?'

'I propose,' said Peroni, without the slightest idea of how he was to go about it, 'to find out where Loris went this morning.'

'An excellent idea, *dottore,*' said Guerra, leaning forward and indicating to his driver that he wished to return to Verona.

'Oh, there is one point that perhaps should be borne in mind,' he added, apparently as an afterthought.

'What's that, *dottore*?' Peroni asked.

'The Pillipopoli family possess a large villa and a great deal of land on Lake Garda.'

The dark-blue, ministerial-looking car moved majestically off, leaving Peroni in the middle of the road.

The telephone started to ring just as Peroni's sister, Assunta, was locking up the flat to go down to the hairdresser's. She thought of letting it ring, but then, deciding it might be something important for Achille, she reopened the front door and went in to answer it.

'*Pronto?* Is *Commissario* Peroni at home, please?'

It was a woman's voice, and just the sort that Assunta trusted least. Moreover, it had a faint but recognisable Neapolitan accent, and experience had taught her that Neapolitan women were bad for her brother. If only he would make up his mind to settle down with some pleasant girl from the north! She made up her mind to speak to Giorgio once again about finding the right girl.

'*Pronto?*' said the voice again without the least edge of sharpness.

'*Pronto,*' said Assunta. 'No, he's not here at the moment.'

'Then perhaps you'd be so very kind as to ask him to ring me some time this evening if he has a moment. My name is Regina.'

Assunta took down the number which the Neapolitan voice dictated, then said, 'I'll tell him,' and rang off immediately. After that, having scribbled a message for her brother, she went down to the hairdresser's.

It was pleasantly cool in there after the sweltering heat of the flat, and presently the hands of Carlo, the chief hairdresser, moving about her head with gentle efficiency, the murmur of women's voices, the hum of the dryers, the rustle of magazine pages turning, all combined to soothe away the irritation which the telephone call had aroused in her and replace it with one of total relaxation.

'I daresay your brother's busy on this General Piantaleone business?' said Carlo.

'Yes, he is,' said Assunta, conscious of ears pricking up about her. Most of the women there knew that her brother was the famous Rudolph Valentino of the Italian police, and they were all anxious to pick up titbits.

'Anything to go on?' asked Carlo, who had been a source of helpful suggestions in the past.

'Well, there is one thing,' said Assunta, and the magazine pages instantly ceased to rustle, 'the person Achille's looking for is a boy called Policarpo Pillipopoli. And the interesting thing about *that* is – ' Here she paused for effect and was gratified to notice that even the hair-dryers had been switched off now. 'The interesting thing about *that* is,' she went on, keeping her voice just low enough for everybody to have to strain to catch it, 'that Achille has discovered that this Pillipopoli family are the direct descendants of the Capulets – you know, the ones in *Romeo and Juliet*.'

The effect was gratifying. She paused again to create maximum tension. 'And what's more,' she went on, 'it seems that the Piantaleones come from the other one – the Montagus.'

Murmured expressions of wonder and awe went round the hairdresser's.

'So,' said Carlo, making himself the spokesman for every woman there, 'General Piantaleone was killed *because he was a Montagu*.'

Vaguely Assunta remembered her brother having argued forcefully that this was not the way to think at all, but there was no point in ruining a good story.

'It does rather look like that, doesn't it?' she said.

The family of the second red-head had left Verona. 'But she's still here,' the porter told Toni.

'How do you know?'

98

'I've seen her. She must live in a block of flats at San Zeno – my in-laws live there, and I've seen her a couple of times coming out of them.'

'Do you know the address?'

The porter did, and Toni drove there full of hope. Zeno, the city's patron saint who reconverted the Veronese to the faith, was a negro bishop, and was said to have been so poor that he lived on fish which he caught himself in the river Adige. The area about the basilica in which his body now lies in a glass case is known as San Zeno after him. San Zeno is a stubbornly independent quarter of the city, colourful and inhabited largely by poor people – an ideal place for Red Brigade combatants to have their lair.

The block of flats the porter had indicated was also in keeping – crumbling, untidy, swarming with life. And on enquiry there Toni learned that a red-head was indeed a resident, at flat 11 on staircase B.

According to practically every rule that had ever been taught him, he shouldn't have gone up alone. But impatience, curiosity and enthusiasm made him take the risk, and he climbed up staircase B with his heart racing.

Outside the door of flat number 11 he took a firm grip of the gun beneath his coat. Then he rang the bell.

The door was opened by a red-head. But instead of the machine gun which Toni had more than half expected to find in her arms, there was a very small baby. Two other children were hanging on to her skirt, and a fourth young life was all too evident within her majestically swollen belly.

'Yes?' she enquired.

Faced with the same situation, Peroni would have reflected that the call of politics was inaudible compared to that of maternity, which was what kept Italy alive. Toni just went red and stammered apologetically.

Then, when he finally managed to retreat before this triumphantly overblown symbol of motherhood, he turned his attention to red-head number three.

'I told you so!' said Assunta aggressively. 'The Pillipopolis have got a villa on Lake Garda – just where Loris Piantaleone was killed! Well, obviously, the old family feud has broken out again!'

Assunta's aggressiveness derived from a niggling feeling of guilt. In his preoccupation, Peroni had not noticed the telephone message from Regina and, although she knew she ought to draw his attention to it, she did not intend to do so. As she talked she ladled *tagliatelle* violently out of a bowl and on to the plates of her family. Stefano, meanwhile, was giving a last reluctant look at a tricky chess problem, Peroni was pulling fiercely at a black-market English cigarette as he pondered the multiple problems raised by Loris's death, and Anna Maria was half listening to a news programme on a local radio station.

'Lake Garda,' replied Giorgio mildly to his wife, 'is a big place. Lots of people have villas there. We wanted to get one ourselves if you remember.'

Assunta waved that aside with a contemptuous Neapolitan gesture, *tagliatelle* flying in the air with it.

'The trouble with you,' she said to her husband, 'and with you,' she added, turning to her brother, 'is that you won't accept an obvious explanation just because it also happens to be a romantic one. To me it's quite plain what's happened – the feud between the two families has gone on festering over the centuries, breaking out every so often, and now it's gone to the head of some Pillipopoli–Capulet who's going about killing Piantaleone–Montagus! You said yourself,' she went on accusingly to Peroni, 'that the old Dowager Countess Augusta was mad.'

'Yes, but she can't move from the house,' said Peroni.

'How do you know?' asked Assunta darkly, and then, as Peroni opened his mouth, she swept on, 'And even granted that she can't, what's to stop her getting somebody else to do it for her? Come and eat, everybody.'

'I can't see anybody going round murdering people, particularly in such a complicated manner, just because an old lady tells them to,' said Giorgio, tucking his napkin into the ample folds of his neck under his shirt collar.

'Perhaps they're mad themselves,' said Assunta. 'In these very old interbred families they mostly are anyway.'

'It seems to me that we're getting away from the point,' said Anna Maria.

'I quite agree,' said Peroni.

'What is the point?' asked Assunta. 'A drop of wine please, Giorgio – with mineral water.'

'The point,' said Anna Maria, 'is how Uncle Achille is to find out where Loris Piantaleone went this morning. Until we know that we're just going round in circles.'

'And it's going to be difficult without some other indication,' said Peroni plaintively. 'Garda is preposterously overbuilt.'

'What time did the English car collide with *Signor* Lenotti?' asked Stefano.

'About quarter past nine,' said Peroni.

'And what time did the bomb go off?'

'Twenty-five past ten.'

'Where are you going, Stefano?' called Assunta. 'You haven't finished your *tagliatelle*!'

'I'm coming, Mamma – I want to get a map.'

The family watched in bewilderment mixed with anticipation as Stefano came back with a map, pushed aside his half-finished plate of *tagliatelle* and started to study the map with deep concentration.

'The accident occurred at nine-fifteen approximately – *here*,' he murmured more to himself than to them. 'Now, wherever Loris Piantaleone was going, it is reasonable to assume that he spent some time there, enough to talk to whoever it was he had gone to see, and enough for that person, or some other, to fix a bomb in his car. Let us allow half an hour. Moreover, we must allow a certain amount of time for him to get from the point where the English car collided with *Signor* Lenotti to wherever he was going, and a certain amount more time for him to come back as far as Bardolino where the bomb exploded. Given the geographical position of the accident, he is unlikely to have driven for less than ten minutes. (I am supposing, of course, that he didn't have an appointment out of doors which would have anyway rendered the placing of a bomb highly unlikely.) Pieced together, this data renders it probable that he went somewhere along the shore of Lake Garda not further than *here* and not nearer than *here*.'

He showed them the map, indicating the stretch of lake-side between the villages of Garda and Torri del Benaco. They studied it in a respectful silence which was suddenly interrupted by an Eureka-like howl.

'Anna Maria!' Assunta protested. 'What's the matter?'

'I think I can limit it even more than that!' said Anna Maria. 'Listen.'

Unexpectedly she raised the volume of the radio. '. . . several thousand litres of wine were spilled on the road,' the announcer's voice boomed deafeningly, 'and all traffic was held up for more than an hour while the lorry was righted and towed away.'

'Turn it down!' shouted Assunta, 'and anyway, what's that got to do with it?'

'You missed the beginning!' said Anna Maria. 'A huge lorry carrying wine overturned at San Vigilio at nine o'clock this morning. Look!' She pointed at the map. 'San Vigilio's only just outside Garda on the road to Torri del Benaco. Loris can't have gone beyond Garda this morning.'

'And Stefano's pointed out that he isn't likely to have stopped before it,' said Giorgio.

'So that means – ' said Assunta.

'That he must have gone to the village of Garda itself!' concluded Anna Maria triumphantly.

'There you are, Achille,' said Giorgio. 'Once again they've served it up to you on a golden tray.'

'Well, it's certainly a strong enough piece of reasoning to warrant going through the village of Garda with a very fine toothcomb indeed.' He drained his wine and got up to go to the telephone. 'I'll get it organised.'

'Just a minute, Uncle Achille – ' said Stefano.

'What?'

'If you do that, you may just possibly find out where he went, but you'll raise the alarm in the process and I judge it highly dubious whether you will find anything, and even less likely anybody, when you get there.'

'I don't see any alternative,' said Peroni.

'There is one alternative, Uncle Achille.'

'What's that?'

Stefano told him.

'Oh, no!' said Anna Maria. 'That's much too dangerous!'

Peroni thought so, too. It was an appalling idea, and he would have given a great deal to annihilate his far-too-brilliant young nephew's proposal from the face of the earth. But there it was – solid, outrageous and – he was bound to admit – brilliant.

And the eyes of the entire family – even, indeed above all, those of Anna Maria who had said it was much too dangerous – were fixed on him with a we-know-you-can-do-it expression in them. Oh, yes, Peroni had done things like that before under the coercion of such adoring blackmail. And now it was going to happen again. However much the old Peroni inside him quailed and protested, the intrepid Peroni, the Rudolph Valentino of the Italian police, was going to have to pull him into it by the scruff of his neck.

'Very well,' he said, 'I'll do it. I'll do it this evening!'

Inside him the exclamation mark sounded deathly hollow.

The third red-head was called Monica Branca. The file said she was at the university of Verona and was suspected, without any substantial evidence, of being among the organisers of extreme left-wing meetings. In all his dealings with the university Toni had come across no Monica Branca.

When he arrived at the address given for her, fully expecting her to have become an African missionary, the door was opened by a fading, neurotic-looking woman who clutched her cheek in horror and gasped, 'Oh, Madonna – Monica!' as soon as Toni announced that he was from the *Questura*.

She led him into a soulless, over-tidy living-room where the floor shone like a skating rink and the television set was covered in polythene.

'What's she done?' asked the woman, gesturing feebly for Toni to sit.

'Nothing as far as I know, *signora*.'

'Then why are you looking for her?'

'She may be able to help us in an enquiry.'

'So she *is* involved in something then?'

'Where is she, *signora*?'

'I don't know!' said the woman, biting her handkerchief. 'She left home more than a year ago, and I've no idea where she's been since.'

Monica's chances of being the Red Brigade's gun-woman rose somewhat.

'Why did she leave home, *signora*?'

'I don't *know*!' the woman said again, and the short sentence was full of uncomprehending despair. 'She just walked out and didn't come back! She left a note saying she couldn't bear it any longer and we were not to look for her as she would be perfectly all right.'

'Have you any idea *why* she couldn't bear it any longer, *signora*?'

'No!' Her eyes were welling now. 'She's always had a very good home. Her pappa – my husband – he's the sales director for a very important firm and he earns extremely well. Monica's always had everything she could possibly want.'

'Didn't you notice anything about her in the days before she left, *signora*? Didn't she show signs of – stress?'

'Perhaps – it's hard to say. She's always been a nervy girl.'

'You didn't report her disappearance?'

'I wanted to, but my husband said there was no point. She was twenty-two when she went and free to do what she wanted.'

'You've had no news of her at all since?'

'None whatsoever.' She sounded infinitely dejected.

'Was she at all interested in politics?'

'Oh, I don't know,' she said in a frightened way. 'I don't think so. We never talked about things like that.'

'What did you talk about, *signora*?'

She looked blank. 'Now you come to mention it,' she said, 'perhaps we didn't talk about anything at all.'

'I wonder if I might look at her room, *signora*?' asked Toni.

'If you think it'll do any good.' The woman rose with an effort. 'It's just as it was when she left it.'

She led him upstairs and along a corridor where she opened a door for him. 'I'll wait for you downstairs,' she said. And as she went away Toni heard the sound of muffled sobbing.

Toni looked about him. The room was much what you would expect an average single girl's room to be. There were posters of animals on the walls, a childhood teddy-bear at the foot of the bed, cupboards filled with clothes and shoes. There was a record-player with some old Zecchino d'Oro children's song competition records, a few popular songs and a couple of film soundtrack music. The books were a selection of childhood and adolescent literature with a sprinkling of school texts. All predictable and unhelpful.

There was a chest of drawers with Monica Branca's jerseys, stockings and underclothes, and even though he was unobserved, Toni flushed red as he sorted through it. He was the deadliest Judo and Karate fighter at the *Questura* of Verona and could centre a moving target at 150 metres nine times out of ten, but he was as bashful as a seminarian.

His embarrassment, however, turned to curiosity when he found a scrapbook beneath the underclothes in the bottom drawer. And when he opened it, curiosity gave way to excitement. It was full of cuttings about the doings of the Red Brigade, pictures of all the 'historical founders' of the movement, blood-yearning leading articles from the ultra-left press. Obviously Monica Branca had been a diligent if secret student of the doings of the proletarian combat movement.

Further examination of the room producing nothing else of interest, Toni went downstairs where the mother was waiting for him, her white face with red eyes raised in fear.

'There's nothing to be alarmed about, *signora*,' said Toni, 'I'd like to take this scrapbook back to the *Questura* if I may.

And I wonder if you could let me have a photograph of Monica?'

She went into the room where they had been before and returned with a colour photograph which she handed him. The picture had been taken outside a hotel in the mountains and Monica was wearing trousers and an anorak. Her red hair was striking, her face thin with a slightly too prominent nose. Attractive enough when lit with youth, it threatened to sour with age. Toni put the photograph carefully in his pocket.

'You'll let me know if you learn anything about Monica?' the woman asked anxiously as she took Toni to the door.

'Of course we will, *signora*,' said Toni. 'We shall be in touch with you.' She opened the front door for him. 'Oh, there's one more thing, *signora*,' said Toni. 'Really I should have asked you before. Did Monica have any boy friends?'

'Not really – she was very shy with boys. I was quite worried about it as a matter of fact.'

'You say "Not really", *signora*, as though you weren't quite sure.'

'Well, it's just that she did sometimes talk on the telephone with a boy. She didn't tell me anything about it, but I couldn't help overhearing bits of conversation. And it stuck in my head because he had such a funny name.'

'What was the name, *signora*?'

'Policarpo.'

From behind the counter – on which stood bowls of very small, mercilessly fried fish, now cold as they had been in life with tiny black-bead eyes – Rosa surveyed the back-street *osteria* where she worked. It was one of the few bars in the village of Garda which still bore some resemblance to what it had been before the golden age of tourism. There were wooden tables and benches, and a crucifix on the wall, and Rosa served sharp-tasting wine in old-fashioned glass measures. The place was full, mostly with men playing cards and shouting at the tops of their voices. There were various tourists as well, savouring life as the natives lived it.

All this was the normal evening picture and alighted no

interest in Rosa's dark, slightly sullen face. What did arouse her interest, however, was the man sitting on a stool at the end of the bar. She had a vague impression that she had seen him somewhere before. He was not one of the locals, but he was certainly not a tourist either, and he didn't look as though he were on holiday. He was dark and very good looking in a southern way, and it seemed to Rosa's professional eye that he was slightly drunk which did nothing to lessen his fascination. She noticed he was smoking English cigarettes.

Rosa was wondering how she could find out more about him without seeming inquisitive when he gave her the opportunity by ordering some more wine just as a lull at the bar afforded a natural excuse for a chat.

'You on holiday?' she asked, allowing him a view of her magnificent breasts as they swelled below the neckline of her black dress.

'No, no,' said the southerner, his eyes raking the display enthusiastically. 'I'm here on duty.'

'Duty?' she said. 'You make it sound as though you were a policeman.'

'I am,' he said.

Then she realised where she had seen him before – on television. This was the famous Achille Peroni, the Rudolph Valentino of the Italian police. She felt a surge of excitement and, turning away for a second, she modestly wriggled her breasts just a little further out of their casing in his honour.

'I suppose you're here about that bomb business this morning?' she said.

He glanced over his shoulder, presumably to see that nobody was listening. 'Yes,' he said in a tone which implied that he wouldn't have admitted it to everybody. 'Yes, as a matter of fact I am.'

'But that was over in Bardolino,' she said. 'What brings you to Garda?'

'Ah,' he said with a smile that made her stomach tilt in excitement, 'that is the point.' Again she had the impression that he had drunk too much.

'The point?' she urged him gently.

'The point,' he confirmed. 'He was blown up in Bardolino all right, but *I* have discovered that before being blown up in Bardolino he was here in Garda. *And I know where he was!*'

'No!' Her dark eyes were looking at him with admiring awe.

'Yes,' he said, apparently basking in it.

She leant closer towards him. 'And where was he?' she asked.

He opened his mouth and then shut it again. 'Forgive me,' he said, 'but I really mustn't – not even for you.'

The 'even' made up for a lot, and when Peroni left the bar a few minutes later, Rosa felt that, although she had not got all the facts, she nevertheless had the makings of an excellent story. She set about spreading it with a will.

After Peroni had repeated the performance a couple of times for good measure he felt that, always assuming Stefano's calculations were correct, the story now had ample opportunity of reaching the right ears. Or rather the wrong ones. He started to wait for the results with a feeling of sick trepidation in his stomach, and his normally affectionate feelings for his nephew soured to bitter resentment.

Indro Montanelli, journalist, historian and founder-editor of *Il Giornale*, was eating a plate of Tuscan beans in the restaurant he frequented when he was called to the telephone. It was the office.

'We've had a call from Verona,' said the night editor. 'It seems that the police have uncovered a theory that General Piantaleone was a descendant of the Montagu family, the ones in *Romeo and Juliet* – the play I mean.'

'Yes,' rumbled Montanelli, 'I have read it.'

'And apparently a boy who's suspected of the shooting – name of Pillipopoli – is descended from the Capulets. And the man who was blown up just outside Bardolino this morning, being the General's son, was also a Montagu – if the theory is correct.'

'The inference being that, rather than a mere political affair, this is a revival of the historical family feud?'

'That's the idea.'

'Is there any evidence for all this?' asked Montanelli.

'Not what you'd call evidence. I've been on to the police about it as well as the two families. No comment from everybody, but I had a distinct impression that the families knew all about it all right.'

'Well, that's quite enough to run a story on – after all, it's not libellous, is it?'

'No, but I don't quite know how to handle it. It's a page three story really, but page three's been locked up for hours.'

'Then put it on page one,' said Montanelli, rumbling again, 'If nothing else, it's amusing – and one should never despise the amusing in journalism.'

That settled, Indro Montanelli went back to his beans.

It was very dark. In the narrow slit of sky above him between the houses, Peroni could see some stars, but there was no moon. He walked, stumbling deliberately every so often, with the prickles rising on the back of his neck like a terrified hedgehog's. Safety was only a quick sprint away, on the well-lit lake front where the tourists were still strolling, boosting up Italy's sagging economy in the bars and restaurants and shops. *Giornali, Zeitungen, Newspapers, Journaux. Ice's Cream – Own Product. English Tea Like Mother Makes It.* Peroni visualised it longingly as he moved in the dark alleys, expecting every second – what? He didn't know, but if Stefano was correct that the villa couldn't have been left totally unguarded, then whatever it was, it was certainly very dangerous.

Yet again Peroni was tempted to make a bolt for safety, but at once he visualised the disappointed eyes of Stefano and Anna Maria and that, coupled with the thought that he might be missing another startling Peroni coup, made him overcome the temptation.

Besides, Stefano might be wrong. He looked at his watch and decided to give it another quarter of an hour, after which he would decide that Stefano *was* wrong and make for home. Just a quarter of an hour more. The idea of a quick escape consoled him briefly, but he remembered that Stefano so rarely was wrong, and consolation vanished, leaving behind animal panic. Peroni breathed a fervent emergency call to St Janarius.

Then he sensed rather than heard a movement behind him. He whipped about and caught a hunk of flesh and hair and sinew which was bearing down upon his skull with some heavy iron object. The man was heavy and powerful, but he lacked Peroni's peculiar training, and before long he was on the ground making a bubbling noise in his throat as though something inside were broken.

Peroni got out his gun, hoisted the man to his feet and started walking him towards the lakeside town's little police centre where he had earlier warned a plump, fussy urban policeman that he might be arriving with company. This official had put his own office at Peroni's disposal, and into it he now pushed the man.

Seen in the light, he appeared to be a fisherman. Unshaven, none too clean, dressed in jeans and grubby shirt. He had a large, stupid, scowling face with leathery skin burnt dark by the sun.

'Your name?' said Peroni and got no answer. 'You realise,' he went on amiably, 'that I can use torture?'

This wasn't true; well, hardly true, but the mere mention of it could be effective.

It wasn't now. The fisherman just sat staring at Peroni in a hostile way.

'Why did you try to attack me just now?'

No answer. No change of expression.

'You heard, didn't you,' went on Peroni, 'that I'd discovered where Loris Piantaleone went this morning just before he and his car were blown up by a bomb?'

There was still no answer, and Peroni felt a surge of irritation. He had risked his neck to put Stefano's outrageous plan into action. Most improbably it had produced results, creating yet another sensational Peroni episode for the media. And now when everything appeared to be accomplished, he was to be frustrated by this obstinate silence.

Peroni drew his breath to attack again, and just at that moment the door opened and the tubby urban policeman whose office it was came in, saw Peroni and started to back hastily out again.

'Come in, come in,' said Peroni. 'Perhaps you can help me. I can't get a single word out of this man – not even his name.'

The policeman glanced at Peroni's prisoner. 'I don't wonder,' he said. 'He's deaf and dumb.'

Peroni was a compulsive narrator. He needed to recount his exploits, even embellish them. Not that he was a liar. He was a Neapolitan artist who knew that plain facts needed heightening here, shading there to give them their full value. This process gave him great satisfaction and consequently when he arrived home, having had the deaf-and-dumb fisherman transferred to custody in Verona, he was exasperated to find the family all in bed, and the flat in darkness.

Then his attention was caught by a pale glow of white by the telephone. Looking closer, he saw it was a note, and switched on the light to read it. 'Achille – call Regina', it said with disapproving brevity, adding a telephone number. Peroni felt a surge of excitement which swept away tiredness and frustration. He looked at his watch. It was late. She was probably asleep. Nevertheless he dialled.

The high-pitched ringing tone sounded loud in the silence. Eeeee – eeeee – eeeee. He thought he would let it ring ten times, then give it up and go to bed, but when he got to ten, he decided to let it go ten more.

She answered on the seventeenth. '*Pronto?*' It wasn't the voice of somebody wakened from sleep.

'*Pronto,*' said Peroni.

'Achille!' She sounded pleased.

'I'm not disturbing you?'

'No, no. I couldn't sleep, so I just went out for a walk.

When I got back I heard the phone ringing. What are you doing so late?'

He told her. If he had had the entire family sitting about him, he could not have asked for a more appreciative audience. She listened with rapt attention, only interrupting with little gasps of astonishment or admiration.

'Achille,' she said when he had finished, 'you're terrible – you really are! You should never have done a thing like that! You could easily have been killed!'

'If I hadn't done it, I might never have found out where Loris Piantaleone went this morning before he was killed. And remember that wherever *he* went may well be the same place his father went the night he was killed.'

'And you have found out?'

'Not yet. But the police at Garda told me all they could about Minelli – that's the fisherman's name. Tomorrow I'll question him as soon as we can get an interpreter, and then it shouldn't be too difficult to find out what person or organisation he was so concerned about as to try and kill me.'

'Yes, of course! And then the whole business will be cleared up?'

'Perhaps.'

'You're brilliant, Achille!'

'No, no – it's just the luck of the Neapolitans. By the way, when you put me on to the Dowager Countess Augusta the other night – you knew what she was going to tell me?'

'About Montagus and Capulets? I guessed – it's her mania.'

'Why didn't you tell me yourself?'

'I thought you'd like to hear it "from the horse's mouth" as the English say. Besides, you said you were interested in the past, and she really is the one who knows most about that.'

'Thank you then, Regina.'

'You're welcome, Achille.'

'Was there any special reason you wanted me to call you this evening?'

'Oh, yes – of course there was! With all your news it went

right out of my head. I said I'd ring you to fix a lunch date. How about tomorrow?'

'Tomorrow would be perfect,' said Peroni, determining to make it so however many Pillipopolis or Piantaleones might meet with violent death during the coming twelve hours. 'Where shall we meet?'

'You're the busiest – you decide. Somewhere quiet.'

'Well, I shall probably be out at the lake following Minelli's traces – shall we meet there?'

'Lovely.'

'Lazise? There's a *trattoria* on the harbour where they grill lake trout. One o'clock?'

'I'll be there.'

Before she rang off, Peroni caught an almost imperceptible sound at the other end of the line which sounded like a kiss. He went to bed that night a happier man than he had ever been since his arrival in Verona.

When the coffin containing the remains of the late General Orazio Piantaleone was carried out of Verona Cathedral there was such a large crowd that it took the hearse a quarter of an hour to get out of the square with a great deal of undignified hooting.

Few interments have caused so much public interest since the star-crossed lovers were carried to their tomb. This was partly due to the fact that the Montagu–Capulet story had broken publicly that morning in *Il Giornale* and was now the talk of Verona. The tourists, in particular, were delighted to learn that one of the most famous stories in the world was, so to speak, taking place before their very eyes.

Big though it was, the Cathedral was not able to hold the crowd which was now spilling out, past the two griffins bearing the two columns of the portal, into the cathedral square in the wake of the coffin.

In the presence of all the civic dignitaries, the funeral Mass had been said by the bishop, and although he made no direct reference to the Capulets and the Montagus, he showed by reference to the evils of internecine strife that he was aware of the story.

Peroni, who was present, enjoyed a good funeral, though he preferred them Neapolitan style with plenty of uninhibited wailing and tearing of hair, and a gargantuan meal afterwards going on into the small hours of the morning when the grief-stricken mourners would finally reel senseless to their beds. Although second to none in his admiration for things English, Peroni did not appreciate the British-style phlegm displayed at upper-class northern Italian funerals which debased them from high melodrama to mere social functions. Nevertheless, he was bound to admit that this one had its points. A current of high drama was almost tangible in the air.

When the hearse had finally made its way out of the square, the long procession through the streets of Verona began, with Peroni's red Alfa flashing in and out of the interminable and solemn line of cars as he overtook, impatient of the funereal pace.

Having reached the cemetery, he parked beside a flower stall and then went up the steps between the two lions *couchant* and in through the gates with RESURRECTURIS in gigantic letters above them, and was just in time to follow the coffin as it was carried into Verona's eternal suburb.

The Piantaleones had their own private funeral monument, an imposing rococo affair with an almost Michelangelo-esque dome and two heavy wrought-iron gates, now opened to reveal the gloomy interior where a concrete aperture in the wall had been made ready for the General, while another was in preparation for Loris.

Among the crowd Peroni was able to recognise representatives of all the leading aristocratic families of Verona. Or rather all but one. The Pillipopolis were conspicuous by their absence.

What with the crowd and the concealment afforded by neighbouring monuments, Peroni was able to observe the family mourners without being seen. Although the classical Piantaleone profiles were borne high, Peroni sensed that they were all in a state of unnatural tension. Something besides political enmity was threatening this family, like some inexorable Greek doom hanging over it. Even Gabriele seemed affected, though perhaps it was because for once, in deference to custom, he was wearing a dark suit.

When the melancholy ceremony was done Gabriele submitted himself impatiently to the task of shaking hands and receiving condolences, but as soon as he was able to, he broke away from the family group and set off towards the cemetery gates.

Watching him, Peroni felt an instinct to follow. But common

sense said that there was a great deal of practical importance to be done, so the *commissario* in him – who almost always got the upper hand in these internal clashes of opinion – sternly overruled any Neapolitan indulgence in mere instinct.

Later Peroni realised that the *commissario* was wrong.

Outside the cemetery Gabriele got into his car and drove to the Verona headquarters of the ACI – the *Automobile Club Italiano*. Here he enquired for an acquaintance of his who, he was told, was available. Gabriele had acquaintances in every public office in the city and he cultivated them assiduously, for not only did they eliminate for him all bureaucratic formalities, queues and waiting lists, but they also provided him with valuable information. It was information he was after now.

'*Ciao!*' said Gabriele going into his acquaintance's office, hand outstretched.

'*Ciao!*' said the acquaintance, stretching out his hand and remembering the bottles of finest Reciotto he had received from Gabriele the previous Christmas. 'Is there anything I can do for you?' he asked when the congenialities were done.

'As a matter of fact there is,' said Gabriele. 'I want to find out who owns the car with this registration number.' He passed over the piece of paper on which he had written the number of the car that had driven away from the villa in Garda the day before.

'No trouble,' said the acquaintance. 'Make yourself comfortable and I'll be right back.'

He was gone five minutes, and he returned with the same piece of paper which he passed to Gabriele.

Now, written below the Verona registration number, was a name in block capitals, and as he read it Gabriele gave a low whistle.

'An accident?' enquired the acquaintance politely.

'You might call it that,' said Gabriele.

The lake was a burnished sheet when Peroni arrived, and the whole of Garda seemed a different world from the night before.

He parked on the outskirts of the village and walked through it towards an address the local policeman had given him the previous night. It was the address of an old fisherman for whom Minelli worked part-time.

The interview Peroni had had with Minelli that morning before the funeral had not been satisfactory. Even when communication had been established through an interpreter, Minelli had remained gloweringly reticent. He had been drunk the previous evening, he said, and had made the attempted assault under the impression that the victim was a friend of his. And, for all his insistence, Peroni had been able to learn nothing of value from him. In questioning, he thought, the advantages were all on the side of the deaf and dumb. He had therefore decided that, after the funeral, he would see what was to be found out in Garda itself.

As usual the tourists were revealing enough naked flesh to construct half a dozen circus tents. Peroni stared in unbelieving fascination at a Swedish girl – surely she was Swedish? – with a briefer and tighter pair of shorts than he had believed possible. Were such displays not illegal in Italy? He decided to speak to the local Garda policeman about it. But even as he decided, he could hear the policeman's answer: Yes, it was illegal, but too strict an enforcement of the law would be bad for the tourist trade. What hypocrites we Italians are, thought Peroni.

And then he realised that he was following, not the route to the fisherman's house, but the Swedish girl. Naples was running amok within him. The *commissario* took charge of the situation and veered Peroni reluctantly back to the pursuit of truth.

When he reached the address, an old man was sitting on a dilapidated straw-bottomed chair outside the front door. He was rheumy-eyed and stringy, but there was still strength in his arms and shoulders.

'*Questura,*' said Peroni.

The old man's filmy eyes blinked in an effort to focus. 'Eh?' he said.

'*Questura,*' said Peroni louder.

'Not today,' said the old man.

'You have a man called Minelli working for you,' said Peroni loud and clear.

'Vermicelli?' said the old man.

'Minelli!' roared Peroni.

'Ah, Minelli!' said the old man. 'There's a feller called Minelli works for me.'

'I want to ask you some questions about him.'

'You're wastin' yer time – the police took him away last night.'

'I know,' shouted Peroni, 'I am the police.'

'Drunk again,' said the old man, chewing toothlessly.

'Did he work for anybody except you?'

'I just *told* you that he worked for me, didn't I?'

At this point the situation was saved by the arrival of a shrivelled old lady, all dressed in black, with brilliant little eyes set in a face as wrinkled as a prune. 'You won't get any sense out of *him*,' she said. 'Poor old man – it's the arteriosclerosis. Doesn't affect *me* – I'm as sharp as I was when I was a girl of sixteen. But then it's worse with the men, poor things. What was it you were wanting to know?'

'I understand a man called Minelli works for your husband,' said Peroni, assuming a filial air which delighted her.

'That's right,' she said, 'if you can call it work.'

'How many hours a week does he do for you?'

'Depends on the season. Sometimes thirty or so. Sometimes only four or five.'

'Does he have any other work you know of?'

'Oh, no,' said the old man, apparently resentful of his wife's interference. 'Nobody else would employ *him*!'

'There, you poor old man!' she said, 'you told me you saw him with your own eyes!' She turned to Peroni. 'He doesn't remember a thing,' she said. 'Only a week ago it was – he told me about it himself. The poor old man saw him coming out of a villa. And he looked so shifty that the old man thought he must have been stealing something. But I made enquiries later on and I found out that he was a part-time caretaker.' She turned back to her husband. 'Now do you remember, you poor old man?' she said.

At this he suddenly looked as abashed as a little boy who has wet himself, and Peroni felt quite sorry for him. 'Where is this villa?' he asked with a prickle of excitement at the nape of his neck.

'I'll take you there,' said the old man, sounding eager. And so, with the old woman's approval, they set off.

Arterio-sclerosis didn't prevent him from finding his way about, and a few minutes later they stopped outside heavy iron gates in a high stone wall. 'That's her,' said the old man proudly.

'Who lives there?' asked Peroni.

'No idea,' said the old man cheerfully. 'City folks I daresay.'

Peroni thanked him and then, on the spur of the moment, gave him a thousand-lira note. Tipping witnesses wasn't in the spirit of the modern Italy, and the Italian Communist Party wouldn't have approved, but it was well received.

When the old man had gone, Peroni walked around the walls, but was unable to get a glimpse inside or find any sign of life. So he went back to his car and started to drive up towards the village of Albisano. Somewhere along the way, he reckoned, there must be a point from which he could view the villa from above. And sure enough, rounding a corner, he saw the place below him on his left. He parked and got out a pair of binoculars.

Even from this position the villa was not laid bare, for it was surrounded by large trees, but Peroni was able to make out a little of it. It was a large, dark, nineteenth-century building, and it was unequivocally closed up with heavy wooden shutters at all the windows. Strange, he thought, that a lake-side villa should be shut up during the peak holiday month of August.

Then, having seen all that there was to be seen, he drove down to the Garda police headquarters where he found the plump official whose office he had used the night before and asked him whether there were not a law in Italy forbidding displays such as he had seen a little earlier.

'There is,' said the plump functionary, looking unhappy, 'but it's impossible to apply. What would happen to our tourist trade if we arrested everybody who was indecently dressed?' He spread out sweaty palms in a gesture of appeal.

'That's what I thought,' said Peroni. 'I just wanted to hear it confirmed. And now,' he went on, 'there's a villa I want to know something about.' He described its position in detail.

'I know the one,' said the fat policeman. 'Owned by a lawyer – name of Verdi. *Avvocato* Verdi.'

'Pity,' said Peroni, 'things never tie up as neatly as they ought to. I was hoping to find it belonged to the Piantaleones or the Pillipopolis.'

'Piantaleones?' said the policeman, frowning in concentration. 'Now you come to mention it, I believe *Avvocato* Verdi's wife is a Piantaleone.'

There was only one proper course of action. Peroni would have to make an official application to the magistrature to search the villa. This would take several hours, and if *Avv.* Verdi and his Piantaleone wife carried any weight, it might take longer. Besides, *dott.* Spinelli, the deputy public prosecutor, would be hostile towards the application simply because it came from the police. What with one thing and another, by the time Peroni was officially permitted to enter the villa, anything in it pertinent to the deaths of the General or Loris would have disappeared. Such things happened as Peroni well knew. He had been involved once in a case which came up for trial in Venice, and at the last moment documents containing vital prosecution evidence 'accidentally' fell into the Grand Canal.

An alternative to the formal application did exist, but the *commissario* wouldn't hear of it. Besides, it was time for lunch with Regina.

He drove fast to Lazise and parked on the lake front. She wasn't at the taverna where they had agreed to meet, so he sat at a table outside overlooking the miniature port and ordered a Chivas Regal.

She arrived ten minutes later wearing enormous dark glasses, flared white trousers and a red shirt, open at the neck to the fourth button. Peroni realised that he had only seen her once before, and then by night and in eighteenth-century costume, but she still reminded him of a Goldoni actress.

'*Ciao*, Achille!'

'*Ciao*, Regina!'

'What'll you drink?'

'Vodka and Campari, please.'

He ordered it for her, together with another Chivas Regal for himself. 'Shall we eat out here?' he suggested when they were comfortably into their drinks.

'Oh, yes please!' she said. 'I love watching the boats.'

They started with risotto made from a century-old secret recipe with tench from the lake, and they drank a cellar-cool Soave poured from a large jug painted with flowers.

'Achille,' she said when the risotto was done and they were waiting for their trout, 'why did you become a policeman?'

It was a question he usually dodged, and he would certainly have dodged it now if she hadn't been Neapolitan. Even so he was reluctant to answer.

'It's a long story,' he temporised.

'I like long stories.'

He swallowed half a glass of Soave in one and decided to risk it.

'I have not always,' he said, 'been a police *commissario*.'

'I had imagined that,' she said smiling.

'What I mean is,' said Peroni, 'that I haven't always been on the side of the law.'

She watched him with heightened interest, her lips slightly apart.

'When we were children, my sister and I were *scugnizzi* – the gutter kids of Naples. We had no father, and our mother – ' He let the sentence go unfinished as he saw sympathetic understanding light in her eyes.

'We lived as best we could – stealing, pimping, working the black market. Not many people make a fortune out of that sort of life, but the funny thing is that I think I might have done. I was good at it, and I liked it. If things hadn't happened the way they did I might be a Mafia boss by now.'

'You don't look the type.'

'There is no special type.'

'I'll take your word for it. What did happen though?'

'Well, one day –'

Their trout arrived at that moment, and they had a salad with it, pouring on vinegar that still tasted of wine through the sharpness.

'Go on!' she said.

'One day we ran into a hungry-looking young man who looked like a slightly older version of myself. It was cold, and he offered us a bed for the night and some food, but he said there was just one thing we ought to know about him before we accepted.' He paused for effect and a mouthful of trout.

'What was that?'

'He was a priest. I probably wouldn't have gone when I heard that, but it was very cold, and we both felt that if there were free hand-outs we might as well take advantage of them. The place he took us to was a pleasant surprise. It wasn't one of those institutions with dormitories and polished floors. It was just another tumbledown Neapolitan house, very roughly furnished and none too clean. He told us that we were free to come and go as we liked. There were no rules, but when we wanted there would always be food and somewhere to sleep for us.

'You know I've often cursed the subtlety of that priest. If he'd tried to convert us or rehabilitate us or anything like that, we'd have been out of the place like lightning, and today I might be all of a piece, instead of being a Neapolitan gutter kid dressed up as a policeman.'

'But what did he do?'

'That was it – he didn't do anything! He let you come and go, and listened when you wanted to talk. Then one day one of the other boys there happened to say he rather fancied the idea of working on the railways. A couple of days later the station master of Naples arrived to talk the idea over. He just happened to be a friend of Don Pietro – that was the name of the priest. Don Pietro had the most unlikely friends in the most unlikely places. If one of the kids found he had a talent for cooking, the head chef of one of the smartest restaurants in Europe just happened along. If somebody else thought he'd like to write, then somehow or other we'd find the editor of the *Corriere della Sera* dropping in for lunch the next day.

'After a while it became catching – even my sister went to work in a hotel. But I didn't know what I wanted to do. So one day I mentioned it to Don Pietro, and he just said, "Oh, you ought to be a policeman, Achille." I almost jumped out of my skin. If there was one class of people I trusted even less than priests, it was policemen. Just for once Don Pietro was wide of the mark, and I told him so. "I don't know so much, Achille," he said. "I've noticed something about you – you have an irresistible urge to get at the truth. It's stronger than anything else in you." To my surprise I realised he was right. "Just think about it," he said. Well, of course, once he'd planted the seed I couldn't think of anything else, and a couple of days later the chief of police in Naples happened to drop by. He was a friend of Don Pietro, too. . . .'

They were having coffee when the story came to an end. 'I think that's absolutely wonderful, Achille!' said Regina, looking at him with something like awe. Then she glanced at her watch and the expression changed. 'Heavens!' she said, 'I must go – I've got a lesson at three.'

Peroni walked her to her car. 'When can I see you again?' he asked.

'Call me tonight,' she said. 'We'll fix something then.'

She kissed him lightly on the cheek, got into the little car and accelerated quickly off in the direction of Verona.

As he watched her go, Peroni wondered uneasily whether he was falling in love.

When Peroni was slightly drunk the *dottore/commissario* was at a disadvantage. This was the case now. Peroni had consumed two large Chivas Regals before his lunch, a great deal of Soave with it and some grappa afterwards. As a consequence the moral imperative of applying to the deputy public prosecutor for a warrant to search the villa seemed less urgent. The respectable part of him put up some resistance, but it was quickly overcome.

He drove back to Garda, parked and walked to the heavy iron gates the old fisherman had shown him that morning. The lock presented no particular problems to a man of Peroni's skill, and within a few minutes he was inside the grounds.

He looked warily about him for dogs of which he was terrified. There was no sign of one, and he calculated that with such a vigilant guardian as the deaf and dumb fisherman there would have been no need.

He walked towards the heavily built, mid-nineteenth-century villa. The grounds were large and well kept, though gloomy with overhanging trees which was a relief in the August blaze.

The make of the lock on the front door surprised Peroni. It was sophisticated and very expensive, and suggested that *Avv.* Verdi was particularly anxious to protect himself against burglars. Special tools would have been required to open it and more time than Peroni cared to dedicate. He examined the rest of the front. The windows all had heavy wooden shutters and there was no other door.

At first sight the back seemed as invulnerable as the front, but then his attention focussed on a small iron door. It probably opened into a cellar and stood within a small porch which would allow him to work unseen by anybody who didn't come right up to it. He stepped into the porch.

As he had suspected, the door did lead into a cellar containing logs and gardening tools. There was another locked door at the other side of it, and when he had dealt with that Peroni stepped into a long corridor with doors opening off it. Lighting his way in the pitch darkness with a torch, he tried the nearest door and found that it opened into a sitting-room with old-fashioned furniture which nobody, he decided, could envy. But close examination revealed nothing of interest.

Some while later he had to admit that close examination of the entire house had also revealed nothing of interest. It was just the stuffy country villa of a comfortably-off Veronese family. So why did it need a watch-dog like Minelli and expensive, bank-type locks?

He was on the point of giving up the whole thing as a bad job when he began to be vaguely aware that perhaps he had found something after all. Something very intangible that went before him as he moved through the dark house. When he went into a room, he felt that it had only just been left. When he turned a corner in a corridor, it was as though it had just rounded the next corridor ahead of him or disappeared down the stairs.

As soon as he was conscious of it, this presence became overwhelming. He caught himself listening for footsteps and movements in the dark. But this was a trick of the senses. The physical presence was no longer in the house. It was the imprint of somebody's psyche on the atmosphere. Somebody who had spent a great deal of time in the villa.

And, he realised in a sudden flash of blinding clarity, it was *somebody he knew.*

Then all of a sudden the lunchtime intake of alcohol went to his bladder. Expert by now in the layout of the villa he was able to move swiftly to the nearest lavatory. Then, as he was fumbling desperately to unbutton, his pocket torch fell to the ground, and even his extreme physical urgency did not prevent him from understanding from the noise it made in falling that the space of floor he was standing on was hollow.

In his impatience it seemed that the mighty gush which brought relief would never end. Not for the first time he marvelled at the gargantuan capacity of his bladder. But slowly the torrent diminished to a trickle and Peroni, careless of last drops, buttoned himself once more and knelt down.

He quickly found that four floorboards could be made to shift with his hands. These were held in place by nails which were easily prised out allowing him to lift the floorboards.

But, as soon as he had lifted them, Peroni's elation vanished. The room or space below, which his torch revealed, was empty. Whoever or whatever had been kept in it had been removed.

There was a ladder going down from the lavatory, and Peroni got on to it with a sense of anticlimax accentuated by the now quickly dissipating fumes of alcohol. But when he reached the bottom, he saw that there was something after all. Not much compared with what he had hoped to find but something just the same. As his torch moved round the walls he saw a complicated network of racks and frames and, although they were empty, he knew beyond doubt what they had contained. And that made everything a great deal clearer. A key-piece of the jigsaw puzzle slipped into place. If it could only be linked now with the identity of the person whose psyche was so clearly stamped on the atmosphere of the villa, then perhaps the whole picture might be clear.

Now he ranged through the villa in a new way, searching for some trace of the person which would give him the identity. But whoever it was had been punctilious in clearing up traces, and Peroni could find traces of nobody except the stuffy, comfortably-off family of *Avv.* Verdi.

Then, when he was in a little study at the back of the house, his torch picked up a sudden gleam. Switching back on to it, Peroni went over and knelt to pick it up.

It was a tiny gold pencil of the sort that go with pocket diaries, but it was much more expensive than the common run of such pencils. It was not something you would expect to find in *Avv.* Verdi's family, so it stood a good chance of belonging to the other person.

Peroni stood looking at it in the torch light. Possessions, he knew, could tell you about the identity of their owner, but, though he had his flashes, Peroni wasn't that psychic. He gripped the pencil hard and tried, but it told him nothing.

Suddenly he felt frightened. What he had stumbled upon was big and although one of its watch-dogs, in the shape of the deaf and dumb fisherman, had been removed, there might be others and, like Minelli, they would be ready to kill. It was time to get out quick. Breathing a hasty invocation to St Janarius, Peroni headed back towards the cellar he had come in by.

When his receptionist announced that two officers from the *Questura* wished to see him, *Avv.* Verdi felt a stab of panic. He had been dreading trouble ever since the beginning. And now it had come.

Or perhaps, after all, it hadn't. He tried to calm himself with the reflection that the police often did come to see him about his clients. Maybe this was just another routine visit.

'Ask them to step in, *signorina*,' he said on the internal telephone.

Three seconds later the receptionist was opening his office door and two policemen were entering. One he knew personally – a melancholy, dyspeptic-looking man. What was his name? Lenotti. But it was the sight of the other one which upset the lawyer. He didn't know him personally, and didn't wish to, but he had seen him on television and his picture in the papers. He was *Commissario* Peroni, the Neapolitan so-called Rudolph Valentino of the Italian police. *Avv.* Verdi had no liking for southerners, but it was not Peroni's provenance that upset him now so much as the fact that he was in charge of the enquiry into General Piantaleone's death.

'*Buon giorno*,' the three men murmured at each other with ritual politeness, shaking hands.

'Please be seated, gentlemen,' said *Avv.* Verdi, gesturing towards two chairs in front of his desk. 'Can I help you?'

'I understand,' said Peroni, giving a disconcerting impression of a skilled lawyer at the outset of a lethal cross-examination, 'I understand that you have a villa in the village of Garda.'

Avv. Verdi felt a sickening lurch in his stomach. So it had been discovered at last. He saw professional ruin looming ahead of him, social ostracism, almost certainly prison.

'My family possess one,' he said, managing to keep his voice steady.

'Do you go there frequently?'

'Not recently, no. The place is mostly closed up.'

'Does anyone else, to your knowledge, go there?'

'The villa has always been at the disposal of my wife's family. I believe some of its members occasionally go there.'

'For any particular purpose?'

Again *Avv.* Verdi had the unpleasant sensation of being in the witness box, ruthlessly stripped of all reserves. 'For weekends,' he said.

'Did the late General Piantaleone go there?'

'I believe so.'

'And his son Loris?'

'Yes, I think so.'

'Purely for relaxation?'

'As far as I am aware.'

'*Avvocato*,' said Peroni. The tone had unexpectedly changed. It was no longer cuttingly forensic, but had a hint of warmth in it. *Avv.* Verdi felt a lift of hope, though in what he could not tell. '*Avvocato*, I know what's been going on at your villa in Garda – quite enough to establish a case. But naturally there are points which escape me. If somebody who was in on the whole affair from the beginning were to help me with these points, I daresay such a person might escape prosecution.'

Miraculously *Avv.* Verdi saw his life and career, which a few seconds before had lain about him in a desolation of rubble, rebuilt and gleaming in the sun. He would be a traitor, of course. But to what? Piantaleone was dead. Loris was dead.

'It was my wife Norma who came to me in the first place,' he began, and there was a general slackening of tension in the room with the realisation that the decision had been made. 'She told me that her cousin, the General, had started a movement whose ultimate aim was to combat Communism and instal a right-wing government which would put a stop to the galloping decay in the Italian body politic. She asked me if I wished to adhere to the movement, and I said I did. My convictions tallied exactly with those of the movement, and I was certain General Pianta-leone was the only man in Italy with sufficient prestige to attract followers. Preliminary meetings were held at my house in Verona.'

'When was this?' asked Peroni.

'About eighteen months ago.'

'Go on.'

'It became evident that a place was needed for combat training and exercise, somewhere easily accessible and yet well protected, large and with ample grounds. My family villa was proposed. I opposed the idea adamantly, but my wife – well, she is very much a Piantaleone, and she was determined the place should be put at the disposal of the movement, so I was obliged to give way.'

'What exactly went on there?'

'Physical training, weapon handling, courses in Judo and Karate, political instruction.'

'Organised by the General?'

'Towards the end of his life he was a trifle – mentally disturbed and he became more and more of a figurehead. I understood that most of the organisation was done by his son Loris, who also travelled about making contact with groups and individuals who might give their support.'

'When did all this training and activity take place at the villa?'

'Mostly at weekends.'

'Who was there the rest of the time?'

'Frankly, I don't know. The whole thing had got out of hand. It was as though the villa were no longer my property. New locks were put on the doors, and I didn't even have the keys to them.'

'But you did know who the other members of the movement were?'

'Oh, yes, I knew them.'

He checked momentarily when it came to giving their names, but as it was amply clear that there was no going back now, he licked his lips and gave them. They were names which made Lenotti, a great respecter of persons, blink in astonishment. They included leading local businessmen, politicians, headmasters, senior state functionaries. The scandal would be enormous.

Only one thing was really bothering *Avv.* Verdi now and he brought it up when, at long last, Peroni came to the end of his questions. It was swelteringly hot in the office by then and dark, too, for nobody had bothered to turn on the light.

'There is just one thing, *commissario*,' said Verdi as the three men rose.

'Yes?' said Peroni.

'I should be grateful if my wife were not to know of the source of your information.'

'I daresay that can be managed.'

'It's a great honour being married to a Piantaleone,' said Verdi, 'but it can be very uncomfortable at times.'

It was the hottest evening of the year which was all very well for the tourists who were crowded into the great bowl of the Roman arena listening to a performance of *Aïda*. It was not so pleasant if you were on duty at the entrance to the *Questura*. The policeman glanced at his watch. Another hour and a half and he'd be off duty. He visualised himself at home, stripped down to pants – perhaps with the *bimbi* in bed he could even take them off – and getting a bottle of wine out of the fridge.

Then he checked his thoughts. They weren't the sort you could permit yourself when you were on duty outside a police headquarters in Italy where, however quiet things might look, you were always in the front line of an endless battle. At any moment a car might round the corner. Just like any other car except that its occupants would be Red Brigaders. Then as it passed a gun would suddenly be pointed from the window and you'd be sprayed with bullets before you even had time to reach towards your own holster. It happened almost every day.

Just then a car did round the corner, and the policeman's fingers stiffened towards his gun. But then he recognised it as a police car. It slowed to a halt in front of him and *dott*. Peroni got out followed by *dott*. Lenotti. Peroni looked excited about something. The policeman saluted.

'Why don't you go and get some supper?' said Peroni to Lenotti.

'Thanks,' said Lenotti with a reproachful expression which seemed to imply that Peroni should know better than to think he could eat an ordinary supper with his stomach in the state it was. But he went off just the same.

Peroni went to the reception desk and got an envelope, then he took a small gold pencil out of his pocket, put it in the envelope and sealed it.

'Give this to Simoni when he comes in, will you?' he said to the policeman, handing him the envelope. 'I want to know anything he can find out about this pencil.'

'Yes, sir.'

'Is *dott.* Guerra in?'

'Yes, sir – he's in his office.'

'I'll go and see him. No, wait a minute, first I must make a phone call.' And Peroni moved off in the direction of his office.

The policeman on duty at the entrance to the *Questura* decided that the call in question was to a woman.

'*Pronto?*'

'*Pronto* – Regina?'

'Achille – *ciao*! Aren't you nearly dead in this heat?'

'Heat? I hadn't even noticed it.'

'That shows you've got something more interesting to think about.'

'I have.'

'Then tell – if it's not a secret.'

'As a matter of fact, I suppose it is. But it'll be public knowledge tomorrow. I've uncovered a clandestine fascist movement which was run by General Piantaleone.'

'Achille, how wonderful! However did you do it?'

'Well, before I met you for lunch this morning I went to Lake Garda . . .'

Cradling the receiver between chin and shoulder, he got out and lit a cigarette and settled down to the soothing and yet stimulating activity of recounting his exploits.

'Oh, Achille,' she said when he had finished, 'you really are brilliant!'

He didn't bother to contradict her. 'Now I must go and tell it all to *dott.* Guerra,' he said.

'Who's he?'

'Oh, I forgot you don't know about the workings at the *Questura* – he's the head of everything here.'

'Then I'm sure he'll be very pleased with you.'

'Just before I go,' said Peroni, 'when can we meet?'

'Oh, tomorrow I hope, Achille. I've got a terribly busy day, though – can I ring you?'

'Yes, of course. I'll be waiting for you. *Ciao*, Regina!'

'*Ciao*, Achille!'

The Father Christmas-like head of the DIGOS was feeling the heat, too. The ramshackle electric fan in his office did nothing to prevent the formation of huge drops of sweat which gathered and fell on to the papers before him if not quickly mopped up by an already soaking handkerchief. The heat increased his general sense of frustration at the way things were going. Or rather were not going. But he allowed none of this to show in his expression which beamed Yuletide geniality when there came a knock at the door and Toni, the youngest of his men, came in.

'Sit down, sit down, my boy,' said the head of the DIGOS. 'Help yourself to a cigarette. Oh, of course, you don't smoke – how very wise of you. Now then, what's your news today?'

'I haven't any I'm afraid, sir. I can't find a trace of either Policarpo Pillipopoli, or the red-head, Monica Branca.'

'It looks as though they've left Verona.'

'It does rather, sir.'

'On the other hand, we haven't got a single, even minimally positive report on them from anywhere else. And that's odd in view of the detailed descriptions we have sent out of them both.'

'Maybe they've managed to get abroad, sir? Or just holed up somewhere.'

'Maybe. Whatever it is, I think we're going to change our approach. Take the day off tomorrow and think about it.' He said it as though he were producing a particularly splendid toy train from a sack.

'The day off?' said Toni staggered.

'That's right,' said the head of the DIGOS beaming. 'The day off.'

'Thank you, sir.'

The benignity of his chief seemed to waft about Toni like a cloud as he left the office.

But the head of the DIGOS wasn't benign at all. He knew that Toni had been working round the clock for more than a week, and that a free day magnanimously conceded now might save ten days later if the boy cracked up. The *Questura* was dangerously short of men.

If *dott.* Guerra minded the heat he didn't show it. His tie tied, his jacket buttoned, he sat listening to Peroni's report with polite interest.

'My congratulations, *dottore*,' he said when Peroni came to the end.

'Thank you, *dottore*,' said Peroni, trying and failing to sound modest.

'Of course, this new development gives us a great deal to occupy ourselves. All these people,' and he tapped the list Peroni had given him, 'will have to be brought into custody simultaneously which will require careful organisation. It is interesting to reflect,' he continued, looking up at Peroni with what might have been a hint of a smile, 'that this discovery of yours, *dottore*, will deprive the Veronese professional classes of a large number of their leading members. I fear it will not make them feel any more warmly inclined towards the south of Italy.'

It was the first time Guerra had ever referred to Peroni's origins, and Peroni felt it must be a sign of approval.

The coolest place in Patti's flat was a small balcony which, surrounded as it was by huddles of reddish-brown roofs, was only reached by the sun briefly at midday. This made it a welcome refuge in July and August. She was sitting out on it when she saw Gabriele arrive on foot and disappear into the front doorway below. A minute later the bell rang.

'Where's the car?' she asked opening the door.

'Battery's being charged,' said Gabriele.

She observed him more closely and decided he must be a little drunk. 'What's the matter with you?' she asked.

'Nothing,' he said. 'Nothing – except that I've got there at last.'

'Where?'

'Where I've been trying to get for so long. I know who's behind the whole business.'

'Congratulations,' she said, giving him a martini. 'How did you do it?'

'I told you I got the number of that car I saw leaving the villa in Garda. Well, I found out who it belonged to. And I watched them.' He paused for a moment and then laughed. 'It was the place that made me think – it was so completely out of character. Anyway, there's a little bar just down the road from it where I could watch without any fear of being seen. And that's where I got the reward for all my hard work.'

'What?'

'I saw somebody else going in there.'

'And who was that?'

'The big fish,' said Gabriele tauntingly. 'The biggest fish of all.'

'I suppose that means you're not going to tell me who it is?'

'You suppose right.'

Patti sighed. 'What did you do then?'

'I went home. Then I made a phone call and fixed an appointment.'

'And when is this appointment?'

'In about twenty minutes. I must go. I just thought I'd drop in on my way and tell you the good news. I'll call back afterwards and we'll celebrate.'

'You sound very sure there'll be a reason to celebrate.'

'I'm absolutely certain.'

'But is it safe, Gabriele?'

'Perfectly. The mastermind is at the opera in the arena tonight. So I made my appointment in the piazza outside during the interval. I'll be surrounded by several thousand people. You couldn't be safer than that, could you?'

134

'Oof! It couldn't be hotter in Naples!' said Assunta. 'After midnight, and there isn't a breath of air.'

The family was sitting out on the balcony eating an enormous water melon. The children were in their pyjamas, but with the plausible excuse that it was too hot to sleep, they had gained permission to wait up for Uncle Achille, if he wasn't too late.

'That's him now!' said Anna Maria, jumping up as she heard the front door opening. She and Stefano ran into the hall.

'*Ciao*, Uncle Achille!'

'What's the news?'

'We saw General Piantaleone's funeral on television!'

'What did you find out from the deaf-and-dumb fisherman?'

'And what have you been doing all day? You might have telephoned!'

'Children!' said Assunta, 'let your uncle sit down first. Water melon, Achille?'

'Please.'

'Now, Uncle Achille – tell all!'

He paused for effect. 'I have uncovered,' he said, 'a clandestine fascist movement organised by General Piantaleone.'

'Well, well, well,' said Giorgio, wiping juice from his chin, 'so the old boy was up to something after all! And that's what he was doing when he was supposed to be looking after his estate in Rosaro!'

'Exactly,' said Peroni.

'How did you do it?' asked Anna Maria.

Peroni recounted the day's events from the General's funeral to the recent interview with *dott*. Guerra, only omitting his lunch with Regina which was not for the children's ears, or for Assunta's either, come to that. He let himself go with the description of his visit to the villa, but when he came to the bit about the psyche which he had felt so strongly stamped on the air he was brought up sharply by Stefano.

'Forgive me saying so, Uncle Achille, but this is not evidence.'

'I know it's not,' said Peroni, trying not to look offended, 'but you know very well I've had impressions like that before and they've always led to something.'

'I think,' said Stefano with a sceptical air, 'that if you analyse the incidents carefully you will find that it was not so much the impressions as the facts surrounding them that led to something.'

'That's very unfair, Stefano!' said Anna Maria, rushing to Peroni's rescue, 'Uncle Achille's instinct has always been terribly important!'

'You say that because you rely on instinct yourself,' said Stefano. 'Personally, I prefer not to have my reasoning influenced by anything other than solid fact.'

'Well, it's just as well you're not the only one,' said Anna Maria, 'or we'd never get Uncle Achille's cases solved for him!'

'Children, children!' said Assunta, 'let your uncle go on with his story!'

They let him have a clear run until he came to the shelves and racks in the little room under the lavatory.

'But if they were empty,' said Giorgio, 'how could you know what they had contained?'

'It was obvious from the form of them. They'd clearly been constructed to hold weapons.'

'Ah, I see!'

While Peroni was describing his interview with *Avv.* Verdi, he was interrupted once again by Stefano. 'That would seem to explain one thing,' he said.

'What's that?'

'Loris's movements at the time of his father's disappearance. He said he was visiting agricultural machinery factories in Milan which you found out wasn't true. What this lawyer says would appear to indicate that he probably was in Milan all right, but on behalf of the movement.'

When Peroni finally reached the end of the account Anna Maria said, 'Well, I think that's simply wonderful, Uncle Achille. I bet there isn't another policeman in the whole of Italy who could have done all that in one day.'

'It's certainly impressive,' said Stefano, 'but – '

'But?' said Anna Maria. 'You seem to be doing nothing but criticise this evening!'

'I'm sorry if I give that impression. It's just that I'm bound to point out that, as far as the deaths of General Piantaleone and Loris are concerned, we're not a great deal further forward.'

'Oh yes we are!' said Anna Maria. 'We know they were involved in this movement, and that explains why they were killed!'

'Does it?' said Stefano.

'Well, of course it does! The General was the head of a clandestine fascist movement – if that's not asking to be killed, I'd like to know what is!'

'But was he?'

'Was he what?'

'Head of a clandestine fascist movement?'

'I thought that was the whole point of what Uncle Achille's found out today!'

'I must disagree. At the very outset of the whole affair Uncle Achille discovered that General Piantaleone was in a state of advanced senile decay. How could such a man organise a clandestine movement?'

'All right, granted,' said Anna Maria. 'He was the figurehead then, which amounts to the same thing.'

'So who organised it?'

'Loris.'

'Loris was a fanatic, but as Uncle Achille has also told us, he was stupid – he couldn't have run something as complex as that by himself.'

'All right then, clever, what did happen?'

'I believe,' said Stefano slowly, 'that there is somebody else behind this movement. Somebody who is neither senile nor stupid. Somebody who calculatedly used General Piantaleone as a figurehead to further his own ends. Then, I believe, the General became increasingly difficult to handle as his state of senile decay was exacerbated. Probably he threatened to reveal the real organiser's identity if his demands were not met with, and by so doing he signed his own death warrant. On the night of his disappearance he was induced with promises to the villa at Garda where he was killed.'

'Wait a minute,' said Assunta. 'What about the Red Brigade? They did, after all, claim his murder for themselves.'

'It's never been proved that it was the Red Brigade,' said Stefano, 'and it wouldn't have been impossible to simulate the circumstances – enough to produce a stencilled communiqué with a five-pointed star on top. In fact,' he went on, turning to Peroni, 'you told us that the typewriter used was not one known to belong to the Red Brigade.'

'But if this is so,' said Giorgio, 'why didn't the Red Brigade deny responsibility?'

'Why should they? It would have been a feather in their caps.'

'And what about Loris?'

'Assuming my reasoning to be correct, he somehow discovered that his father had gone out to Garda on the night of his death and drove there – followed by *Signor* Lenotti – to demand an explanation. Plainly, he could not be allowed to return to Verona alive with that knowledge, and so the bomb was put in his car.'

'Why didn't they kill him there like his father?' asked Anna Maria.

'At the moment I can make no conjecture about that,' said Stefano, 'and this is partly why I said we are no further forward as far as the murders are concerned. With his swoop today Uncle Achille has caught the body of the serpent, if I may use the metaphor, but the head has escaped. I think you'll find, Uncle Achille, that *Avv.* Verdi and his wife and indeed all the other members of the movement have no more idea about who was really behind it than we have.'

'So I'm left with a fistful of mist,' said Peroni gloomily.

'It's not as bad as that, Uncle Achille,' said Anna Maria. 'There's your impression of somebody's psyche stamped on the air of the villa.'

'That's not going to help me get to the person whose psyche

it is,' said Peroni. Then he took another slice of water melon and brightened somewhat. 'There's just one thing that might, though,' he said.

'What's that?' said all the family, looking at him.

'The gold pencil.'

Policarpo

When Peroni got to the office the next morning there was a note asking him to call *dott.* Simoni, the colleague to whom he had entrusted the gold pencil. He dialled.

'Simoni speaking.'

'Good morning, *dottore*. Peroni.'

'Ah, good morning, *dottore* – lovely day!'

'You've got news about my pencil?'

'Indeed I have. You're lucky this time. Or don't they say that you're always lucky? What is it the papers call it? The Neapolitan streak?'

'That's right,' said Peroni, hiding his impatience. Simoni was a nice little man and could be very helpful, but he did run on. 'The pencil?' Peroni hinted.

'Ah, yes, the pencil. Well now. It comes from a pocket diary which is produced in Switzerland by a Geneva firm of luxury stationery manufacturers called Pierre Ronceaux et Cie. It's an expensive product, but the interesting thing about it is that it's not exported. So whoever you're looking for must have been to Switzerland last Christmas.'

'Or had a friend who was there,' suggested Peroni.

'Yes, of course, there's that to it, isn't there?' agreed Simoni.

'Anything else about it?'

'Only that just over 15,000 of these diaries were sold in Switzerland for this year. At a price for which you could get a meal out for a whole family over here, too.'

'Lucky Swiss,' said Peroni.

'Oh, they've got nothing on the Neapolitans! Good morning, *dottore*!'

'Good morning, *dottore*.'

Barbara awoke with a feeling of elation, and just for a second couldn't remember the cause of it. Then it came back to her – Toni's call the previous evening to say he had been given the whole coming day off. She would have him to herself from morning till evening.

Being engaged to a policeman was a wonderful thing, much more exciting than a bank employee or a teacher. But it had its disadvantages, and not the least of them was that you saw so little of him. Lately, in particular, what with the Red Brigade and the General Piantaleone business, Toni had been working almost uninterruptedly. So the prospect of having him for an entire day was particularly exciting.

She got ready as quickly as she could and went down to the kitchen where her mother had the coffee on.

'*Ciao*, Mamma!'

'*Ciao*, darling. You're looking very bright.'

'Well, of course I am! I've got the whole day with Toni!'

'Oh yes, so you have. What are you going to do with it?'

'Oh, we'll see what he feels like.'

Quarter of an hour later Toni called for her in his car and they set off. The sun was bright, she knew she was looking her prettiest and she was head over heels with the man sitting beside her. The world couldn't have seemed a happier place.

'I've got an idea,' said Toni. 'Why don't we buy ourselves something to eat and then go out to the lake. We could spend the whole day at San Vigilio and just swim and lie in the sun until evening.'

'That would be lovely!' She would probably have said the same if he had suggested going to Hell. 'There's the PAM – we can get some food there.'

They went into the supermarket, got a trolley and went round the shelves choosing their lunch. This added a new dimension to Barbara's happiness because it made her think of what it would be like when they were married.

'Let's have a bottle of Valpolicella.'

'Can we afford it, Toni?'

141

'Of course we can. Now all we want's some cheese and – '

He stopped short and she could feel his interest in their lunch suddenly die on its feet. 'What's the matter, Toni?'

'Nothing. I just want to see – ' He left the sentence unfinished and then suddenly left her, wheeling their trolley.

Barbara found herself alone in the alley surrounded by tins of peeled tomatoes and bottles of oil. She couldn't understand why he had abandoned her, but she had a nasty presentiment that something was wrong.

It was more than justified when she started in pursuit and, rounding the corner at the end of the alley, caught sight of Toni again.

He was following a red-head.

He was being subtle about it, but there could be no doubt. Every time she stopped, he stopped and, although he appeared to be carefully examining the goods on the shelves, Barbara could see that his attention was entirely on her.

When the red-head came to the cash desks, Toni took a place in the slightly longer queue beside hers. Then when she had paid and gone out he followed her, abandoning the trolley with their lake-side lunch in it.

Barbara felt as though the sun had gone out.

The chemist was a jovial man, well known and well liked, and nobody could have been more surprised than his own assistants when he was taken away by the police. They couldn't imagine what he could possibly be involved in. They knew that his views were right wing. He had never hidden his belief that the country needed a stronger government which would take firmer measures to prevent the spread of Communism.

But what his assistants didn't know was that for more than a year he had been spending all the spare time he could at week-ends at a villa in Garda, training to take an active role in the overthrow of the government.

He had gone pale when the policemen had arrived and asked him to accompany them to the *Questura*. But by the time he arrived there he had recovered some of his customary equa-

142

nimity. He had known all along that it was a risk and, besides, with the legal system that prevailed in Italy the thing would drag on for a long while and probably end up with suspended sentences. And the many millions of lire he had made in his shop would comfortably absorb even such a shock as this. On the whole, he decided that it was in his interest to be co-operative.

This decision was reinforced when he was taken into the presence of a southern-looking detective who had an extraordinary relaxing effect upon him. Although this detective didn't say it in so many words, the chemist had the impression that he was a political sympathiser and would do all he could to make things easy.

The detective took him through the whole story from the day when a fellow member of the neo-fascist MSI party in Verona approached him in a roundabout way to find out whether he would be prepared to do something concrete to bring about a new order in Italy. He made no bones about his excitement at the discovery of such a possibility – an excitement which mounted when he learned that the new movement was headed by General Piantaleone.

'Perhaps you'll agree with me,' said the chemist, 'that we should all be a great deal better off if there were one or two men like him in the government today.'

He told about the training he had received, the security measures taken at the villa, the cautious recruitment of new members, the spirit of hope and enthusiasm which had pervaded the new movement. He agreed that the ultimate aim of of it all had been to seize power.

As for the General's death itself there was obviously no doubt that it was the work of the Red Brigade. Nobody else would be capable of what, for the chemist, practically amounted to deicide.

Yes, he had understood that the General had become slightly arterio-sclerotic towards the end, but he had assumed that Loris was running things in his place.

'Did you ever suspect that somebody other than General

Piantaleone and Loris might be behind the movement?'

'No,' said the chemist looking puzzled. 'Such an idea had never occurred to me.'

Nor had such an idea occurred to the school-teacher or the bank employee Peroni had interviewed previously. It was beginning to look as though Stefano might be right once again.

Toni had abandoned Barbara in the supermarket with the utmost reluctance, but the sight of the red-head had left him no alternative. He couldn't be entirely certain it was Monica – presumed terrorist and accomplice of Policarpo Pillipopoli – but the resemblance was sufficient to warrant following her. It made it no easier to know that Barbara was certain to see he was following a red-head and to draw her own conclusions for, in strict accordance with the rules of the DIGOS, Toni did not discuss his work with anyone outside, not even Barbara.

Manoeuvring so as neither to lose the red-head nor be seen by her, he consoled himself that things would easily be patched up with Barbara if this really were Monica, if she led him to Policarpo, if the DIGOS could arrest the pair of them. Always assuming he didn't get killed in the process.

Still wheeling her trolley, the red-head took the supermarket lift down to the garage. Toni went by the stairs. Without looking right or left, he made for his own 600, but he saw her from the corner of his eye as she unloaded purchases into the boot of a shabby-looking Fiat 125. It had a Rome number plate, he saw. This may have meant that she'd come from Rome, but if it was Monica it was more probable that the car was stolen. The Red Brigade always used stolen cars which could be abandoned in complete anonymity.

Toni drove out after her. Several other cars were mounting the ramp at the same time, so there was no danger of being noticed. She drove away from the town centre towards the outskirts, and finally came to the least fashionable, poorest and most overcrowded quarter of the town which tourists in search of Romeo and Juliet never came to see.

She stopped in front of a large, down-at-heel-looking block, considerably pre-Mussolini in date, its age marked by dust and grime and smoke.

He drove on past her, stopped outside a horse-meat butcher's and watched in his mirror as she unloaded the boot and then went into the block with her purchases. Toni climbed out of his car, crossed the road and walked back. You went in, he saw, through an open courtyard hung with washing and then took one of the entrances to the various staircases. He was too late to see which one she had taken.

A little further down the road was a bar with a yellow dial-sign outside indicating you could telephone. Toni went into the bar which was rowdy and none too clean, and asked for a telephone token. As he dialled, he blessed the noise which would prevent any snatch of conversation from being overheard.

'*Questura.*'

Toni gave Father Christmas's internal number, was put through, identified himself and described what had happened.

'Splendid, my boy!' said Father Christmas, benevolence humming over the wires. 'Stay there and I'll be right with you. It looks as though you're fated not to have a day off, doesn't it?'

'I don't mind about that, sir,' said Toni, 'I'm only worried that perhaps it isn't her after all.'

'We'll think about that when we've had a closer look at her,' said the head of the DIGOS ringing off.

Patti was not given to worrying, least of all about Gabriele. He was one of those people who always survived. Or so she'd thought. But now she was beginning to wonder. It wasn't so much that he had failed to come back as he'd promised the previous evening – he'd done that dozens of times. It was rather the nature of what he was handling that worried her. She knew it was dangerous. So had he really been as safe as he thought in the piazza outside the arena surrounded by several thousand people?

She wished he hadn't kept the anonymity of the person or people he was after quite so strictly. If she had known who they were, she might have had some idea of where to look for him.

But as she didn't she decided, after much anxious thought, to telephone his home.

Gabriele's young cousin, Paolo, answered and she recognised his voice, grateful that she hadn't got the General's widow.

'May I speak to Gabriele please?'

'He's not here,' said Paolo.

'Have you any idea when he went out?'

'That's just it,' said Paolo, 'he hasn't been back all night.'

Suddenly Patti began to feel frightened.

There were no sirens or police cars. The Father Christmas head of the DIGOS and his squad permeated the street noiselessly and, in so far as it was possible, invisibly. One moment Toni was by himself, the next his chief was standing by him, and he was able to spot a dozen of his colleagues, all totally part of the background and all at strategic points. He had taken part in such operations, but he had never seen one from outside before, and the efficiency of it impressed him.

'Any movement?' asked the head of the DIGOS.

'No,' said Toni.

'Then we'd better find out the lie of the land. After that we'll decide how to handle it.'

A few minutes after that a girl with large yellow-lensed glasses and too much make-up went into the greengrocer's. 'I wonder if you could help me?' she said.

'I'll do my very best,' said the young male greengrocer who had no aversion to too much make-up.

'I'm a representative for Euroclub books. I've got a client somewhere here, but I've lost her schedule, and I'm going to get into trouble if I can't find her – apart from losing my commission.'

'What's her name?'

'That's just it – I can't remember.'

'What *do* you know about her then?'

'Well, she's got red hair, and I think she lives in that block over there – I'd ask the porter, but there isn't one.'

'There certainly is a red-head lives over there,' said the young greengrocer who obviously had a good eye for such things, 'B staircase, but I can't tell you which flat.'

'Do you know the name by any chance?'

'Tommasi – Tommasini – something like that.'

The girl with too much make-up wasn't unduly worried by the fact that the name was different. Terrorists change their names as often as they change their cars.

'You've been very helpful,' she said, 'I should be able to trace her now.'

'You're very welcome at any time.'

Half an hour after that a polite young gas inspector went into the courtyard of the block. He was armed with the formal identity card which the municipality of Verona issues to all its gas inspectors to prevent impostors making their way into private homes with the pretext of reading meters. And in fact, on his first two calls, he did no more than read the meter. Then on his third call he found a chair-ridden old lady, seated at the window of her living-room looking out over the courtyard.

'I wonder if you could give me some information,' he said when he had read the meter.

'If I can.' She sounded delighted.

'I'm looking for a customer – name of Tommasi, Tommasini. She lives here somewhere and she has a query about gas consumption, but I don't seem to be able to find her.'

'Yes, that would be the red-headed girl, wouldn't it?'

'I'm afraid I don't know the colour of the lady's hair,' the gas inspector lied suavely.

'Well, there is a Tommasi over on B staircase – the top-floor flat.'

'*Signorina* Tommasi,' said the inspector, carefully writing down the information.

'Oh no – *signora*,' corrected the old lady. 'There's a husband, too, though I think he may have something the matter with him.

147

A very thin, pale face he's got and he hardly ever goes out. They're altogether a very quiet couple.'

'Thank you very much, *signora*.'

'You're welcome.'

'It's beginning to sound,' said the head of the DIGOS when the contents of this interview were reported to him, 'as though it just might be them at last.'

'What's the matter, Achille?' asked Regina.

'I have a feeling that we're not getting anywhere with this business of your uncle,' said Peroni, 'and it depresses me.'

They had met in a bar overlooking the river Adige, and they were now sitting with their drinks in its tiny, shaded and, at the moment, deserted garden which was concealed by the building itself, by creepers climbing densely on ironwork and by a parapet overlooking the river.

'But that's just not true!' said Regina warmly, 'it was only yesterday you discovered poor uncle's clandestine movement!'

'That's just it,' said Peroni, 'there's no lack of sensations. Thanks to you I discovered the Montagu–Capulet tie-up which everyone got so excited about. Then Loris was blown up in his car, and the media went wild. And then, as you say, I found your uncle's neo-fascist movement. But it's as though they were all – theatrical explosions, and somewhere behind the smoke and din of them, the truth is as safely hidden as it was at the beginning.'

'I don't believe that, Achille,' she said. 'Somehow I feel you're very near the truth.'

Peroni looked at her doubtfully, and then all of a sudden she kissed him. The kiss tasted faintly of the vodka and Campari she was drinking.

'Does that make you feel less depressed?' she asked at length.

'Considerably,' said Peroni.

The agency which let the fifth-floor apartment was surprised at the customer's haste to move in immediately. But the money was paid cash down, and the reason (that he was currently staying in a hotel and didn't want to waste any more money) was plausible. So they handed over the keys and the young man drove off.

When he arrived outside the block where the new apartment was, he was joined by two friends with suitcases, and together they went up the stairs.

Once inside the flat, however, they didn't seem so much concerned with moving in as with the observation of another fifth-floor apartment across a dividing roof-top. Nor did their suitcases contain clothes or linen, but radio equipment, powerful binoculars and guns. While two of them mounted the radio equipment, the third cautiously observed the window of the other flat. He could make out a kitchen table and stove, but no people.

'One, two, three, four, five – testing, testing,' said one of the men at the radio.

'*Pronto*,' crackled a jovial voice which the listeners knew to be the head of the DIGOS, installed in a florist's van parked in the street just outside that other block whose fifth-floor window they were observing. 'All well?' the jovial voice enquired.

'All well, sir,' said one of the men.

'Can you see anything?' the DIGOS chief wanted to know.

The young man at the window abandoned his binoculars and went over to the radio. 'Only the room, sir – it's a kitchen.'

'That you, Toni?'

'Yes, sir.'

'Well, keep watching then. If it's a kitchen, they're bound to go into it sooner or later.'

'Yes, sir.'

The radio clicked silent. For what seemed like a long time nothing happened. A fly buzzed noisily about, every so often banging against the window-pane. Toni continued to train his binoculars on the window opposite. Somebody's stomach rumbled.

'One of the boys might bring us up a sandwich or something,' complained one of the men at the radio, but he stopped short when he saw Toni stiffen suddenly.

'It's her,' said Toni.

'What's she doing?' asked the hungry man, reopening radio contact with the florist's van.

'Wait a minute – she's getting out some plates and glasses – a couple of cans of beer . . .'

'Is it her?' came the voice of the DIGOS chief.

'Say I think so,' said Toni over his shoulder to his colleagues, 'say that as far as I can tell judging from photographs it is her.'

'And the man?'

'No sign of him so far.'

There was another heavy silence, broken only by the crackling of the radio. Then Toni said, 'She's saying something – I think she's calling him in to eat.'

Even the crackling seemed to stop in the suspense, and you could hear the breathing of the DIGOS chief in the van.

'Here he comes!' said Toni excitedly. Another pause.

'Well?'

'No doubt about it,' said Toni, 'that's Policarpo Pillipopoli!'

'Mamma?' said Paolo Piantaleone somewhat diffidently.

'Well?' said his mother. The deaths of her husband and son had aged her beyond recognition, but they had also given her a hardness which she had lacked before.

She and her younger son Paolo were sitting at table in the dark, formal Piantaleone dining-room where the polished eighteenth-century table and the silverware gleamed in aristocratic silence. Veal cooked in Marsala had been served, but neither of them seemed hungry.

'Don't you think perhaps,' Paolo went on choosing his words carefully, 'that we ought to do something about Gabriele?'

'No,' she said, 'I don't.'

'But there's been no sign of him since yesterday evening.'

'Gabriele has always been accustomed to coming and going as he wanted.'

'Yes, but under the circumstances – suppose something's happened to him?'

'Paolo,' said the General's widow looking up from her plate, 'under the circumstances you refer to I have lost my husband

and my elder son. That is enough for me – I am not concerned with what may or may not have happened to your cousin who, unlike them, has never brought anything but disgrace and anxiety to this house.'

'Yes, Mamma,' said Paolo.

Even when organising an anti-terrorist operation which could involve the loss of several lives, the head of the DIGOS did not believe in sacrificing his stomach. From inside the florist's van which was his campaign headquarters he had ordered a meal from the world-renowned 12 Apostles restaurant. He had started with Parma ham, gone on to *tortellini* and was now enjoying slices of creamed chicken with asparagus. He ate slowly for there was no hurry. He had scheduled the attack for three in the morning, the hour when resistance was at its lowest and when he would be most likely to surprise the two terrorists asleep. He had organized many similar operations, and in practically all of them at least one person had been killed. He was going to do all he could to avoid it this time. If possible. Unfortunately, it often just wasn't.

The chief of DIGOS finished his chicken and went on to strawberries.

The menu was less exotic in the fifth-floor observation flat. Toni and his colleagues had had to make do with salami or cheese rolls from a nearby bar. At the same time they were able to observe the meal which, at the other side of the roof-top, Monica and Policarpo were having.

'There's just one thing that unites all Italians,' observed one of the men, 'irrespective of religion or politics.'

'What's that?' asked Toni.

'Spaghetti.'

At 2.30 a.m. the attackers, including Toni and commanded by the DIGOS chief, were crowded into the florist's van receiving their final instructions.

'If they make the slightest move in the wrong direction, shoot

– I'd rather have them killed than you. But try and only shoot to wound. We want them alive for more reasons than one.'

They all knew that only too well. A living terrorist could always lead to others, but a dead terrorist was no more than a dead end.

At five to three they started to move in. A sickle moon was setting in a velvet blue sky. It was a lovely night and many of the people who had been to the opera in the arena would still be about. But not in this part of the city. The street was deserted, and so was the courtyard as the men made their way across it. Their guns already out, they stepped inside the entrance to B staircase which was stone and smelt strongly of cats and cooking. As soundlessly as it could possibly be done they started to climb it.

When they got to the top they grouped themselves about the door leading into the flat where they hoped that Policarpo Pillipopoli and Monica Branca were fast asleep. The timing of the next few seconds was vital and had been rehearsed until it reached an almost atomic precision. But when you were dealing with terrorists, not even that much precision guaranteed you against things going wrong.

The left hand of the DIGOS chief was raised. For a long second it stayed in the air. Then it dropped, and several things happened simultaneously. In the darkness a gun blasted at the lock of the door and somebody kicked violently against its flaking panelling. At the same time a portable searchlight ripped through the darkness. It was appallingly brilliant, intended to stun anyone who suddenly awoke to it into total immobility.

By its light the door crashed open, and the men could see the couple lying on an improvised bed on the floor with a rug over them and two cushions for pillows. The attackers fanned swiftly into the room.

'Up!' the DIGOS chief ordered, his Father Christmas-like geniality for once attenuated.

Slowly the couple, both wearing trousers and shirt, stood up, and for the first time Toni saw them, not so much as terrorists, but as human beings who have been brutally awoken from sleep.

Policarpo, he realised, must have been almost exactly his own age. It seemed strange to be pointing a gun at him.

But Toni had no time to reflect on the strangeness of it. Almost as though by sleight of hand Policarpo had whipped a gun from beneath his shirt. It was pointing towards Toni.

The DIGOS chief took the decision to shoot, but in the split second between his taking it and pulling the trigger, Monica threw her body in front of Policarpo's and the bullet tore its way into her stomach.

At the same time another bullet, from Policarpo's gun, shattered the searchlight glass and the room was plunged from the nightmare glare into total blackness. There were shouts, the sound of stumbling and collision, another gunshot followed by a cry, and then after what seemed like a long time somebody turned on the light which seemed as dim as a candle after the searchlight.

Monica was huddled on the improvised bed. In the doorway one of the DIGOS men had collapsed on to his knees.

Policarpo had gone.

It took long seconds to organise a pursuit. Somebody had to attend to Monica and somebody else to the wounded DIGOS man, but finally the chase began. They could hear Policarpo's feet one, maybe two floors below them. As they ran they saw lights snapping on beneath doors and heard frightened, excited voices.

Fortunately, there were men in the courtyard and street below so Policarpo couldn't get far. The men plunged wildly down the stairs and then along the ground-floor corridor out into the courtyard.

Whoever had stopped Policarpo, it wasn't the men in the courtyard. And as they ran out through the main entrance they saw he wasn't in the street either.

For a moment everything broke down into swirling confusion. The men of the DIGOS were highly trained and disciplined, but when things went as wrong as this, they could show that they were also Latin.

There had been police behind Policarpo on the stairs, in front of him in the courtyard and the street. Somehow, between them, he had disappeared.

Toni was the first to re-trace the way they had come. When he came to the other end of the ground-floor corridor where you turned right up the stairs he saw what nobody had noticed before in the dark. There was a window, and it was open. Toni climbed through it and found himself in a courtyard at the other end of which was a wall with a gate in it. The gate was locked, but with the help of a tree you could scramble up the wall. Which was what Policarpo must have done.

Toni got to the top of the wall just in time to see a car starting off in the narrow street below. He was also just in time to pull himself flat on top of the wall as a bullet singed above his head and splattered into brickwork.

Pursuit was out of the question as there was no other car, so Toni climbed down and went to the florist's van where he radioed the *Questura* and arranged for road-blocks to be set up all round Verona. Then he climbed the steps up again to the fifth floor.

The wounded DIGOS man was in pain, but not seriously wounded.

Monica Branca was dead. But the red hair still seemed alive about her white face. And her right fist was clenched in the symbol of proletarian defiance.

'She sacrificed herself deliberately for him,' said the DIGOS chief who was kneeling beside her. 'Who would have expected her to do a thing like that?'

'A fly couldn't get out of Verona without being seen,' said *dott.* Guerra with something like satisfaction. 'There are road-blocks at every conceivable exit of the city.'

A conference had been hurriedly convened to deal with the new situation. Apart from Guerra himself, it was attended by the DIGOS chief, by Peroni, various police and *Carabinieri* officers, and the officer commanding the city's urban police.

The first sun was beginning to shimmer on the water of the Adige outside.

'I,' said the DIGOS chief with his customary air of holly-and-mistletoe benignity, 'have known the Red Brigade to get through without being seen when even a gnat shouldn't have been able to.'

'What do you suggest then?' asked a *Carabinieri* officer some-what irascibly, for it was the *Carabinieri* who bore the main brunt and faced the main dangers in manning road-blocks.

'No, no,' said the DIGOS chief, waving a finger genially at him, 'you misunderstand me. I implied no criticism whatever of the arrangements made. I'm merely saying that Pillipopoli and the Branca girl were not autonomous. They were a part of the Verona column of the Red Brigade. So I suspect that now he will not *try* to leave the city, but will make for one of their urban hideouts where he will be as safe as a mouse under the floorboards.'

'*If* he manages to get there,' *dott.* Guerra pointed out. 'Such a comprehensive operation within the city itself has never been mobilised before.'

'Then let's hope we're lucky.'

Peroni followed the exchanges with a certain detachment. Although Policarpo formed part of the general investigation, he was nevertheless a political criminal and therefore the direct concern of the DIGOS. On hearing the previous evening that Policarpo and Monica had been run to earth, Peroni had con-gratulated himself that he was, for once, out of the front line. Any gun battles that might be involved he would watch on television.

A phone rang and Guerra picked it up. 'Yes?' He listened intently, nodding every so often. 'Very well. Thank you,' he said at last, ringing off.

'Well, gentlemen,' he said, 'we have him.'

A murmur of interest went round the office. 'He was spotted by two of your men, Colonel,' Guerra went on to the officer commanding the city's urban police, who looked gratified. 'They recognised him at once and intimated to him to stop. He pro-duced a gun and they took refuge behind a car. He used the momentary respite to run into the twelfth-century Romanesque church of St Cunegonda, barring its doors behind him. It was plainly a hasty decision, and he presumably counted on leaving the church by another exit. But there was something he didn't know.'

'What?' asked several people who were not as well versed in Veronese ecclesiastical monuments as was *dott*. Guerra.

'There is no other exit. Or, rather, the only other door of the church leads into a cloister which, in its turn, used to lead through to a monastery. But that entrance was blocked up shortly after the monks left it in the last century.'

'So all we have to do now,' put in a *Carabiniere* officer, 'is to get half a dozen men with bullet-proof shields to smash in the main doors.'

'If you will forgive my saying so,' said *dott*. Guerra urbanely, 'you are plainly no Veronese. The panels on those doors are among our most priceless artistic treasures. If every terrorist in Italy were in that church, it would still be more than all our careers are worth to touch one of them.' He rose preparatory to going.

'Just one thing,' said the commander of the urban police. 'What time did he go in there?'

'Shortly after seven o'clock.'

The commander of the urban police looked relieved. The early-morning mass, he explained, would have been over, so the church would have been empty.

'Unless,' pointed out somebody else, 'some early-rising tourist had gone in.'

They paled at the thought. Tourists were even more precious than sculpted panels. If one of them were held as hostage or, worse still, killed, tourism, which was Italy's biggest industry, could be irreparably damaged.

'The best we can do, gentlemen,' said Guerra, 'is to go and see for ourselves.'

Peroni followed them out, foreseeing an agreeable morning's entertainment.

The miniature square in front of the church of St Cunegonda

had been sealed off and a large crowd had gathered in the two streets which led into it. An excited murmur rose as sirens were heard howling in the distance and then coming nearer. The crowd was pressed still further back to make room for the five cars which now drew up.

The men who got out of them, the crowd recognised, were top brass who had come to swell the already large numbers of police and *Carabinieri* in the area. Some of them recognised Peroni and waved at him, but the *commissario*, firmly in charge this morning, restrained any impulse there might have been to wave back.

'He doesn't seem to be short of ammunition,' said a young *Carabiniere* officer coming to meet Guerra and his party. 'He shoots if anybody so much as puts their nose out.'

'Has he got anybody in there with him?'

'Apparently not. I've spoken to the sacristan and he said that the church was deserted. He'd have been in there himself if he hadn't gone out to buy a paper at the moment the man went in.'

The news that there were no tourist hostages produced a movement of relief among the senior officers. At least the national economy wasn't threatened.

'I'd like to speak to the sacristan,' said *dott.* Guerra.

'Yes, sir.'

While he was waiting for the man to arrive, Guerra moved cautiously, but with his usual disregard for his own safety, to look into the little square in front of the church. Immediately there came the whine and smack of a bullet, but he returned as calmly as he had gone and made no comment on the incident.

'I seem to remember,' he said when the sacristan had come, 'that the only alternative entrance to this church is the door into the cloister.'

'That's right.'

'But there's no way into the cloister except through the church?'

'Not unless you were to climb in.'

'Climb?' said Guerra looking up sharply.

'Well, there's a wall round the back and from that you could

157

get on to the sloping roof over the cloister walk. If somebody was to go down that to the guttering he could probably swing himself down by the arches.'

'I suppose we could send up a group of men,' *dott*. Guerra mused, half to himself and half to the *Carabiniere* officer beside him.

'Not a group you couldn't,' said the sacristan, 'you wouldn't find a group that was good enough climbers for the job, and even if you did that tile roof wouldn't take the weight of them. It's one man or nothing.'

'Yes, but what good is one man going to do?' mused Guerra.

'A considerable amount perhaps,' said the *Carabiniere* officer. 'He'd have the advantage of surprise. If we create sufficient diversion at the front he might get right up behind Pillipopoli without being spotted.'

'It would be a considerable risk.'

'Less than you might think. The church is packed with good cover – heavy stone columns and so on.'

'I suppose so.' Guerra seemed uncertain. 'It would have to be a volunteer.'

'I'm sure somebody would offer himself for such a job.'

Suddenly Peroni began to feel uncomfortable.

'It would have to be somebody,' Guerra pointed out, 'who was good at climbing.'

'A marksman, too.'

Now Peroni felt that everybody was looking at him and, not for the first time, he cursed his own legend. He was famous both as marksman and climber. Everybody knew about his cat-like exploits. What they didn't know about was the terror they had caused him. The trouble was that he had never been able to resist the call of his own legend.

'Would anybody care to volunteer?' said *dott*. Guerra, looking about him.

There was a heavy silence. In the midst of it Peroni heard himself saying, 'I could try, *dottore*.'

Without a word Guerra gripped him by the hand. Somewhere a camera clicked and it was an index to Peroni's inner desolation that he was totally indifferent to it. He resolved that if he got out of this in one piece he would have the largest candle that human skill could make set up and lit before the shrine of St Janarius in Naples.

Escorted by Guerra and a group of senior officers he went round to the back of the church.

'This is the wall,' said the sacristan, as though he were presenting a work of art to a group of tourists.

For a moment Peroni thought he was expected to crawl up the sheer face of it like a fly, something he could not accomplish even for the sake of his legend.

'The fire brigade,' said Guerra, putting him right on this score, 'will put you up on the top. The rest is up to you.'

While they waited for the fire brigade Peroni lit what he was convinced would be his last cigarette.

The red van arrived without any wailing sirens which would alert Policarpo. The ladder was erected against the wall, and the senior officers all shook Peroni's hand in what he felt was a distinctly valedictory way. Then he started to climb.

The wall was a high one and he felt extremely queasy by the time he was halfway up. What would it be like at the top? And even if he did get safely down on the other side, instead of applause and a large Chivas Regal he faced a gun battle with a terrorist.

Doing his best to put all this out of his mind, to resist the temptation to look downwards and the even greater one to go downwards, he reached the top and looked over the other side. There was indeed a sloping, tiled roof, though the tiles looked as though they would require no more than a light wind, let alone a man of eighty-five kilos, to dislodge them.

As he scrambled on to it the headlines swam before his eyes. PERONI PLUNGES TO CLOISTER DEATH. PERONI'S LAST ADVENTURE. Or perhaps GUNMAN SLAYS POLICE VALENTINO.

He forced himself to concentrate on the downward climb, spreadeagling himself so that his weight was supported by the largest possible number of tiles. He edged slowly towards the cloister below like a snake, reflecting that the tiles were firmer than they looked.

But even as he thought it, the support slipped from under his right hand and the whole delicately poised balance of his body was thrown into anarchy. Clutching and scrabbling desperately with his fingers, he managed to regain a precarious equilibrium while the loosened tile slithered down the roof and came to a stop at the guttering.

Five minutes later, without further mishap, Peroni caught up with it. From there he was able to see the whole cloister laid out beneath him with all the peace of medieval stonework. On the other side was the door into the church through which he would have to go.

The guttering had been recently installed, which meant he could put some reliance on it. Gingerly he edged a leg over and found a stone ledge with his foot. Below him, to judge by the other three sides, was a line of slender columns. He felt for them with his feet. If the guttering gave way now he would break his neck. But it held, and his foot came into contact with rounded stone. He managed to twine his ankles about it, then lower himself until he could embrace it with his arms. It was like climbing down a massive stone rope.

Beneath this range of columns was another, but they were too thick to climb down. So he had to perform a Tarzan-like operation, lowering himself from the upper order of columns and then swinging down. This accomplished, he was only a jump from the ground. He jumped and landed on grass.

Peroni ran silently to the door, getting out his gun as he went. There was a heavy iron latch which Peroni eased up with his handkerchief. Then with the tips of his fingers he edged the door open a centimetre. It creaked, and although it wasn't loud it sounded to him like the scream of a pig having its throat cut. Fortunately his colleagues were creating a deafening diversion out front with a loudspeaker invitation to Policarpo to give himself up, recited to an accompaniment of howling sirens.

Centimetre by centimetre he widened the opening until it

was large enough to squeeze in through. Then he closed the door behind him.

It was dark inside. Like all early Romanesque churches it allowed the very minimum of light to filter in. There was just a faint glow from some candles somewhere out of sight.

Immediately in front of him Peroni saw a massive stone pillar which must have completely hidden his entrance to the church. That was a large chunk of luck. He moved up to the pillar and edged his head cautiously around it. Now he was able to see Policarpo, who had climbed up beside a low window at the other end of the church out of which sporadically he fired.

It might just be possible to immobilize him by shooting his right wrist, or at any rate arm. Difficult in the semi-darkness, but worth a try. He edged forward into a position from which he had a clearer view of Policarpo and, as he moved, his foot knocked accidentally against some sort of box stacked against the wall of the church. Fortunately the noise of it was imperceptible against the din that was going on outside and Peroni ignored it. He aimed, waiting for Policarpo to raise his right arm again.

'Welcome,' said a female voice in English somewhere just behind him, 'to the eleventh-century church of St Cunegonda. The earliest Christian church on this site dates back to the seventh century, though recent excavations have shown remains of an earlier pagan temple . . .'

In his horror, Peroni had no idea for a second of what it could be. Then he realised that what his foot had knocked against accidentally and somehow switched on was a recording machine intended to describe the church for tourists in Italian, English, French or German.

Policarpo had heard it, too, and a split second later a bullet smacked into a pillar and Peroni felt a stinging pain in his cheek which he realised must have been caused by a fragment of flying marble.

Just a little way to his right a shape loomed up in the darkness. A confessional. Peroni dived for it.

'The façade,' the voice went with him, politely impersonal,

161

'is a particularly fine example. It is constructed of alternating tufa and marble . . .'

As Peroni knelt in the comparative safety of the confessional he heard another bullet biting into the hard oak above his head. His position reminded him that he hadn't been to confession for over two years, and he vowed that he would do so if ever he got out of the church of St Cunegonda alive.

The immediate problem was how to do so. And how to get Policarpo out alive as well, if that were possible. From the confessional he looked out in search of inspiration. Now he could see the source of the glow he had first seen on entering the church. It emanated from a little bunch of candles burning before the image of a saint opposite him.

Idly Peroni wondered what saint. Certainly not St Francis or one of the well-known ones. A bishop to judge by his dress. And what was he holding in his left hand? A box of some sort from which liquid was emerging. Dark-coloured liquid.

Blood.

Peroni stiffened with excitement. It looked very like a representation of the miraculous liquefaction of blood which could only be connected with one saint. Confirmation came as he made out the lettering over the figure's head. JANARIUS EPISC NAP. Janarius bishop of Naples.

How could this fail to bring him luck? thought Peroni. He looked to St Janarius for inspiration, and as he looked the inspiration came. It was chancy, but then miracles were chancy things.

He lifted his gun, aimed and fired and then watched with satisfaction as the large candle-holder opposite toppled over backwards. Now everything depended on the candle flames catching the hangings. Drapings such as those would have hung there for years, even generations, and should be as dry and combustible as a mountain of spiders' webs. Provided the candles hadn't gone out in the fall.

Seconds later a flaring and crackling and spluttering told him they hadn't. Smoke began to billow out in a satisfactory way. And the wooden organ loft above St Janarius promised an indefinite supply. In a few minutes the church would be filled with one enormous, impenetrable cloud of smoke.

He tied his handkerchief over his mouth and nose and abandoned the confessional, feeling his way silently through the cloud.

'The north wall of the church is covered with a series of frescoes depicting scenes from the Old Testament,' the voice continued monotonously out of the darkness. 'Many of these date back to the eleventh century, but they are almost unrecognisable . . .'

Then Peroni heard another sound which he didn't like at all. Footsteps were moving towards him. He had assumed that Policarpo would stay where he was, near the window at the bottom of the church. Why should he deliberately come into the cloud? In a second Peroni knew the answer.

'It's not going to be that easy, policeman,' came Policarpo's voice out of the choking blackness. 'You were just waiting for the applause of your bourgeois, multi-national masters, weren't you? Clever policeman to find a trick like that to catch the bad terrorist! But don't be too sure! You see, I know I'm finished now, so I've got nothing to lose. All I want is just one more stinking, capitalist life before I go. Your life, policeman!'

Peroni felt a prickle of terror down the back of his neck. Policarpo had the courage of desperation and he knew from experience that there was no limit to what people could do when they had that.

His only hope now lay in silence. If Policarpo could neither see nor hear him there was a chance. Peroni stood in the inky, burning darkness forcing himself not to cough. He had the unpleasant feeling of having changed role from hunter to hunted.

With infinite precaution he edged his way down the church, pausing every few seconds to listen. He heard a chair shift on the stone floor. It was too near for safety. And then through the smoke there came the sound of Policarpo's raucous breathing. It was moving straight towards him.

Hesitant which way to move, Peroni felt rather than saw that he was standing beside a pew. He lowered himself silently and crawled snake-wise into the foot space. A couple of seconds later Policarpo's steps passed exactly where he had been standing before.

There was a new fear now. The fear of being overcome by the fumes. The handkerchief was not doing much good any longer, and the thought that Policarpo was no better off was no consolation.

But Peroni forced himself to wait until the footsteps had passed. Then he wriggled cautiously forward till he came to the end of the pew. With difficulty he got to his feet again, realising that he must be in the central aisle.

'The annunciation on the main altar is of a considerably later date . . .'

There was only one feasible plan now. Everything depended on his not collapsing for just a few minutes more. And on Policarpo not looming suddenly up on him out of the darkness.

Supporting himself on the benches, he tottered rather than walked ahead. Consciousness began to slip. It seemed as though he had been walking through the smoke for ever, and it had got thicker and thicker as he went.

A shape reared up just ahead on his right. Policarpo. Peroni jerked up his gun to shoot. Then he realised, just in time, that it was a holy water stoup.

He must be near the door. Then unexpectedly his foot knocked against stone, and he realised it was the steps leading up to the door. Practically on all fours he scrambled up them and found himself touching the wood of one of the huge doors which was the obverse side of the world-famous panels.

He pulled himself up by a heavy block of wood in front of him which could only have been the bar used to bolt the door. It was firmly wedged in, too, and he felt he could never push it up. It would have been a good enough weight under normal circumstances, but weakened as he was by the smoke the task became Herculean.

Desperately, regardless of noise, Peroni struggled with it and had the satisfaction of feeling it come unwedged. One heave should get it free. He was bracing himself to make it when a bullet slapped into the wood by his ear.

Policarpo was moving back towards the door shooting.

Fear gave Peroni strength. He put his shoulder to the wood and gave a last mighty heave.

The bolt came up and away with a noise like thunder. The heavy door swung open, letting air flood in and smoke billow out. Peroni realised that he would now provide a perfect target framed against the brilliant sun outside. He jumped quickly aside.

As he did so he heard another gunshot, and it took him the best part of a second to realise it hadn't been fired in his direction for once.

As he staggered out of the church, gasping for air, he heard the same polite, impersonal voice a long way behind him. 'We hope,' it said, 'that you have enjoyed your visit to the church.'

Policarpo had shot himself through the palate and the back of his head was blown off. But when they got to him they found that his left hand – as Monica's right had been – was still clutched in defiance of the whole world.

Gabriele

'There's a *signorina* asking to see you,' the voice of an elderly policeman on the desk squawked into Peroni's ear over the internal telephone.

The word *signorina* covered a lot of ground. 'A young lady', which was the nearest you could get to it in English, at least told you she was young. But Italian, with greater courtesy perhaps, gave you no clues at all. It could be a stringy old spinster of seventy or a willowy and voluptuous creature of seventeen. Certainly, thought Peroni, the word created suspense.

'Show her up,' he said, and sat back to wait.

Forty-eight hours had passed since Policarpo's death and, so far as progress was concerned, they had passed uneventfully. There had been a great uproar, of course, but Peroni had been too tired and drained, physically and emotionally, to appreciate it. He recovered sufficiently to spend part of the evening with Regina. Unfortunately, she had to go off for a class at nine o'clock, but her kiss at parting told him that the moment of truth between them was near.

As no further developments had followed immediately on Policarpo's death, the papers had made do with the reconsecration of the church of St Cunegonda, made necessary by the suicide which had taken place in it. It was to be held by the bishop that morning and Peroni hoped to attend.

He had already arranged by telephone for a gigantic candle to be fashioned in Naples and placed before the shrine of St Janarius.

There were footsteps in the corridor outside and a knock at the door. The *signorina* was about to be unveiled.

'Come in,' called Peroni rising.

As *signorinas* went, he could have done a lot worse. It was Patti. But a very different Patti from the one he had seen a week before at the fancy-dress ball. The sparkle was gone from her cornflower-blue eyes and a scared look had taken its place.

'I didn't want to come to you,' she said after Peroni had solicitously sat her down.

'People seldom do,' he agreed reassuringly. 'What can I do for you?'

'Gabriele has disappeared.'

He looked up quickly. 'When?'

'On Tuesday night.'

Four days ago, the same day that Peroni had uncovered the General's neo-fascist movement. 'Why didn't you tell me before?'

'I thought he'd come back. Besides, I knew the last thing he would want me to do would be to go to the police.'

Peroni took it in good part; after all, it was natural enough. 'And his family?'

'They don't know anything about him either.'

'Why didn't they get in touch with me?'

'They don't care what happens to him.'

'Why should anything happen to him?' Patti was silent. '*Signorina*,' said Peroni, 'I understand your reluctance to come to the police, but now you have come, you might as well go all the way. I shan't be able to help you otherwise.'

Still she hesitated. 'He'd discovered who it was that was behind the General's fascist business.'

'What?' The shock of it catapulted Peroni out of his chair. 'How do you know?'

'He told me.'

'Did he tell you who it was?'

'No.'

'But if he really does know, if he isn't making it up, he's in a nasty position. Look what happened to Loris.'

'Why else do you think I came to you?'

'Tell me the whole story.'

Reluctantly she did so. She started with the General's letter

167

to Loris saying where he was going on the night of his death which confirmed what Stefano had already deduced. She then described how Gabriele had put the letter among the mail on Monday morning thus precipitating Loris off to his death. She told how Gabriele had taken the number of a car coming out of the villa gate and traced its owner.

'The same person who he says is behind the whole affair?'

'No, it can't have been. He called whoever *that* was "the biggest fish of all." And he only saw that person later. He followed the owner of the car somewhere or other – '

'Where?'

'He didn't say. He just said it was – so out of character.'

'Whose character? The car owner's?'

'That's what I understood.'

'Go on.'

'Well, he watched this place, and that was when he saw the other person go in.'

'The biggest fish of all?'

'That's right.'

'What did he do then?'

'He said that he went home and then made an appointment with whoever it was.'

'That was a dangerous thing to do.'

'He said it was quite safe. He fixed it during the interval at the arena in the square outside. He said they'd be surrounded by several thousand people.'

'So whoever it was must have been at the opera?'

'That's right. He said quite clearly. "The mastermind's at the opera in the arena this evening." And then he went off to see him.'

Not as helpful as it might sound, thought Peroni. Several thousand people were at the arena that night and, as it was a fashionable event, they would have included most of the Piantaleones and Pillipopolis.

'Did he say when he'd be seeing you again?'

'That same evening. He said he'd come back when he'd finished. To celebrate.'

If Patti hadn't been so tough, Peroni would have suspected a break in her voice. He took her through the whole story again, carefully questioning her about every detail. Finally he shook hands with her. 'I'll do everything I can to find him,' he promised.

'You'll keep in touch?'

'As soon as there's any news at all, I'll let you have it.'

But in spite of his optimistic tone, Peroni was convinced that Gabriele was dead.

Peroni reported the conversation with Patti at the morning conference with *dott.* Guerra.

'This Gabriele seems to be a highly unsavoury character, does he not, *dottore*?' said Guerra.

'Indeed he does, *dottore*.'

'However, if he really knows the identity of this so-called "mastermind",' said Guerra, fastidiously putting the melodramatic word between inverted commas, 'he is running the gravest possible danger. At all costs we must trace him before somebody else does.'

'I think he's already dead,' said Peroni.

'Possibly,' said Guerra, 'possibly. But so long as there is a chance of him being alive we must concentrate on seeing that he is kept so. Is that tie Neapolitan, *dottore*?'

'Yes, *dottore*.'

'Extremely colourful.'

Patti had said that Gabriele was slightly drunk that evening. That and the general elation, Peroni believed, had led him to a fatal tactical error. It was true that he would have been safe with the big fish-mastermind in the square outside the arena surrounded by several thousand people. But he would have been far from safe *on the way there or on the way back.*

Peroni was sitting on top of a ladder in front of a large-scale map of Verona which covered an entire wall at the *Questura.* He was hovering over the Roman arena. From it his eye went to the street where Patti's flat was. A five minutes' walk, he estimated, and one that was obliged to follow a more or less set course. He worked it out carefully and saw that it included a network of intersecting narrow streets which were always fairly deserted after dark. Gabriele, who had been on foot that evening because his car battery was being charged, had walked that way both going to and coming from the arena. Assuming that he did start the return journey.

And then Peroni realised that he must have done. Whoever it was could not have known, however masterful his mind, which direction Gabriele would arrive from. But he could have seen which direction he went away in. And he could have followed him. Or had him followed.

Peroni telephoned the arena and enquired the time of the interval on the previous Tuesday night. A quarter to eleven, he was told.

'And how long did it last?'

'Half an hour.'

Which made it look as though Gabriele had been somehow done away with in that particular area some time between eleven and eleven-thirty the previous evening.

'Just you tell me something,' said the playful old man who had been a non-commissioned officer with the celebrated Italian Alpine corps. 'What did you have for lunch yesterday?'

'I'm afraid I can't recall,' said the detective patiently, remembering you should always be polite with members of the public, particularly old ones.

'In that case,' said the old soldier triumphantly, 'how do you expect me to remember what happened last Tuesday evening? Eh?'

'I meant if anything unusual happened,' said the detective.

'Unusual things don't happen when you're my age. Now when I was your age it was a different matter – every girl I met was likely to turn into an unusual thing, if you see what I mean. But I'm too old for that sort of thing now.'

'Now then, now then,' said his wife, adding to the detective, 'You'll have to forgive him – he's a terrible tease.'

The detective smiled understandingly. 'Of course,' he said. 'Can *you* remember anything out of the way that happened on Tuesday evening?'

'Well, let me see now,' she said, 'if we look at the telly programmes it might give me a hint. Tuesday, Tuesday. What time did you say?'

'Any time after about eleven o'clock.'

'That's right,' she said. 'We were watching the end of that American gangster film, weren't we, Attilio?'

'Bang, bang, bang!' said the old soldier, and laughed when the detective looked startled. 'Well, that's what it was,' he went on. 'All shooting at each other they were.'

'That's right,' said the old woman, 'because we heard the bang out in the street, didn't we, Attilio?'

'Ah, so that's what you're after, is it?' said the old man. 'Bangs in the street?'

'Was there one?' asked the detective, who had pricked up his ears.

'That's right, there was. But there's no need to get all excited, young fellow, it was only a car.'

'Are you sure of that?'

'Well, what else would it have been I should like to know? We don't have shootings around here. Besides, Marta went down just after that to put the cat out and there weren't any bodies outside, were there, Marta?'

'But it *could* have been a gun?' the detective persisted.

'If it's going to make you any happier, young man,' the old soldier said, 'I suppose it could.'

One or two other people in the immediate area thought they remembered something like the back-firing of a car on the previous Tuesday evening, and one or two others said it must have been the shooting in the film. Nobody was more definite. One woman said she had looked out of the window and seen a dark-coloured van disappearing round the corner, but nobody else claimed to have seen anything.

Lenotti was one of the men scouring the area Peroni had

isolated as the possible site for an assault on Gabriele. His investigations had produced nothing, as he had confidently expected them to do, when he rang the door-bell of a second-floor flat. The door was opened by an elderly, diminutive and cross-looking woman who looked like, and in fact was, a retired school-mistress. She studied Lenotti irritably, as though he were a particularly dull member of the class, while he identified himself.

'It is, of course, one's duty as a citizen to collaborate with the authorities, but I must warn you against taking advantage of the public's good-will,' she said snappily.

'I beg your pardon, *signora*,' said Lenotti, not knowing what she was talking about.

'*Signorina*,' she corrected him, obviously punctilious about her unmarried status.

'*Signorina*,' said Lenotti, 'I wasn't aware that I was taking advantage of your good-will.'

'You come asking me if I heard or saw anything unusual on Tuesday night when one of your colleagues has already been here making similar enquiries. I call that gross inefficiency.'

'Oh,' said Lenotti mournfully. That was the sort of thing that did happen to him, and now she would probably make a report about it. 'When did he come to see you, *signora* – I mean *signorina*?' he asked.

'The day before yesterday,' said the retired schoolmistress.

'But we didn't know then – ' he began. And then the significance of it dawned on him. 'I should be grateful, *signorina*,' he said a little more confidently, 'if you would describe this person who called on you.'

'Do you mean to say you don't know your own colleagues?' she snapped.

'Whoever this was,' said Lenotti lugubriously, 'he wasn't a colleague of mine.'

At about the same time Peroni got the break-through he had been hoping for.

Inge Rotterheim had been brought up in Verona and nothing remained of her German origins but a slight accent which, it was generally considered, lent her a touch of chic and helped in the business. The business in question was a novelty goods shop, a line which Inge had more or less pioneered in Verona. She sold things like diminutive wooden models of genitalia, freaky jewellery made out of twisted wire, ash-trays with naive reproductions and posters of such subjects as lavatory pans with black gorilla paws waving up from their depths. She asked ridiculous prices for these things, but as there were a lot of Veronese with more money than sense, she got what she asked.

She was about to close for lunch when the bell – a device fitted into a miniature Victorian chamber-pot on the door – rang, and a dark, very good-looking man came in. Inge had a voracious appetite for men of practically all sorts, and this one looked special.

'*Buon giorno,*' she said politely, the 'r' in *giorno* betraying her origin.

'*Questura,*' said the man.

Inge's stomach heaved with misgiving. Was there some regulation she had overlooked? Running a business could be a very complicated thing in Italy. 'How can I help you?' she asked, flicking delicately tinted eyelids.

'Do you live here?'

That sounded a promising beginning. 'No,' she said, 'I've got a flat in Borgo Trento.'

He seemed disappointed by this. 'And you weren't here by any chance on Tuesday night?'

'Tuesday night? Yes, as a matter of fact I was – I stayed here late stock-taking.'

'How late?'

'Oh, till some time after eleven.'

'And did you hear or see anything at all out of the way around this area?'

The detective, who was having a liquefying effect on her inner parts, picked up a large felt-tip pen and then put it down again hastily when he realised what shape it was made in. She carefully refrained from smiling.

'Out of the way?' she said.

173

'Unusual.'

One highly unusual thing had happened to her that night and, although she had told various friends about it, she was reluctant to tell the police. She hesitated and he seemed to catch on to her hesitation.

'There was something?' he said.

'We-ell . . .' She could hardly deny it, she thought, and besides it could do no harm. 'It was about half past eleven,' she said, 'and I'd already closed up the shop. I was going to my car outside when a young man came up to me. A very good-looking young man with golden hair.' She felt as though a high-tension current had suddenly shot through her from the detective. 'Is something wrong?' she asked.

'No, no,' he said, 'please go on.'

'Well, as I say, he came up to me and asked me if I'd give him a lift. I told him to jump in.'

'Weren't you afraid he might – do you some harm?'

'Men don't frighten me – I've got a Karate black belt.' Even as she said it, she wondered if it was a mistake; Italian men didn't usually like their women tough.

'Did he say why he wanted a lift?'

'Yes. He said somebody had shot at him. But I didn't pay much attention to that.'

'Why not?'

'Men will think of the oddest excuses when they want to get to know a woman.'

He studied her appreciatively. 'Yes,' he said, 'I suppose they do. So what happened next?'

'Well, he asked me to drive him into the country – said he'd tell me the way as we went. I was quite amused by the idea, and it was a lovely night, so I played along with him. We drove for about half an hour and then he told me to stop. So I pulled off the road and stopped.'

'And then?'

'We stayed in the car for a while – you know, talking and so on.' The memory of it made her nostalgic, and the 'so on' was heavily weighted with meaning. She paused for a moment, sighed lightly and then continued. 'After a while I said "Shall we go back to Verona now?" and he said, no, that was where he was getting out. I asked him if he lived there and he said "Not really", which seemed a funny sort of answer. Anyway, it was his business, so I let him out. And that was the last I saw of him.'

'Where was it that he got out?'

She frowned in concentration. 'There was a sign pointing off the road some way ahead of us. It was the name of a village I think – that's right, something to do with roses.'

For the second time she felt the current of high tension pass through her.

'Rosaro?' asked the detective.

'That's right,' she said. 'Rosaro – that's what it was.'

'You've been very helpful,' he said, giving her his hand.

She watched him go with disappointment. There was no doubt about it, she decided, it had been a mistake to mention the Karate.

Ever since he had first visited the village of Rosaro and drunk sour red wine with the parish priest, Peroni had had an obscure feeling that he was not finished with the place. But his pleasure at the prospect of going back there was slightly eclipsed when he got back to the *Questura* and learned of Lenotti's discovery confirmed by subsequent interviews. Somebody else, purporting to be a policeman, had been asking questions in the area before Peroni had learned of Gabriele's movements on Tuesday night. And whoever it was had been trying to find out where Gabriele had gone.

From the schoolmistress and the other witnesses they had been able to get a good description of the man. He was about sixty years old, of average height but lightish build, balding, with a sallow complexion, small somewhat sunken eyes and a slightly receding chin. One witness had said that he had too smooth a way about him.

In some ways it was a frustrating description, for it had no smack of Pillipopoli or Piantaleone about it. Nor indeed did it resemble anybody they had come across since the start of the affair.

'The important thing,' said *dott.* Guerra, 'is whether this person approached your German woman, *dottore.*'

'She would certainly have told me if he had – she was quite frank about everything,' said Peroni, 'Besides, he wouldn't have thought of going into a shop. I only went in there myself out of sheer scrupulousness.'

In fact, he had only gone in because of the sight of Inge Rotterheim glimpsed through the shop window, but it amounted to the same thing.

'However,' said Guerra, 'you say that she recounted the adventure to several of her friends so it would not be impossible for the story to reach the ears of whoever is after Gabriele. The sooner we get up to Rosaro the better, *dottore*, and we'd better take some men with us in case we're obliged to search the countryside.'

Five minutes later they were on their way with Peroni, somewhat flattered, driving as a passenger with the Verona police chief.

'It certainly makes sense,' said Guerra driving fast and incisively. 'The Piantaleone estate up there would be just what Gabriele needed. After the shooting episode he no longer felt safe in Verona, but up there he would be out of reach of whoever was pursuing him, and at the same time he would be able to continue his blackmail scheme.'

Peroni felt a lift of pleasure as they drove into Rosaro. The village street leading to Don Adriano's neat little church was deserted in the midday heat except for a dog outside the *osteria* which looked up as the caravan of police cars came into sight and then, dismissing it as unworthy of interest, went back to sleep.

'Where shall we start, *dottore*?' asked Peroni.

Guerra waved a manicured hand politely. 'It's your investigation, *dottore* – you tell me where to go and I'll go there.'

'In that case,' said Peroni, 'I think we might start with the Piantaleone peasants.'

'An excellent idea.'

As they drove through the undulating, wooded countryside with its olive and cherry trees and the wild rose bushes which gave the village its name Peroni heard a crack of gunshot outside.

'What's that?' he said, startled.

'Hunting,' said *dott.* Guerra imperturbably. 'This is splendid hunting country, you know. People come from as far as Milan for a day's shooting.'

'What do they shoot?' asked Peroni, on whose Neapolitan horizon such things had not infringed.

'Birds mostly.'

They stopped where Peroni had stopped on his previous visit and the same big dog came barking towards them, but faced with half a dozen policemen it decided the opposition was too heavy and slunk growling to the side of the path.

Peroni and Guerra went into the farmhouse. The father of the family, with bloodshot eyes and mottled face, and three strapping lads were having dinner in the stone-flagged front room, each hunched over his plate. The mother, who had given Peroni wine, was standing by the fire ladling steaming, yellow polenta out of a large pot. They all of them froze like statues as Peroni and Guerra entered.

'Good morning,' tried Peroni.

The father muttered something indistinguishable into his plate.

'We're looking for Gabriele Piantaleone,' said Peroni, feeling that it sounded, for some reason, foolish. 'Have you seen anything of him?'

The words ran into a solid wall of silence.

'Come along now,' said Guerra, giving Peroni a look which seemed to say forgive my discourtesy, but I know how to handle these people. 'It's for his safety that we're trying to find him. You heard what happened to his cousin Loris? Well, the same sort of thing may happen to him if we don't find him quickly.'

Peroni had to admit that Guerra did know how to handle them. He used their own dialect and spoke in a hectoring, paternal tone which seemed to have its effect for they all shifted uneasily and glanced at each other.

'I know all about your loyalty to the family,' Guerra went on, 'it does you credit. But here it's misplaced. If you know of Gabriele's whereabouts and keep silent about them, you might be responsible for his death.'

The woman took a step towards her husband, her mouth open to say something, but he stopped her with a gesture, standing up.

'He's upstairs,' he said and, jerking his head, he invited Peroni and Guerra to follow him. They went through a curtained entrance and then up a narrow flight of stone steps, with the wife and the sons cautiously curious behind.

At the top of the stairs the man went to a door and opened it. An expression of slow surprise came over his face as he looked in.

'He's gone,' he said.

'When did you last see him?' asked Guerra.

' 'Bout half an hour ago.'

'I was just going to take him some food up,' said the mother.

'Is there any other way out of the house?' asked Guerra.

'Through the hayloft,' said the eldest boy.

'Show me.'

Opposite the door they had just opened there was another, crudely made and older than the rest of the house with a heavy wooden latch. The boy opened it and they went into a hayloft stacked full with hay. A ladder went down to the floor below where a large door opened into the open country behind the house.

'When did Gabriele come to you?' asked Guerra.

The family looked at one another. 'Couple o' nights ago,' said the mother.

'Tuesday?'

'That's right – Tuesday night it was,' confirmed the eldest boy.

'And he asked you to put him up?' They nodded. 'Did he say why?'

178

'Well, he said like as someone was after him down in Verona.
'He had no vehicle with him?'
'No.'
Guerra turned to Peroni. 'It's as well,' he said, 'we brought some men with us.'
They walked round the house to the front where the policemen were waiting.
'He's probably not been gone long,' said Guerra, getting out a military map of the area, 'but it's easy to disappear in this sort of country – the partisans made very effective use of it during the war. Now then, I suggest we proceed like this . . .'
Guerra briefed the men and Peroni as though for a military operation, giving each of them a slice of the country to cover. He obviously knew the land well, and his directions were brief and efficient so that minutes later Peroni and his colleagues were fanning out into the countryside.
Mercifully it was not so hot as it had been in Verona. They were nearly 600 metres up and there was a slight breeze, but it was still very warm and before long Peroni, who was not accustomed to cross-country treks, was beginning to feel uncomfortable with his shirt sticking to his back, sweat trickling and then pouring down his face, and his shoes, which were made for elegance, beginning to pinch cruelly.
The countryside was beautiful with sweeping mountain vistas, undulating woods and fields and little villages in the distance snuggling harmoniously into it. All this meant less than nothing to Peroni who was urban to the soles of his aching feet. As far as he was concerned, the country was no more than the space between two towns. 'Once you've seen a tree,' he had remarked on another occasion to Assunta who agreed with him, 'you've seen them all.' For him streets were a *sine qua non* of existence.
And to make matters worse for him now there was the shooting. So long as he was out in the open it was reasonably safe, for however wild these hunters were they were presumably not deliberately homicidal. But in the unavoidable wooded areas, it was a different matter. Shots cracked on all sides, and there was no telling that the next one wasn't going to hit him as some

crazed huntsman caught a flash of his shirt through the dense undergrowth and mistook it for a rabbit. You read about these hunting accidents in the paper every day. Dozens of people got killed; as a sport it was every bit as lethal as Italian politics.

Rounding the shoulder of a hill, Peroni saw in the distance the village he was supposed to be making for. It couldn't be more than two kilometres away. But not, of course, two kilometres of hard, sensible pavement which you could cover comfortably in twenty minutes, but two kilometres of up and down, of vicious brambles, of barbed wire fencing erected to prevent the passing of a Houdini, and of unexpected boggy patches into which you had stepped ankle deep before you were aware of them.

And of adders. Peroni remembered them with a shock. There was a large poster about them in the *Questura*, illustrating the various sorts of terrain in which you were most likely to come across them, and Peroni realised he was travelling through them all. The dry stone walls he was obliged to scramble over were ideal nesting places for them. Eighty-five per cent of adder bites, said the poster, were on the hands, a fact which in the adder-free surroundings of the *Questura* had aroused no more than academic curiosity, but now that he was obliged to use his hands to get over the walls it became a matter of alarming topicality.

During the summer months the local paper was full of stories about people being bitten by adders, but they usually seemed to have a serum ready to hand, or at least a car which would take them to a doctor. But Peroni had neither car nor serum. You could, he had read, cut a deep hole in the flesh and suck out the poison, but he would as soon have been capable of biting the adder back.

What with adders and hunters, the prospects of sudden death seemed numerous, but he nevertheless managed to reach the village he was heading for, where he drank two clandestine beers, and set off back on a different route for the starting point.

He never expected to find Gabriele, and so it came as a complete shock to him when, stumbling exhausted through a copse, his eye was caught by the mop of golden, angelic hair, bright against the brown earth.

Gabriele was dead.

There was a small black hole just above his left ear, and from it a gush of blood had spurted across his cheek and down to colour his expensive white shirt a dull red which still glowed in the afternoon sunlight.

Francesca

It was just in time for the evenings.

ANOTHER MONTAGU SLAIN, said one. MONTAGU–CAPULET CONFLICT: ANOTHER VICTIM, said the other.

'It's all they ever think of,' grumbled Peroni.

'You can't really blame them,' said his brother-in-law, Giorgio, thoughtfully hunting fragments of boiled mutton with a toothpick. 'After all it makes a wonderful story. And they don't know that the whole thing's exploded.'

'But has it been exploded?' said Anna Maria.

Peroni looked at her horrified. 'Well, of course it has,' he said. 'For heaven's sake don't let's start chasing that hare again!'

'It's a hare we never did catch, Uncle Achille,' she pointed out.

'You can't catch ghost hares,' said Peroni.

'I wonder,' she said meditatively.

'I'll get coffee,' said Assunta, looking pleased, for she had always been a supporter of the Montagu–Capulet theory.

'What do you wonder?' asked Peroni resignedly.

'It's just that when you first heard about them being Montagus and Capulets, you were naturally suspicious because you were afraid that the hard facts might get lost in a smokescreen of legend. Now I wonder if we're not making the contrary mistake.'

'And what would that be?'

'Letting the legend get lost behind the facts.'

'Nonsense,' said Stefano ungraciously. 'We know that the General was killed because he had become an embarrassment for whoever was the effective power behind the neo-fascist organisation. Not because he was a Montagu. And we know, too, that Loris was killed because he found out about his father's death. And now Gabriele's been killed because he knew the identity of the person behind it all.'

'The fact still remains,' said Anna Maria obstinately, 'that all these people belong to one or other of the two families. All right – the facts have been explained up to a certain point. But we still don't know whether the legend has some bearing on them. My instinct tells me that we're not going to get at the final truth until we go back to the Montagus and the Capulets.'

The family was silent. Anna Maria's instinct was as much an object of awe as Stefano's intellect.

'But how?' said Peroni helplessly.

'If I were you, Uncle Achille,' said Anna Maria, 'I should look very carefully into the movements of all the Pillipopolis over the last twelve hours. Just in case one of them was up in Rosaro.'

Under the circumstances nobody believed it for a moment, but there was a theory that Gabriele had been killed in a hunting accident. It was suggested by the area in which he had died and by the fact that the weapon used had been a hunting rifle. Lenotti and various other men from the *Questura* and the *Carabinieri* had stayed up in Rosaro to search the countryside about and question everyone they came across. Peroni expected no sensational results from this, and so, although he was not particularly enthusiastic about Anna Maria's idea either, he set up a routine enquiry into the movements of the Pillipopoli clan that day.

It was a monotonous job which took a lot of cross checking, and it was in banal and apparently quite unsuspicious circumstances that the metaphorical bomb was uncovered.

Francesca Pillipopoli had told an enquirer from the *Questura* that she had left her home at about three (confirmed by the servants) and gone to the cinema to see a replay of *Il Gattopardo*. But when a routine check was made of this statement it was learned that the cinema in question had been closed that afternoon as a result of a minor fire in the projector room.

Peroni remembered the pretty, shy seventeen-year-old on

whom his charm had so surprisingly failed to work at their first meeting, and for the first time he began to wonder whether Anna Maria's instinct might not be right after all. He sent for the file on Pillipopoli, Francesca Emilia Teodora Isabella, and when it arrived he started to read it with avidity.

All Francesca's life was there from the moment of her birth in a luxury clinic in the hills outside Verona through to the present day, and there was nothing to give rise to suspicion. She moved with the staider Liceo set – bright, friendly, attractive young people almost all of good families who frequented certain *pizzerie*, certain bars, walked together in Via Mazzini, went skiing together in the winter and swimming in the lake during the summer. Not for her the fringe groups of drug-taking, promiscuity and political violence. Her only rebellion, small but successful, had been against her family's reluctance to allow her to ride a scooter, and she had acquired a red one (VR 86233). Nothing much to go on there.

Or so it seemed.

For now a theory was beginning to take monstrous shape in Peroni's mind. Suppose Francesca was not what she appeared? After all, she and her brother, Policarpo, had been very close, and the ranks of the Red Brigade were crowded with pretty young girls of good family. Why not?

At that moment the phone rang on Peroni's desk. The police and *Carabinieri* had returned from Rosaro and were waiting to give their reports. Peroni went into the large room which had once been a ballroom to listen to them.

With much flipping through notebooks and clearing of throats the reports were made. They had interviewed everybody who had been hunting in the area that day. Some of these people were local peasants who had shot over that country since they were boys. Others came from Verona and other towns round about. Their guns were being checked ballistically, but they all declared themselves innocent of having shot at anything which could have conceivably resembled a human being.

The entire population of the village of Rosaro seemed to have been interviewed as well, and Peroni had to listen patiently to all their negative statements and, remembering that Berlinguer – secretary of the Italian Communist Party – was known by his associates as '*cul di ferro*' or 'old iron arse' for his ability to sit through endless meetings, he decided that the same might be said of him.

'Rosa Zanichelli,' droned on Lenotti, 'wife of the village tobacconist, aged sixty-two, reports that she was taking some rubbish to throw away at a tip when she noticed ...'

Another holiday-maker, thought Peroni to himself. The village was full of them, as most of its families let rooms during the summer. His conscious mind had momentarily switched off to form the thought when his unconscious mind, which continued to monitor Lenotti, flashed through to him that against all probabilities something of vital importance had been said. He played it back. '... a girl riding on a red scooter.'

Rapt attention took Peroni with such suddenness that Lenotti, immediately convinced he had said something wrong, began to stammer.

'Did she say anything of this girl's appearance?' questioned Peroni almost passionately.

'I – er – I interrogated her upon that point,' mumbled Lenotti, 'but she said that all young girls looked the same to her.'

'The number plate – did she get the number plate?' They never did, but the question had to be asked.

'I enquired about that,' said Lenotti unhappily, baffled by Peroni's sudden interest. 'She said it was a Verona licence number. She didn't get the number, but she thought that the last two figures were both threes.'

Not even his closest collaborators suspected that behind the rubicund benignity of the DIGOS chief's expression undiluted irritation seared as insistently as a dental drill. It had begun when a bullet had exploded through the palate of Policarpo Pillipopoli and had continued unabated ever since. For with the death of Policarpo (and that of his mistress, Monica Branca, several hours before him) he had lost the only two major leads he possessed into the heart of the Red Brigade column in Verona. And the fact that he had been personally responsible – however inadvertently – for the death of Monica did nothing to alleviate the irritation.

So now the announcement that *dott*. Peroni had called an unexpected meeting aroused no cordiality within him. Apart from anything else he resented Peroni's position of dominance in the Piantaleone affair. It was a political matter and, as such, should have been handled by the DIGOS. Intrusion by the Public Security Police only made for confusion.

None of this showed in his beaming countenance as he entered *dott*. Guerra's office, summed up the number and rank of people present and decided that something unusual must be afoot.

'Gentlemen,' said Guerra when everybody was seated, 'as a result of investigations into the death of Gabriele Piantaleone this morning something has come to light which may be of fundamental importance. If you would outline the facts, *dottore*?'

'Certainly, *dottore*.'

The dental drill within the DIGOS chief's mind jabbed with renewed viciousness as he observed Peroni's ill-concealed relish of what was obviously to be a dramatic moment. But as the story of Francesca Pillipopoli unfolded, the mental anguish became somewhat alleviated in spite of Peroni's self-satisfaction.

It was possible, he thought, just possible. She just might have been indoctrinated by her brother, and the lack of any supporting evidence about her commitment to the terrorist cause meant nothing at all, for they would have demanded first and foremost that she should remain to all outward appearances an unimpeachable little bourgeois until the right moment came.

'Of course, there may be some other reason for her having lied about the cinema,' Peroni was saying, 'but taken in conjunction with the fact that a young girl on a red scooter with a Verona licence number probably ending in double three was seen in Rosaro at about the time of Gabriele's death, it seems worthy of attention.'

'It certainly does,' said Guerra.

'We seem to be forgetting the fact,' said the *Carabiniere* General irritably, 'that a person whose description in no way resembles that of a young girl and who purported to be a policeman was enquiring about the movements of the Piantaleone youth on the night he disappeared.'

'We are not so much forgetting,' said Guerra with smooth courtesy, 'as acknowledging the possibility of another alley for exploration.'

The *Carabiniere* General hurrumphed.

'Consequently,' Guerra continued, turning to Peroni again, 'I think we should proceed to call in Francesca Pillipopoli for immediate interrogation.'

And run the risk, thought the DIGOS chief, of another suicide or misdirected bullet. Two vital leads had already gone that way – did they want to lose a third?

'If you'll forgive me, *dottore*,' he said to Guerra with even more of his usual bonhomie, 'I think that would be a mistake. If she is what *dottore* Peroni has suggested then she could well lead us sooner or later to the headquarters of the Red Brigade in Verona. But if we bring her in now – assuming that we succeed in getting her alive – we may lose our last chance for a while.'

Guerra considered this. 'What do you say, *dottore*?' he asked, turning to Peroni.

'Naturally, I should like to question her as soon as possible,' said Peroni, 'but I do see the other point of view. We might just learn more from her movements if she were free.'

Guerra thought again. 'Twenty-four hours,' he said at last. 'At the end of that period we will reconsider the whole position. But please ensure the maximum surveillance. Remember that we are knowingly letting a potentially dangerous terrorist loose on the public. If that were to reach ministerial ears, gentlemen, heads would fall.'

Toni was glad that his fiancée Barbara was not with him. To anybody else it would have been evident that his assiduous attention to the movements of the pretty, dark-haired girl were purely professional. But Barbara was incurably jealous, and she would have been quite capable of assuming that his casual but unswerving observation had subtly changed from professional to emotional.

Two of Toni's colleagues were with him on the job, but none of them gave any sign of recognition for each other. Toni himself looked like a student with his first 600 car. One of the others was a woman who might have been an elementary-school teacher while the third seemed to be a businessman with an unobtrusive Fiat.

For three such highly trained members of the anti-terrorist police following a ruthless political killer, it was being a very uneventful morning. Francesca had emerged from the Pillipopoli home on her red scooter shortly after nine o'clock. She had met a group of other boys and girls and driven out to the swimming pool. The DIGOS female agent had followed her in, looking as though she had come to pick up a child, but found that Francesca did nothing more unpredictable than swim.

After that the party drove back into the centre where they parked their scooters and walked in Via Mazzini. Then the girls of the party went off by themselves to buy some clothes, meeting up again with the boys in Piazza Dante about an hour later for ice-creams and more talk. Then they all walked back down Via Mazzini and split up to go home for lunch.

These movements were all duly reported back to the *Questura* by radio from the businessman's car, and the three were told to stay with Francesca. They took it in turns to have hurried snacks at a nearby bar, but they needn't have hurried, for Francesca didn't come out after lunch.

The long, hot afternoon burned itself slowly towards evening. The student, the businessman and the elementary-school teacher sat in their respective cars watching the Pillipopoli home patiently and unavailingly.

The sun started to go down, but the heat didn't.

Back in the *Questura* all the functionaries who weren't on night duty went off to their assorted wives, mistresses, mothers or solitudes. Peroni and the head of the DIGOS sat in their respective offices waiting for news. *Dott.* Guerra's twenty-four hours had nearly expired.

And then a phone buzzed in Peroni's office. A radio report had just come through that Francesca had left her home for the second time that day.

Running to the radio room Peroni almost bumped into the DIGOS chief. The two men smiled with their teeth, shook hands hurriedly and went in.

'. . . behind her,' the voice of the businessman was saying. 'She's just turned into Via Cavour. No chance of her spotting us in this – the traffic's heavy. She's turning right. Now she's doubled back into Via Roma. It looks like she's making for Via Pallone . . .'

Peroni and the DIGOS chief looked at one another, both struck by the same thought.

'It could be,' said the DIGOS chief.

'We'll know in a minute,' said Peroni.

And in almost exactly a minute the voice came over the radio with an inflection of excitement. 'She's on the road to Rosaro!'

'Careful she doesn't spot you,' said the DIGOS chief and gave instructions for the three cars to break up their positions and routes in order to be as unobtrusive as possible.

For twenty minutes nothing more came over the radio than confirmatory monosyllables indicating that Francesca was following the expected route.

Then: 'She's going straight through the village and out again,' came the voice, and Peroni followed her progress along the darkling road in his mind's eye.

'We can't stay close to her any longer – she'd see us. I'm stopping just outside the village. We can see her across the valley for at least a couple of kilometres.'

There was a long silence garnished only with the crackling of the radio and the DIGOS chief's heavy breathing. Then the businessman's voice came again. 'Wait a minute – she seems to have turned off the road. She's making for some sort of old ruin. I think she's going inside. Yes, she is – '

Suddenly the voice tensed with excitement. 'And there's a light in there – It's gone now, but there must be somebody else in there with her!'

The ruined villa had been there from the very beginning, Peroni thought as he drove towards Rosaro with the DIGOS chief and a contingent of armed men with bullet-proof shields. He remembered seeing it that first day as he drove up to interview the Piantaleone peasants. An architectural corpse, too remote in time, too far gone in decay to have anything to do with a twentieth-century murder investigation. (But the Capulets and the Montagus were even more remote in time, whispered a voice in his head which might or might not have been Anna Maria's.) And now it seemed as though the old villa was being cast for the role of headquarters of the Veronese column of the Red Brigade.

It was well chosen for the part, too – remote, fairly inaccessible, above suspicion. There was just one thing wrong with it as a terrorist centre. It belonged to the fascist Piantaleones.

Was it possible that a column of the Red Brigade, numbering among its members two of the Pillipopolis, could have deliberately chosen a Piantaleone villa, however ruined? It would be appropriately ironical, but surely the Red Brigade didn't waste time on irony?

Or didn't they? Peroni thought of their macabre gesture of leaving the body of the Christian Democrat president, Aldo Moro, in the boot of a car parked in the very heart of Rome, exactly equidistant from the headquarters of the Italian Communist Party and the Christian Democrat Party. You couldn't take cruel irony further than that. And certainly the villa would be safe enough for it had been long abandoned and none of the Piantaleones ever went there.

Peroni, the DIGOS chief and the armed striking force got out in the village. It was dark now and the inhabitants had all retreated to bed or television, so nobody saw the party move out from the houses as silently as so many stalking cats.

They were halfway towards the villa when a shadow detached itself from a low wall beside the road. It was Toni.

'She's still in there,' he said, 'she and whoever else is with her.'

'Then there's no point in waiting,' said the DIGOS chief. 'The longer we delay in country like this, the more chance they have of realising we're here. We'll go straight in.'

Peroni's stomach bucked convulsively.

Hidden from the villa by a clump of trees the whole party, including the businessman and the elementary-school teacher, worked out a plan of campaign. The idea was to get into the building in silence if possible. As long as their approach went unrecognised the initiative was to rest with Peroni and the DIGOS chief. But if it came to trouble the men with the bullet-proof shields would be ready for instant action.

Shadow-wise they moved towards the ruined villa.

When they got there they saw what had once been a path from a long since removed gate to the low steps leading up to the front door. It was not more than a couple of hundred metres, but it seemed to Peroni to go on for ever. Every second he expected the flash and crack of gunshot from one of the windows above his head. But there was only silence.

After a seemingly endless time-lapse they reached the front door, and Peroni and the DIGOS chief stood one on either side of it with their guns ready, the others grouped about them.

With his left hand Peroni turned the massive door handle as delicately as a *pizzaiolo* putting black olives into mozzarella cheese. Then with his left foot he pushed insinuatingly, almost amorously at the door. It moved open, creaking slightly. The whole party tensed in silence, waiting for an answering spit of flame. But none came. Peroni pushed again.

When the door was opened wide enough and still nothing but silence had come from within, the party stepped quietly inside. The place smelled musty and damp. At first Peroni could make out nothing in the darkness, but gradually he perceived that they were in an ample hall. The place must once have been magnificent, but now, in its total abandon, they were almost as much in danger of falling masonry as they were of terrorist bullets.

Men fanned silently out to right and left, but met with nothing but silence and darkness. There was nobody on the ground floor, so the party made for an enormous stone staircase which yawned at them from the other side of the hall.

Feeling their way gingerly, they climbed the stairway as it swept round and up to the first floor where a corridor stretched off to right and left. They stood for a moment in silence, uncertain which way to go.

And then, for the first time since they had entered the house, they heard a sound which was not made by themselves. It was a scarcely audible murmur of human voices and it came from the left.

They moved like bulky ghosts towards the sound which came from a room leading off the corridor. And as they drew near it they saw a faint light emanated from under the closed door.

They ranged themselves about this door, guns ready. Peroni winged a petition to St Janarius. The DIGOS chief nodded. The door was thrust open and the party erupted into the room.

What they saw was the last thing in the world they expected. By the glow of a torch on the floor a couple were locked together on a low camp-bed, totally absorbed in the act of love.

The men goggled unbelievingly. And Peroni's incredulous surprise was increased a hundredfold when the couple broke apart and he was able to see who they were.

The girl was Francesca. The man, or rather the boy, was Paolo Piantaleone.

Nobody said anything for a moment. The anticlimax was too great. Francesca fumbled for clothes to cover herself. Paolo started up and then, restrained either by the cohort ranged against him or his own nakedness, fell back again.

'I think it's time for a little explaining,' said Peroni, aware just how lame it sounded.

'I think it is!' said Paolo, struggling angrily into jeans. 'What right have you got to burst into private property like this?'

'The *signorina*,' said Peroni mildly, 'told me a – ' He was going to say a lie, but the sight of Francesca rumpled and half-clothed stopped him. 'The *signorina*,' he corrected himself, 'gave me a misleading account of her movements yesterday. She said she was at the Corallo Cinema when in fact it had been closed down because of a fire in the projector room.'

Francesca made a feminine moue of irritation.

'Since she was in fact up here and since, moreover, Gabriele Piantaleone was killed, also up here and at about the same time,, you will forgive us if we jumped to a false conclusion.'

Francesca and Paolo looked shamefaced.

'Perhaps,' said the DIGOS chief, Yuletide geniality in full flood, 'it would make matters easier if there were not quite such a martial display.' And he nodded to his own contingent to leave them. But, Peroni noticed, he kept his own gun unobtrusively ready.

'Would you like to start at the beginning?' said Peroni, as though he were offering them the first go in a game.

'Paolo and I are in love!' said Francesca defiantly.

'I'd gathered that,' said Peroni. And indeed it explained a lot – Paolo's guilty behaviour at their first meeting and Francesca's almost unnatural invulnerability to the Peroni charm. 'But why,' he went on, 'the secrecy?'

'Don't you know who we are?' said Francesca, wide-eyed as though he had questioned the existence of the sun.

'What do you mean, who you are?' asked Peroni, taken aback.

'He's a Montagu,' said Francesca, 'and I'm a Capulet.'

And that explained a lot, too, thought Peroni – particularly the shifty reaction of each family at the mention of the other. At the back of their minds, and not so very far back either, they all believed in it. And what was more, it looked as though Anna Maria were once again to have the right of it.

'All right,' said Peroni tolerantly, 'let's assume for the sake of argument that you are a latter-day Romeo and Juliet. What's wrong with that?'

'The legend,' said Francesca.

'What legend?'

'It's a lot of nonsense!' broke in Paolo.

'It's not a lot of nonsense!' said Francesca hotly. 'Look what happened!'

'We've been into this a thousand times,' Paolo shouted back at her, 'and it's still a lot of nonsense.'

'What is this legend?' said Peroni hastily, realising that if there wasn't an intervention they would soon be as closely locked in combat as they had been before in love.

'It's an old story in her family,' said Paolo. 'Whenever a Capulet and a Montagu fall in love, it says, the family feud will start again.'

'I see,' said Peroni. 'So when your father was killed, you assumed – '

'*She* assumed,' corrected Paolo.

'I think,' said the DIGOS chief, 'you'd better start at the beginning.'

'We – ' said Paolo and Francesca together.

'Ladies first?' said Peroni, who, all other things being equal, preferred to hear things from a woman.

'It all started earlier this year,' said Francesca, 'in February. It was cold and very foggy.' Peroni nodded; he knew those Verona fogs.

'I went to eat a pizza with some friends. Not a sit-down pizza, but one of those slice-pizza places where you eat it wrapped in a piece of paper standing up at the counter – you know?'

Again Peroni nodded. He knew the places well and visualised the owner behind the bar racing backwards and forwards with huge trays of pizza, cutting it into slices and handing it over the counter towards a dozen waving hands.

'Lot of people of our age go there,' Francesca went on, 'and there's a juke-box, so they often dance and it turns into a sort of impromptu party. Well, that particular day . . .'

Peroni recognised on her face that tender, distant expression that women often have when recalling an occasion of falling in love.

'On that particular day,' Francesca went on, 'several people asked me to dance and I said no. I felt sort of – apprehensive, and thought it must be the weather. And then I saw a boy standing in front of me . . .'

She smiled at Paolo and he smiled back at her, both of them caught up in the moment of that first meeting in a stand-up *pizzeria* in fog-wrapped Verona. (And Peroni wondered if Shakespeare, or rather Count Luigi da Porto, would have described it like that if he had set the story in the twentieth century.)

'I'd never seen him before. He asked me to dance, and this time I didn't say no. We danced for a while and then we went out into the fog and just walked about. I'd never liked fog before, but that day I loved it, with people looming mistily up at us and then disappearing, and little votive lights at roadside shrines flickering at us as though the Madonna, or whoever it was, approved. It was quite by accident that we saw a clock and realised we'd been wandering about for three hours. Do you remember?'

'Uhum,' said Paolo.

'So I said I'd have to go home. They'd be worried to death about me I knew – Pappa would ask endless questions and there'd be a terrible scene.'

So for all his Communism, thought Peroni, Count Gino Pillipopoli was still just an old-fashioned Italian father.

'Paolo took me home, and when we got there he said wasn't that where the Pillipopolis lived, and I said yes. And that was how we realised.'

'As far as I was concerned it didn't mean anything!' said Paolo, anxious to uphold masculine common sense, 'but she kept on about this legend in her family. It sounded rubbish to me, but I agreed not to tell anyone and to meet in secret. That's why I thought that when the spring came this old villa would be useful. I knew that nobody ever came here, and I thought that with time Francesca would get over this fear of the legend – '

'And I did, too,' Francesca went on with the story. 'At any rate partly. And although we didn't exactly go round shouting it out to the world, we started meeting more or less normally. We didn't go in Via Mazzini or any of the other places where everybody would see us, but I was a bit less scared. And then Paolo's father was killed.'

'I told her it was nothing to do with us,' said Paolo. 'How could it be?'

'And then a week after that,' said Francesca, 'my grandmother sent for me.'

'Your grandmother?' said Peroni. 'Ah yes – the Dowager Countess Augusta. Please go on.'

'Well, she really does believe in the legend. She's always been steeped in the whole Capulet and Montagu business. She warned me about it, and she said that she'd been talking to you only the day before. She said it was dangerous, and there would be more deaths. Well, that scared me, and I said what could I do about it. She said I'd have to leave Paolo, and I told her I would never do that!'

She and Paolo gripped each other by the hand, as though defying, not only Peroni and the DIGOS chief, but all the generations of dead Montagus and Capulets and the sinister legend which forbade their love.

'When,' asked Peroni, 'had you told your grandmother about Paolo?'

'When?' said Francesca. 'Never. We didn't tell anybody.'

'In that case how did she know about you?'

Francesca looked baffled. 'I don't know,' she said, 'I've always somehow assumed that Grandmother Augusta just did always know about everything.'

'Neapolitan I may be,' said Peroni, 'but I draw the line at magic!'

The death of his son had taken all the resilience out of Count Gino Pillipopoli, and he showed neither surprise or resentment at Peroni's late night visit.

'My mother?' he said dully. 'No, I don't think she'll be in bed. She sleeps very little.'

Neither did he show curiosity as to why Peroni should wish to visit the Dowager Countess at nearly midnight. He just led him up the stairs to the doorway of the little apartment and then, having handed him over to the nannie, left him there, walking heavily down the stairs again.

As before, the nannie left Peroni in the crowded drawing-room with its glass case full of porcelain statues, and then went to wheel in the Dowager Countess.

'So the Handsome Neapolitan Policeman has returned,' said the old lady, holding out her hand to Peroni, and he, as he kissed it, felt himself caught up once more in that unreal, nightmare world where the old Capulets and Montagus were more real than the living Veronese. But this time he would have to keep his head in it.

'And what can We do for you?' she went on.

'How did you know about your grand-daughter Francesca, and young Paolo Piantaleone?' asked Peroni.

If it took her by surprise, she didn't show it. 'How did I know *What* about my grand-daughter and this young man?' she countered.

'That they were in love,' said Peroni.

'I know of no such thing,' she said.

Coming from anybody else such prevarication would have called for rough handling, but not with the Dowager Countess. 'Your grand-daughter told me herself,' said Peroni with diplomatic courtesy.

'Told you?' She cocked one bright, bird-like eye at him.

'That she was in love with him.'

'And?'

'That you had sent for her and warned her of the consequences which would result, according to the family legend.'

The Dowager Countess reflected for a second, then reached a conclusion. 'Well?' she said.

'I need to know how you learnt of your grand-daughter's relationship with this young man. It could be of vital importance.'

Again the Dowager Countess paused. Then she said, 'I was Informed.'

'By whom?'

'A Well-wisher I believe is the term.'

'And who was this well-wisher?'

'I have no idea.'

'You mean you received an anonymous letter?'

'I received some Photographic Prints.'

'Of what?'

'Of my grand-daughter and the young man you mention in compromising situations.'

'Sent to you anonymously?'

'If you Care to Put it that way.'

Peroni thought there was no other way in which it could be put, but let the point pass.

'Were they sent through the post or delivered by hand?'

'They were Dispatched by means of the Postal Service.'

'Do you still have them?'

The Dowager Countess Augusta eyed Peroni as though he had made an improper, though not wholly unacceptable offer. Then she rang a little silver hand-bell and waited until the nannie appeared.

'Trombetti,' she said, 'The Photographs.'

The nannie disappeared and returned with an envelope which she passed to the Dowager Countess who handed it to Peroni as though it were a bestowal of largesse.

He opened the envelope and took out five photographs. A quick glance through them showed the Dowager Countess's idea of compromising situations to be some half-century out of date. All five photographs showed Paolo and Francesca in various parts of the city, hand in hand or with their arms about each other and, in one case, kissing lightly.

The question was, why had these photographs been sent to the Dowager Countess, and Peroni believed he knew the answer to it. Somebody, knowing of her obsession with the legend, had hoped in this way to spark off the old family feud anew, thus diverting attention from the real motivation behind General Piantaleone's death.

Who? Peroni's thought plunged into a black sea, and when it surfaced again there was a coral-chipping of the truth in its teeth.

'Do you have the envelope in which the pictures arrived?' he asked.

'Certainly not!' said the Dowager Countess with an air which said that whoever else might have kept dirty old envelopes, she certainly did not. She had not noticed the postmark, but she believed that the address was typewritten.

'May I take these photographs to the *Questura*?' The law made no doubt that he could, but Peroni deemed it fitting to put the Dowager Countess above the law.

'You may,' she conceded regally.

Peroni had kissed her hand and got as far as the door when he remembered something and turned. 'Please forgive the question, *contessa*,' he said, 'but in view of our previous conversation, why didn't you think of telling me about this?'

Her look raked him from head to toe. 'One does not wash one's Dirty Linen in Public, *commissario*,' she said.

Peroni thought that the original Lady Capulet all of seven hundred years ago perhaps looked on the family vicissitudes then as no more than dirty linen.

The scientific specialists were able to tell Peroni no more next morning than that the pictures had almost certainly been developed privately, a conclusion his own common sense had already reached. Was it possible, he thought in frustration, that five photographs could give no clue as to the identity of the person who took them?

He started to brood over them, picking at the minutest details. They had been taken in various parts of the city, all in relatively uncrowded streets and squares. And it seemed from the angle that at least three had been shot from a vehicle. It seemed, moreover, that the camera lens had been more or less level with Francesca and Paolo, as though the vehicle had been not so much a car as a van.

Next Peroni studied the two pictures which appeared to have been taken on foot. The first was the one of the kiss. They were sitting on a stone bench by the river, her head resting on his arm while he, bending down, appeared to be brushing her lips lightly with his. The picture must have been easy to take as there were so many tourist views in the vicinity that the photographer could easily have given the impression that he was photographing one of them.

Peroni turned to the other photograph that had not been taken from the van. Paolo and Francesca were looking into the window of a toyshop, hand in hand. He must have just made a joke, for she had turned her head towards him, laughing, her teeth gleaming white and her long black hair furling over her shoulders with the movement.

And then Peroni saw that there was a ghost in the picture.

The ghost of a van. It was parked on the opposite side of the road and was reflected in the toy shop window. It was a black Volkswagen which looked as though it belonged to a shop, business, or firm.

A bell chimed insistently in Peroni's mind and for a second he couldn't understand what it was calling his attention to. And then he remembered. One of the people questioned in the area from which Gabriele had vanished to Rosaro had mentioned seeing a dark-coloured van disappearing round the corner.

It began to look as though the picture were taking shape at last.

Eros Pompi, exclusive Volkswagen agent in Verona, prided himself on being able to sum up clients. As soon as they came through the showroom door he could see, like a sort of psychic emanation about them, the type of vehicle to which they belonged – utility, family, camper, saloon, sports model and so on. Little or no psychic emanation indicated a pedestrian or cyclist.

The man who now came in, for instance, was undoubtedly an expensive sports model. Eros Pompi closed the motoring magazine which constituted his exclusive reading matter and rose to meet him with a smile as bright as a gleaming new chassis.

'Can I help you?'

'I hope you can,' said the expensive sports model, adding unexpectedly, '*Questura.*'

'Oh.' Eros Pompi was taken aback; it must be something to do with stolen cars. 'Won't you sit down?'

'Thank you,' said the expensive sports model, sitting in the soft black-leather armchair designed to make clients feel so comfortable that they could afford anything. 'I want to trace the owner of this van.' And he held out a photograph, indicating a vehicle reflected in a shop window.

'That would be our 1978 model,' said Eros Pompi with swift expertise. 'It could have been bought anywhere.'

'I realise that,' said the expensive sports model, 'but before I start enquiring anywhere, which would take a long time, I'd like to see if it could have been bought in Verona.'

'If you don't mind waiting a moment I'll look in our books.'

'By all means.'

Eros Pompi disappeared into a back room from which he emerged some minutes later with a piece of paper.

'Only three black models of this type were sold,' he said. 'Clients usually prefer brighter colours. One went to a florists in Villafranca. Another went to a fishmonger in Legnago, and the third was sold to an ecclesiastical furnishers here in Verona.'

Eros Pompi felt as though a powerful charge of electricity from the battery of the exclusive sports model had suddenly galvanised him, making him jump perceptibly behind his desk.

'I'll take all three if you don't mind.'

'You're very welcome,' said Eros Pompi nervously, handing over the piece of paper.

The expensive sports model reversed, changed gear and drove out of the showroom at full speed.

It was the phrase 'ecclesiastical furnishers' which had done it. It had instantly put Peroni in mind of what Gabriele had said about a place that was 'out of character'. What could be more out of everybody's character in the Piantaleone affair than an ecclesiastical furnishers?

Common sense said that it could just as well be the flower shop or the fishmongers. Or none of the three. But this time even the *commissario* consented to ignore common sense. After all, there was nothing to lose. And so the total Peroni would begin with the ecclesiastical furnishers.

Quirico Ricordi was his name and his address was in an old, quiet part of the town only a few minutes' drive away. Peroni went there in his red Alfa.

The shop was in an old building down a narrow, little frequented street, its windows displaying a variety of crucifixes, copes, stoles, albs, chasubles, holy-water stoups and candlesticks. It was very quiet.

He parked a little further down the road and then walked back towards the shop. As he came near it, two nuns crossed from the other side of the road and went in. An old-fashioned shop bell tinkled on the door. Peroni moved up to the window and found it was possible to spy into the shop beyond the proliferation of ecclesiastical items laid out like exotic sweets in a luxury confectioners.

He saw the two nuns standing silently in front of the counter, expressionlessly waiting for attention. Then a door opened at the farther end of the shop behind the counter and a man came out, rubbing his hands and smiling unctuously at the nuns. Peroni saw his mouth move in a silent interrogative, and then watched the mouth of the spokeswoman for the two nuns move in a longer speech, presumably describing the purchase she wished to make.

The man's mouth formed another specifying interrogative and, as it did so, Peroni suddenly thought that he had seen this man somewhere before. But he couldn't imagine where. There was nothing remotely Piantaleone or Pillipopoli about him, and yet there was something vaguely familiar about the face.

Now the man was holding his hands out before him, one above the other as though to indicate height. And the spokeswoman nun repeated the same gesture, but holding one hand at a slightly greater height above the other. Peroni wondered what the dumb-show could be about, but the question that really puzzled him was where he had seen the man before.

He was what you might expect an ecclesiastical furnisher to be. No longer young, with a bald pate which looked as though it had been polished with a product especially designed to make ecclesiastical furnishings gleam, he had small, cunning eyes and a weak-looking chin.

Now, having apparently understood the nuns' requirements, he turned and vanished from Peroni's view. When he came back a few seconds later the lesser mystery concerning the purchases was solved, for he was carrying three or four different varieties of candlestick. As the nuns carefully examined these, Peroni continued to ponder the question of the man's identity, even recalling the multitude of identikit pictures which had come before him in Verona, but none of them resembled the ecclesiastical furnisher.

The nuns took their time, consulting together in what Peroni guessed were whispers, carefully handling the candlesticks, holding them up to the light and obliging the shopkeeper to make several more trips to the region cut off from Peroni's view, returning each time with new candlesticks. But after ten minutes the choice was made. The man dexterously made up a parcel while the nuns fished cautiously about in a communal purse for the money.

It was as they handed it over that the truth came to Peroni in a sudden flash. It wasn't that he had seen the man before at all.

He had heard his description.

The ecclesiastical furnisher's appearance exactly fitted that of the man who had enquired about Gabriele's movements after his disappearance to Rosaro.

The nuns were moving towards the shop door and Peroni walked swiftly away towards his own car. He didn't see how the man could possibly recognise him, but he preferred not to risk it.

He drove off in a wave of elation. The probable identification of the ecclesiastical furnishers with the place Gabriele had described as 'out of character' and the other probable identification of the shopkeeper himself with the man who had been enquiring about Gabriele's movements both made it seem as though the truth were near at last.

But a couple of minutes later as he stopped at a traffic lights he realised that behind the excitement there lurked a sense of frustration. The ecclesiastical furnisher fitted the description of the man who had enquired about Gabriele well enough. But there was something else about him. Something altogether nearer, more familiar, and however much he racked his brains Peroni could not get the smallest inkling of what that might be.

Ricordi, Quirico, was listed in the phone book under two addresses. One said *fornitore ecclesiastico*, the other was private. At 7.30 sharp that evening he locked up the former and proceeded to the latter which was a third-floor flat.

At this point two courses seemed open to Peroni. He could visit Ricordi and interrogate him or he could apply for a warrant to raid the shop. Something told him that the first would produce nothing and he was certain that his evidence would not be considered sufficient to carry through the second.

And so once more the protesting *commissario* was bundled away somewhere he could not interfere. His cries of protest echoed faintly in the distance of the endless labyrinth that was Peroni's mind, and then were stifled altogether.

Driving past the shop later that night Peroni saw at once that the front was out of the question. For one thing it was heavily shuttered and for another it was right under a streetlamp. So he drove to the end of the street, turned left and then left again. This street was too far to run directly behind the ecclesiastical furnishers. But halfway down it on the left there was an alley which would have been right behind the shop. Peroni parked and went to investigate.

The alley was dark and deserted, and it led to a very small, anomalous-looking paved opening surrounded by the backs and sides of buildings. It was a dismal place with bits of newspaper on the ground and a couple of plastic containers with stomach-turning food left-overs in them. On one of the walls somebody had sprayed 'Don't force me to start the revolution', while on another some unquenchably militant feminist had applied the circle-cross symbol of her movement under the words 'The witches are coming!' For whom to read? Peroni wondered.

He calculated quickly which of the buildings was the ecclesiastical furnishers and found that it had a balcony on the first floor, reachable via the downstairs window and some guttering. In twelve seconds flat he was on it and examining the shutters which, unlike those at the front, were old and in bad repair. Quietly he set to work. Back at the *Questura* he had checked that the building was unoccupied except by Quirico Ricordi's shop, so there seemed to be little danger in the undertaking.

With the sound of a nut cracking the shutters came open, and the glass doors within presented even less difficulties. Peroni stepped inside and for a horrible moment thought that the large, dark room was filled with a small army of ghosts, all staring at him, silent and motionless. Then he saw that the ghosts were row upon row of ecclesiastical vestments hung on long, running hangers. He pulled the shutters to behind him and then turned on a pocket torch. The vestments looked even eerier by torchlight, like human figures with their heads and arms missing.

There was a door at the other end of the room and Peroni had to pass through the midst of the priests-who-weren't-there to reach it. He walked as though on a tightrope.

He was halfway across the room when he heard something move. Panic exploded silently within him like a Neapolitan firework display. He imagined the prospect of a gun-fight among vestments, dodging from one stiff, richly embroidered shield to the next. Then there came another sound, nearer this time and indirectly visible, too, for he could just make out in the darkness a cope or a stole swaying slightly on its hanger.

He waited in pitch darkness, having turned off his pocket torch at the first sound of movement, not daring to take any initiative yet. Then suddenly something pushed against his leg. There was a gala edition of the Neapolitan pyrotechnics before Peroni switched on the torch again and saw its light reflected brilliantly in two enormous green eyes and heard a confidential mew.

For a couple of seconds he stroked his gratitude, then made

towards the door again. When he reached it, he found that it opened a little creakily to reveal a landing with another door at the end and stairs going up and down.

Deciding to start at the bottom he went down the stairs every bit as silently as the cat would have done. The ground floor was divided into two parts. At the front was the shop itself with a crowd of life-size holy statues which had been cut off from his view when he spied through the window earlier that day. Then at the back there was the door through which Quirico Ricordi had come, rubbing his hands, to serve the nuns.

Peroni listened outside for a moment and then gently turned the knob. The door wasn't locked. Within, his torch revealed the sort of little office you would expect to find in many of the older shops in the city. It was furnished with a desk, two chairs and a cupboard. There was a large and dignified calendar from a wholesale purveyor of ecclesiastical wares, a framed copy of the prayers which priests should say while robing and a poor reproduction of the da Vinci *Last Supper*.

There was a safe, too, and a quick glance told Peroni that there was only one man in the world that he knew who would even attempt to break it, and that man was now in luxurious retirement in the Canary Isles after a brilliant career as the Mafia's number one safe-cracking expert. It was made in Switzerland, cost more money than the majority of safes even contain and was, for its price, surprisingly small.

Peroni was pondering this when he heard the sound of a key in the front-of-the-shop shutter. He switched out the torch and glided out of the office closing the door behind him.

There was only one possible hiding place. Quickly he slipped into the crowd between St Francis and St Anthony, elbowed his way gently through the virgins, martyrs and confessors and was in the very back row (the only place, he would have reflected under less dramatic circumstances, likely to be assigned to him in Heaven if he ever got there at all) when he heard the shutter being pulled up. It was none of your rattle-crash-bang shutters for it went up with a discreet, technocratical murmur which was odd for such a shop.

Whoever had opened it stepped inside the shop and walked across the floor. In the darkness and with the crowded jumble of the Elect in front of him, Peroni could not see who it was, though he assumed it to be Ricordi, Quirico.

Whoever-it-was walked lightly and slowly, feeling his way in the dark, but regularly and without stumbling. Having reached the back of the shop the person opened the door and went into the office, switching on the light.

Still Peroni could see nothing except the glow of the light, but he knew that whoever was in the office was the same person whose psychic imprint he had felt so strongly in the villa at Garda.

From his position in the back row of Heaven, he could hear this person moving about, putting something down, sitting. He waited a minute, then started to edge his way silently through the saints again. When he had emerged from the throng of them, he could see the half open door, but not the person inside. He moved soundlessly towards it, his gun ready. Outside the door he paused for a second and then pushed it open with his left hand.

Kneeling beside the safe, her eyes raised towards him, was Regina.

It wasn't even such a very great surprise. And he remembered how the first time he had set eyes on her she had reminded him of a Goldoni actress. It should have warned him.

Then he saw the confirmation he was looking for. It was on the desk beside her open handbag. Still pointing the gun at her, he picked it up and checked. It was an expensive pocket diary. Inside the cover was printed Pierre Ronceaux et Cie – Geneva, and the pencil was missing.

'*You* put the bomb into Loris's car,' he said. 'You.'

She stood up and shrugged 'I had no choice,' she said.

'And the General?'

'We killed him, too We had to.'

'We?'

'Oh, you'll know it all soon enough – now that you've got

to the centre of the maze. I knew you'd get here sooner or later, Achille. I've been waiting for you.'

The interview began to sound as though it was not going the way he intended. 'What do you mean?' he asked.

'Well, we couldn't go on for ever on different sides, could we?'

'You sound as though you think I'm going to join your side.'

'Oh, but you are, Achille. We've got everything to offer you.'

Peroni murmured an expletive in Neapolitan dialect. 'Everything you had to offer vanished when I discovered the villa at Garda,' he said.

'You're very naïve if you think that,' she said. 'The villa at Garda and the people you arrested were the tip of the iceberg, and a very small tip at that. The movement's still very much alive and it's going to take over Italy. I just want you to be with it when it does.'

Actress or no actress, he could see that she believed what she was saying. 'What makes you think the movement will be able to take over Italy?'

'We've been preparing it for years. Our people are everywhere. The state is visibly crumbling – what opposition can it offer us?'

'Maybe the state can't offer much, but what about the Communists?'

'That's where the Red Brigade has played into our hands. The Communists have been so anxious to disassociate themselves from all this undemocratic violence that they've exaggerated in the other sense. They've been pretending to be just like the other parties for so long that they've *become* just like the other parties. Besides – ' She broke off as though uncertain whether to trust him.

'Well?'

'Not all Italian Communists are quite the comrades they seem to be. Some of them are with us.' She mentioned three names big enough to make Peroni wonder whether there might not be something in what she was saying after all. 'Do you still think we've got nothing to offer you, Achille?'

He couldn't help being curious. 'Just what do you have to offer?'

Locked up in a cell far away in the corridors of Peroni's mind, the *commissario* howled his protest, but it went unobserved.

'A leading position in the whole organisation for a start. You've shown you can do well against us, so how much better will you be able to do for us? In a few months you could be one of the rulers of Italy.'

In the almost febrile state which Regina wrought in him Peroni wondered whether at last he was being offered the bribe he would not be able to refuse.

'What have you got to lose?' she went on. 'You're expected to risk your life every day and then you're treated like a wretched bureaucrat. For all your brilliance the state would sacrifice you at a moment's notice if it needed a scapegoat. You know that's true, don't you?'

He nodded, almost hypnotised by her.

'We don't make mistakes like that. We value our own people. If you joined us, you'd get three million lire a month on top of your existing salary.'

Three million lire! The mind boggled. Something told him that Assunta would not have approved, but he ignored it.

'And that's not all you'd get . . .'

She stepped towards him, heedless of the gun pointed at her, and kissed him on the mouth. Her mouth opened over his like a spreading rose, and Peroni decided that this *was* the bribe he would not be able to refuse.

The kiss became a bottomless chasm into which he was falling. He recognised it as the pit of Hell, but had no desire to escape from it.

And then a face seemed to swim mistily in his mind's eye. At first he was unable to focus it, but then he saw it was the face of Don Pietro, the priest in Naples who had enticed him from the gutter and revealed his outrageous vocation as a policeman. Don Pietro seemed to be pointing to something. Peroni followed the direction in which he was pointing and saw the scene on the road just outside Bardolino when Loris's car had been blown up by a bomb. He saw the fragments of human body blasted in all directions by the explosion and smelled the terrible odour of burnt human flesh, and this sight and this smell checked his headlong fall and pulled him agonizingly out of the bottomless chasm of Regina's mouth.

Still covering her with the gun, he telephoned the *Questura*. *Dott.* Guerra was not there, but Peroni arranged for men and a car to come round and pick up Regina.

They waited together in silence, not looking at each other. Peroni thought that the next time he saw her she would be in the custody of a prison nun as powerful as a tank and probably not much smaller. It was better like that.

After only a few minutes which seemed much longer there was the sound of a car stopping in the street and of doors banging as men got out of it.

When she had gone, Peroni sat alone in the little office for a moment feeling the full desolation of it. Then he got up slowly and went out to his car.

Quirico Ricordi was a jigsaw puzzle fanatic. But not for him the crowded Amsterdam squares with their tricky eaves and cornices, or the Grand Canal scenes with the water glistening in the sun and the gondolas bobbing between their poles or even the Constable reproductions with their elusive skies. They were far too easy. What he liked was purely abstract form in which there was no help from recognisable shapes. And this evening he had the perfect challenge for his skill. For a start it was round which meant that you couldn't make a frame of edges and corners. And then it was a composition of nothing but colours, intricate, soulless and a nightmare to anyone who did not possess the peculiar genius of Quirico Ricordi.

He sat down at his special jigsaw puzzle table and turned on the powerful, jointed lamp which brilliantly illuminated the anarchy of 5000 scattered pieces which he planned to have subdued to perfect order before going to bed.

His pudgy white fingers were moving among the pieces like demented slugs when the doorbell rang. He wondered who it could possibly be at this hour. His only personal friend (though unconnected with the cause) and fellow jigsaw enthusiast, an undertaker named Caruso, was away at an undertaking convention in Turin.

He rose with a sigh and went to open the door. But when he saw who it was he instinctively fell back half a pace. He had never met the man before, but he had heard much of him and seen his photographs. This was the Neapolitan *commissario* in charge of the Piantaleone investigation.

Then he drew himself back on the edge of panic. If the *commissario* had got this far things were bad certainly. But not that bad. The situation was still under control; it would just require a little adjustment.

'Can I help you?' he enquired oilily in his high, somewhat nasal tone as though Peroni had come to buy a missal. Then he saw the *commissario* look at him for a second oddly and guessed that it was because he had recognised his accent.

'I've just come from your shop.'

'And found it closed of course,' said Quirico Ricordi. 'You wished to purchase something of an ecclesiastical nature? I'm afraid you will have to abide in patience until tomorrow morning.'

Peroni stepped into the room and looked about him. 'I want,' he said, 'to talk about the deaths of General Orazio Piantaleone, his son Loris and his nephew Gabriele.'

'I'm afraid you escape my comprehension,' said Quirico Ricordi. 'Who are you?'

'*Questura*,' said Peroni. 'Shall we sit down?'

Quirico Ricordi shrugged and motioned to an armchair. The *commissario* seemed very sure of himself, but he would soon realise that things were not so cut and dried as he supposed. In the meantime it would do no harm to play along with him.

They both sat. Quirico Ricordi folded one plump thigh over the other and looked at Peroni with an expression of polite enquiry on his flabby, beardless face. He waited patiently for the questions. But no questions came. Instead he felt himself being studied with almost surgical precision and he guessed what the object of this scrutiny was.

'You're Neapolitan,' said Peroni.

'Is there anything so surprising about that? Many of us come up to the north. You yourself – '

The expression of dawning awareness confused with anger and distaste on Peroni's face told Quirico Ricordi that he had guessed right. Another little secret had been uncovered.

'What relation are you to her?'

'I'm her father.'

There was a silence.

'I might have guessed she'd grown on a dung-heap,' said Peroni at last. 'All the most beautiful Neapolitan flowers do.'

Quirico Ricordi accepted the insult calmly. It would be paid for in good time.

'What brought you both up to Verona? What was the beginning of it all?'

That was the one thing he couldn't be told. Not yet. Later perhaps when, in one way or another, he had been rendered harmless. But in the meantime a small improvisation was called for. Quirico Ricordi opened his mouth to embark upon it, but at that moment the telephone rang. He rose to answer it, but was surprised and horrified to see that Peroni had moved to get it first.

He was yet more horrified to hear the call being answered in a perfect imitation of his own high-pitched nasal tone.

'*Pronto?*' he heard himself saying with the mouth of the Neapolitan policeman. There was a silence except for the indistinguishable quacking at the other end of the line. Quirico Ricordi knew he should be doing something, but he had been taken off balance once too often and it left him immobile with uncertainty.

Then he heard his own voice again. This time it said, 'I'll go over and see what's happened immediately,' and the receiver was put back in its cradle.

The *commissario* looked up at Quirico Ricordi who saw from

the look that he had understood whose voice it had been at the other end of the line.

For the first time Quirico Ricordi felt that things might be bad after all.

Violence was not Peroni's style, but the painful switch from love to revulsion had aroused emotions which he would gladly have vented on Quirico Ricordi, forcing him through pain to recite the truth. And he would have done so. But it was at that moment that the telephone had rung, and when Peroni had heard the voice at the other end, he realised he would have to arrange for the ecclesiastical furnisher to be taken into custody with his daughter for questioning at a later date. As things stood now, it was essential that everything should be referred to *dott.* Guerra.

Having organised Ricordi's transfer he enquired about Guerra and learned that he had already gone home. The affair had reached a point, however, when the next move must depend on the police chief, so Peroni decided to go and visit him. But first there were one or two telephone calls to be made. Peroni made them and then went out to his car.

Dott. Guerra lived in a house on the *torricelle*, the hills immediately surrounding Verona. The area was a place of entertainment for the Veronese who pilgrimaged there in spring and on various occasions throughout the year to eat and drink, dance, play mini-golf and make love, but it was also dotted with private residences which attested to its earlier history as a more or less exclusive reserve of the better off among the citizens.

The constellations were shining as though they were in a planetarium when Peroni got out of his car and, as he walked up to the house, he reflected that his life had been so urban bound that he did not recognise one of them.

Guerra himself opened the door with a politely enquiring expression which mutely demanded what had occurred of sufficient importance to warrant the infringement of his privacy.

'I hope you'll forgive me disturbing you at this hour, *dottore*,' said Peroni, 'but there have been developments which I think you ought to know about.'

'Of course, *dottore*. Please don't apologise. Come in.'

Peroni stepped into the old, somewhat bare hall. There were no frills, no decorations, no flowers; it was obviously not a woman's house.

'I spend little time here,' said Guerra as though catching Peroni's thought. 'Somebody comes in to clean, but apart from that the place is abandoned. Shall we go into my study?'

The study was monastic in its lack of superfluity.

'Sit down, *dottore*, and let me get you a drink. Chivas Regal, I believe?'

Saying which he was gone, leaving Peroni to wonder how he had known about Chivas Regal. It was one of those little things which reinforced Guerra's reputation for omnipotence.

The police chief returned with a bottle and two glasses. He poured for them both and they toasted each other in silence.

'Well, *dottore*,' said Guerra, leaning back in his chair which he would never have done at the office, 'I am at your disposal.'

'The break-through we've been looking for came last night,' said Peroni, 'or more properly this morning. I learned that somebody had sent photographs of Paolo Piantaleone and Francesca Pillipopoli to the Dowager Countess Augusta, and I surmised that whoever had done so knew of the old lady's obsession with the legend and calculated that her knowledge of the Paolo–Francesca love story would, in one way or another, start the story going again and provide a convenient motive for the death of General Piantaleone. This would be made the more plausible by the fact that one of the two families is Fascist and the other Communist, and moreover that in the Communist family there was a fanatical Red Brigade combatant who would be more than capable of "executing" a leading figure of the extreme right wing like the General.'

'You're assuming,' interrupted Guerra, 'that this person knew the murder would be claimed as their own work by the Red Brigade?'

'Not exactly,' said Peroni, 'I'm assuming that this person already intended to pass the General's killing off as the work of the Red Brigade.'

'I see. Please continue.'

'At this point the story deviates somewhat,' said Peroni apologetically.

'I'll do my best to follow, *dottore*,' said Guerra with grave irony which left Peroni feeling a fool.

'When I examined the photographs more closely this morning,' he went on, 'I saw that in one of them a black, Volkswagen van, parked on the other side of the road, was reflected in the window of a toy shop. Well, another black – or at any rate dark-coloured – van had appeared earlier in the story in the immediate area where somebody had shot at Gabriele Piantaleone before he disappeared up to Rosaro. This seemed to justify a certain concentration on black Volkswagen vans.'

'Indeed,' assented Guerra.

'I learned from enquiries that just such a van had been bought by an ecclesiastical furnishing shop owned by a certain Quirico Ricordi. So, earlier this evening I – forced an entry into that shop.'

'Without authority?' said Guerra, eyebrows raised in polite enquiry. 'I fear that *dott.* Spinelli – '

'Under the circumstances,' said Peroni, 'I don't think that *dott.* Spinelli will be in a position to protest.'

'I am relieved to hear that. Please go on.'

'I found in the shop a young woman who I had believed to be a member of the Piantaleone family. I have evidence that she was at the villa in Garda and she admitted placing the bomb in Loris's car.'

'Sabrina, would it be?'

'Regina,' corrected Peroni.

'Yes, yes – Regina Piantaleone. I've heard of her. But are you implying that she's *not* a Piantaleone?'

'Yes.'

'Good heavens, *dottore*, you have indeed a host of revelations to uncover. Who, then, is she?'

'The daughter of the ecclesiastical furnisher, Quirico Ricordi. That much I learned from him.'

'But how was such an imposture possible?'

'I've discovered that, too. Before coming here I telephoned General Piantaleone's widow and she told me that, some months before the appearance of Regina in Verona, they received an affectionate letter from the girl's father in Naples, identifying himself as one of the Neapolitan Piantaleones and saying that he was anxious to know more about the family in Verona for a genealogical study he was making. The Piantaleones being such a numerous and widespread family nobody bothered to check whether these particular ones were genuine or not. Why should anyone bother to make up such a story? It was only months later that the daughter arrived in Verona with the story of her parents' death. Still nobody thought to check. She was a personable, friendly girl and she was asking for nothing. In fact, it was the General who offered to help her by finding her a flat and getting her to do an interpreter's course. It was only this evening when I telephoned to Naples that I discovered that this branch of the Piantaleone family is non-existent.'

'Very ingenious,' said Guerra, 'so you're suggesting that this – Quirico Ricordi and his daughter came up to Verona where she successfully posed as a Piantaleone and then, having gained the General's confidence, persuaded him to head this neo-fascist movement?'

'Exactly.'

'In other words, it is they who are behind the whole thing?'

'Not entirely,' said Peroni. 'They wouldn't have had the knowledge or the means to organise things on such a scale. No, there was somebody else behind them. And I know who it was.'

'Oh?' said Guerra, eyebrows arched in an urbane interrogative. 'Who?'

'You, *dottore*.'

There was a long silence in the dark study where the two men sat isolated in an island of light shed by a lamp.

'Another glass of whisky, *dottore*?' said Guerra at last.

'Thank you, *dottore*.'

'May I ask,' said Guerra, pouring for both of them, 'if you have any evidence for such an allegation?'

'When you telephoned Quirico Ricordi earlier this evening

to enquire why there was no answer from the ecclesiastical furnishing shop where Regina should have been, it was I who answered.'

Guerra's eyebrows put another question.

'Mimicry,' said Peroni, 'is not encouraged in northern Italian police circles, but in Naples I became very proficient at it.'

'Your reputation with the media is obviously well deserved.'

'Thank you, *dottore*.'

'However, let me point out that not only is the identification of a voice on the telephone not admitted as evidence, but it is even questionable as a matter of mere opinion.'

'I do have other – pointers,' said Peroni modestly.

'Perhaps I might hear them?'

'For one thing, you were stationed in Naples, *dottore*, just at the time the first letter arrived in Verona from the fictitious Piantaleone family.'

'So were a lot of other people. Have you enquired of this couple whether they were – employed by me?'

'Not yet.'

'I think you will find that they deny all knowledge of me.'

'I'm sure they will. So would I in their place.'

Guerra's eyes flickered with the satisfaction of a chess player acknowledging a good move. 'Please go on,' he said.

'The next point is the photographs. I imagine they were taken by Quirico Ricordi at your request. Who but you with your encyclopaedic knowledge of Veronese affairs – ' Dott. Guerra acknowledged the compliment with a little nod. 'Who but you would have known of the legend of the two families and of the potentially explosive nature of a relationship between Paolo and Francesca?'

'A member of one of the families themselves?'

'I don't think any of them is any longer even a candidate for the position we are considering.'

Guerra let that pass with a shrug.

'Then there was the General's disappearance and death. I was surprised you appointed me in charge of the investigation, and then confirmed my appointment in the teeth of the DIGOS and the *Carabinieri*. I had always assumed you took me for a Nea-politan exhibitionist with a profile, and I was flattered to think you considered me able enough to handle such an affair. But I was wrong – you *did* consider me a Neapolitan exhibitionist with a profile and that was precisely why you gave me the job.'

'*Dottore,*' said Guerra, his innate courtesy shocked, 'you do yourself a grave injustice.'

Peroni smiled his thanks. 'We all agree by now,' he went on, 'that the Red Brigade communiqué was faked. But it's not all that easy to fake such a thing, and once again you are one of the few people with the knowledge and the means to do it.'

Guerra nodded appreciatively.

'And then there was the fancy-dress ball of the Veronese nobility. You gave me permission to go there, and there I met Regina who put me on to the Dowager Countess and the whole Montagu–Capulet smokescreen. From the beginning I suspected that somebody had set Regina on to me, but at the time I assumed it was one of the Piantaleones or Pillipopolis. And there's another thing – you, the supreme rationalist, the matter-of-fact northerner, always sustained the Montagu–Capulet theory and encouraged me to follow it.'

'Perhaps I am not quite the rationalist you supposed me.'

'Then there's something else,' Peroni continued. 'The whole business of Gabriele Piantaleone. In one sense it's a mercy you killed him, *dottore*, because he outdid most policemen in his capacity for digging out the truth, and we can't afford to have many people like that about, can we?'

'The police union would never allow it,' Guerra assented.

'Because Gabriele,' Peroni went on, 'found out about you. How exactly he did it, I don't know, but that he did is evident from what his girl friend Patti told me. He telephoned you, and you saw that he represented a real threat to you and your move-ment. You must have agreed to come to terms with him and suggested meeting in the piazza outside the arena during the opera interval where he knew he would be perfectly safe. But at the same time you told Quirico Ricordi to be ready with his van and kill Gabriele when he had left you, probably made careless by exhilaration at your agreeing to all his terms. But he got away, and it must have seemed as though he'd disappeared into thin air. I later discovered that he'd been picked up, in the fullest sense of the word, by the German girl, but at the time it must have seemed as though he'd vanished. He chose his hiding place well. It was near enough to continue his campaign of blackmail and yet far enough to be safe. Or so it must have seemed to him. Did he get in touch with you from Rosaro?'

'You can hardly expect me to answer that, *dottore*.'

'No, of course not. But anyway I discovered where he had gone, and naturally I reported it to you. This put you in an awkward position. If we got to him before you did, then everything was finished. So you took a calculated risk. You organised the search party in Rosaro, sending us all off to look for him. But you were the one who knew the country really well – you had hunted over it before. And when we had all gone, you set off hunting yourself, but this time after human prey. You must have had your own hunting rifle with you in the back of the car when we drove up together. You were taking a big chance, but you've done that throughout your career. It's that which has earned you the reputation for cool daring. And it worked once again. You came upon Gabriele before anybody else and shot him.'

There was another silence.

'So what do you intend to do?' asked Guerra at last.

'What can I do? Make a full report of all this to *dott*. Spinelli.'

'Who will no doubt be delighted to have a policeman to prosecute for once. Very well then – I can't stop you. But I should consider the matter carefully first.'

'Why?' said Peroni with a sense of misgiving.

Guerra shrugged. 'Your evidence is of the thinnest. You will have to make it a good deal more substantial before you can persuade even *dott*. Spinelli to bring a case against me.'

'It shouldn't be impossible.'

'I grant you that for the sake of argument. Let us assume that you establish a case for me to answer. We are in Italy, and you know as well as I do, *dottore*, what happens in Italy when charges are brought against people of any authority. They drag on and on. Witnesses disappear or die unexpectedly. The waters are muddied so effectively that such glimpses of the truth as may have been perceptible at the beginning vanish from sight altogether. And from mind as well, *dottore*.'

Peroni knew it was true.

'And again, if there is any foundation for what you allege, the adherents of what once again for the sake of argument we shall call "my" movement will be everywhere – one or more of the judges before whom the case appears, the jury, the prosecution lawyers. Even *dott.* Spinelli himself – who knows? You couldn't expect a case against me to get very far under those circumstances, could you?'

And that was true, too, thought Peroni.

'The curious thing is in these cases that the only person really to suffer in the end is the policeman who started it all. He has upset the *status quo*. He has put out a lot of important people. He has stirred up a hornets' nest. It's his career which suffers in the end, often irreparably. Whereas silence can often bring promotion with it. Another glass of whisky, *dottore*?'

'No, thank you,' said Peroni.

'Personally,' said *dott.* Guerra, pouring one for himself, 'I have always liked the Montagu–Capulet solution. And indeed it may have played its part in some of the events. It may not fit all the facts, but the vast majority of people have accepted it as the explanation from the very beginning.'

Peroni stood up. 'I must get back to town.'

'Yes, of course. Let me show you out.'

The two men walked in silence to the front door.

'I think I have put the facts before you objectively,' said Guerra, shaking hands with Peroni, 'now the decision rests with you. Good night, *dottore*.'

'Good night, *dottore*.'

The lights of Verona twinkled like those of a fairy town below him and Peroni could make out the dark curve of the river

Adige as it bent round by the church of St Anastasia towards the old Roman bridge. It looked a peaceful and happy town with its opera and the old cattle trough doing service for Juliet's tomb. Not like Milan or Rome or Turin, you would have said. A law-abiding town.

Peroni felt a painful stab of longing for the south where corruption had the advantage of being as recognisable as a running sore. His mind went back to the letter he was about to write when the whole business started. Perhaps he would write it now.

But first of all there was a decision to make.

Dott. Guerra came out into the beating morning sunlight and got into his car. As on every other working morning it was exactly fifteen minutes to eight, which allowed him twelve minutes for the drive and three minutes to park and walk up to his office. He switched on the engine and the large, dark-blue Fiat moved forward, crunching on the gravel.

Guerra was a trifle put out this morning. He had made a serious error of calculation such as a man in his position could not afford. He had under-estimated Peroni.

The previous evening he had naturally denied considering Peroni as a mere Neapolitan exhibitionist with a profile; the most elementary laws of hospitality demanded a denial. But to himself he was obliged to admit that some such thought had been in his head when he had put Peroni in charge of the investigations into General Piantaleone's death. He had, he saw in retrospect, been misled by the flamboyant accounts of Peroni's doings as related by the media.

The dark-blue Fiat swept round the curve in the road just outside Castel San Pietro going down towards the city. It was exactly twelve minutes to eight.

The question was, how to handle matters now? He felt that he had put the situation clearly enough before Peroni and that his reasoning had been extremely cogent. It was plainly in Peroni's interests to be discreet, and then with the passing of a little time Regina and her father could be set at liberty and the whole affair duly hushed up.

But could he trust Peroni to be corrupt? Until yesterday he would have answered unhesitatingly in the affirmative. Now he could not be quite so sure. Indeed, it was possible that a report was already on its way to *dott.* Spinelli. In which case the situation, though by no means irretrievable, would be difficult indeed. But on the whole he felt Peroni was fairly safe. The inducements to silence were irresistible.

The dark-blue Fiat began to mingle with the city traffic. It was nine minutes to eight.

Guerra decided that he would send a memo to Peroni saying that he was recommending him to the minister for promotion. With any luck, the worst should be over in 24 hours, and the whole crisis forgotten in a month.

The dark-blue Fiat was moving up towards the crossroads with Via Marsala and Via Madonna del Terraglio. It was exactly eight and a half minutes to eight.

There was a hanging traffic light in the centre of the junction, but it was at green so Guerra drove straight across. Just at that moment a student with his leg in plaster and using a crutch stepped out on to the pedestrian crossing ahead. As he stopped to allow the student to pass, Guerra wondered vaguely why he was in plaster. It was too early for the skiing season, which was when broken legs abounded among the student population.

The young man was taking an interminable time to cross. As he watched him, Guerra thought that a celebratory dinner might be held in Peroni's honour with the minister as a guest. Neapolitans always found that sort of thing irresistible.

Taken up with this project and tapping his irritation at the student with a manicured finger-nail on the steering wheel, *dott.* Guerra did not notice the grimy off-white Fiat 128 with a Turin number plate that was coming towards the junction from Via Marsala, past the Esso station.

Nor did he notice it as it turned right to come up alongside him, being more taken up with the spectacle of the student, who had suddenly put on an impossible burst of speed and reached the opposite pavement. It took him less than a split second to understand the reason for this, but by then it was too late.

He was just in time to see a young man looking out at him with a smile of triumphant hatred from the Fiat 128 and holding a machine gun. And he was just in time to hear the beginning of the hail of bullets which blasted their way into the gleaming dark-blue bodywork of his car and shattered its windows.

Then he felt an explosion of inconceivable violence erupting simultaneously in the outskirts and city centre of his being, spinning and whirling it entire into a milli-instant of unbearable light followed by a quintessence of blackness which he recognised as eternal.

It was exactly eight minutes and twenty seconds to eight.

The assassination was claimed by the Red Brigade at eleven o'clock that morning in a telephone call to the *Arena* newspaper. The speaker was a man with a flat voice betraying no trace of regional accent.

'The fascist hireling Guerra,' said the voice, 'was executed this morning for crimes against the people.'

They just didn't know how near the truth they were, thought Peroni when he heard of it.

Or did they?

224